COUNTLESS

KAREN GREGORY

BLOOMSBURY
LONDON OXFORD NEW YORK NEW DELHI SYDNEY

Bloomsbury Publishing, London, Oxford, New York, New Delhi and Sydney

First published in Great Britain in May 2017 by Bloomsbury Publishing Plc
50 Bedford Square, London WC1B 3DP

www.bloomsbury.com

BLOOMSBURY is a registered trademark of Bloomsbury Publishing Plc

A CIP catalogue record for this book is available from the British Library

ISBN 978 1 4088 8250 4

Typeset by RefineCatch Limited, Bungay, Suffolk
Printed and bound in Great Britain by CPI Group (UK) Ltd, Croydon CR0 4YY

1 3 5 7 9 10 8 6 4 2

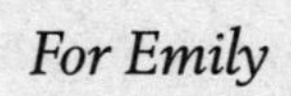

For Emily

PART ONE
THE THING

Chapter 1

The cigarette between my fingers is thin, insubstantial. Like me.

I'm hunched up on a square of frozen grass outside Dewhurst House, waiting. Felicity is always late, which is a joke seeing as I'd catch hell if it were me.

Her car finally rattles round the corner. I take a final drag, watch the lit end flare to my fingertips, then drop it next to the others as Felicity reaches my side.

She pretends not to notice, instead saying, 'What are you doing out here? You'll freeze!' in a fake jolly voice.

We go inside, Felicity's hand on my shoulder blade like I'm about to do a runner. Wouldn't be the first time. Or she might be doing a bone check. We exchange a quick look and I duck my head down.

'Do you want a coffee? You look cold. Black if you must!'

Felicity's rapid sentences are already giving me a headache. Bet she hates our sessions about as much as I do. Which is quite a lot, when it comes down to it. Still, she's lasted longer than most of my key workers – two years and counting – and she's all right really. Better than some.

'So ...' Felicity leans forward with a Concerned Look on her face. 'How are things?'

'All right.'

'And how are you getting on at the Yewlings?'

'Fine.' I try not to let the sarcasm into my voice but here it comes – drip, drip, like it's trying to form a stalactite. An image of my teeny flat in the Yewlings, Tower Block of Dreams, flashes into my head. I attempt a tight smile, the skin forming hard bunches on my cheeks. 'Really well actually.'

Felicity's not buying it.

'OK, shall we get it over with?' she says, and waves her hand at the scales.

I stand on them backwards, making my face into a mask like we're in a play, and listen to Felicity's pen scratch numbers down.

'What have you been up to?' she says.

I crane my head round, trying to spot the figure she's

written, but she's already shifted the book. I slink back to my seat and pick at a loose thread where the chair fabric is ripped and leaking bits of foam. I must have sat here a million times.

'College?'

I look up at Felicity's expectant face. I've been doing this a lot recently, tuning out.

'Sorry, what was that?' I say.

Felicity holds in a sigh. Barely. 'I was asking if you've been attending college?'

My silence says it all. I do mean to go, but half the time I end up circling town or staring out of the window until it's way past the point where showing up might actually make a difference.

I pull my hoodie down lower and curl my knees up to my chest. I can feel my stomach all wrong where I've pressed my thighs against it. I give the thread another tug and it comes away in my hand.

I take a deep breath. I've put this off for weeks, but I'm going to go crazy for real if I don't ask. 'There's something ...'

'Mmm?' Felicity says.

I start to wind the thread on my finger, count how many times it goes round. 'It's nothing really. I just don't feel ... right. Like, more than normal, I mean. I'm tired all the time. And there's something else.' I take another big breath then speak in a rush. 'My stomach … it's kind of swollen. I was thinking, could it be … Have I done something permanent, with Nia?'

'Hedda, we've talked about this. You need to stop referring to your eating disorder by that name,' Felicity says. Which is spectacularly missing the point in my opinion.

'Right, yeah, sorry. But about what I was saying. Could it be … cancer?'

'I don't think … Well, we could certainly arrange for a check-up.' Felicity gives me a closer look, frowns, then glances again at her book of doom. 'Is there anything that's concerning you at the moment? College, home, friends?' I'm already shaking my head when she adds, 'Boyfriends?' Though she's more or less smiling at this last one.

I don't smile. Instead, I feel my face go hot. Silence stretches as wide as an ocean.

When I look up, Felicity has this expression on her face like she's just seen Elvis. Slowly, she leans forward, and in a gentle voice I've never heard her use before she says, 'Have you done a pregnancy test?'

Chapter 2

What. The. F? WTFWTFWTF. No, no, no, no. This can't be right.

I look at the instructions again. The stick I can't hold steady. I'm wedged inside the shopping centre toilets, in the furthest cubicle from the door. I stare at the Boots bag at my feet until it blurs. The seat is beginning to hurt my backside, but I can't move.

There is a cross in the window. I check the instructions one more time. A cross means I'm … but I can't be, can I?

I think there's a chance I might have left my body because my head is expanding and my ears are making the noise that happens before you faint and little black dots are tracking from left to right across my eyes. I lean forward and watch them and think, *Left to right*. It's always left to right. You'd think they might go up or diagonally or something from time to time.

It takes a while for them to clear, but when they do the little blue cross is still there. Then I pull up my clothes, turn round and vomit. A section of my brain makes an automatic calculation: volume of food in versus volume out. Converted into calories, minus resting metabolic rate. Target weight, weight at clinic, actual weight. All the numbers marching in a comforting row, orderly.

I shove the test into the sanitary bin and slam it shut. This is a mistake. It has to be. I don't even have periods most of the time, thanks to Nia.

Except this time, it isn't down to her at all.

I get out of the shopping centre and pace through town, past crappy pound shops and boarded-up windows and jarring spaces where buildings have been knocked down but not yet rebuilt, turning my head at the sickly grease smell of Maccie D's. Sharp wind burns my face. I spot myself, a long smear like a ghost in a shop window, and pull my hat down lower to cover my ears.

I keep going, until I get to the decaying buildings that count as this town's library and duck in. The smell here isn't much better: stained carpets that need to be torn out, damp and mildew round the metal windows. But there's also that good book smell and I try to focus on that. I burrow between shelves, head turned to one side, eyes glancing off the spines, then head for the trolley where the returned books sit waiting to go back on the shelves. I grab one and check it out, face down without properly looking at it. I'll see what I've got when I get back to the flat.

On the way out, I see a woman with a stack of books balanced in heavy arms staring at me. I catch a familiar mixture of disgust and envy battling it out in her eyes. I stare back. *I know what you're thinking.* One of the books tumbles from her arms and crashes to the floor.

I walk fast through an underpass full of graffiti and oily puddles, up a maze of side streets, tatty terraced houses with weeds poking through the front gardens, then on, out of town, along a cycle path. My arms swing in time to my feet. In my head, I count the steps.

The flat's a couple of miles back at an angle from Dewhurst; it's like two neighbouring spokes of a bike wheel, with the town centre in the middle and the adolescent unit sticking out on one spoke, the Yewlings on another. If you add in the detour to Boots, I'll have walked five miles today, but Nia's voice still needles under the thud of my footsteps.

Fat cow. You should do six tomorrow, she says, and I know I will.

I skirt a group of boys kicking a ball over the cracked concrete wasteland at the bottom of the tower block and have to use both hands to get the heavy door to the flats open. No need for my key; the lock is knackered and so is the intercom. The door bangs shut, the sound echoing up the dark stairwell, which smells like wee as usual. The lift doors have a scrawled *out of order* sign taped to them, but I'd always take the stairs anyway.

Eight flights, eight steps per flight, which makes sixty-four. If it was six hundred and four it still wouldn't be enough. Halfway up, a couple of girls sit over a plastic bottle of supermarket cider and I flatten myself against the wall to go past them, head down, then run up the rest of the stairs. They're silent as I go by, but I hear laughter float up behind me.

I'm dizzy again when I get to my door and I fumble the key in the lock, which means I get a big waft of stale smoke and cooking from next door and I swear I didn't even mean to be sick that time. I glance into the toilet, see it's mainly water, stained pink. I run back to slam and lock the front door, take off my rucksack. My shoes. Hop on the scales. Then off. Then back on again. And once more. Repeat the number in my head while I wait for the kettle to boil.

I am not pregnant. I can't be. It must be a false positive or something. You can get those with lots of things, right?

I drink hot tea, black with half a sugar, and take the box back out of the Boots bag. There's two tests left. I guess there's only one thing for it. I rip off the packaging, wee on one and then the other and shove them on the side of the sink before washing my hands, scrubbing knuckles that stand out.

I have a scared little impulse to call Mum, but instead I turn away from the tests and go into the kitchen/living room/whatever space, sit at the tiny table and folding chair. I don't speak to Mum much these days. She wrote me off a while ago, to be honest, and I can't blame her.

My phone goes with a text from Laurel. Now I'm not sure which I'd least like to look at – the message or the tests.

It has to be three minutes by now. I go back to the bathroom and stare at the two unmistakable crosses. My brain begins doing calculations from when it happened: the day they buried Molly. If this is real, that would mean I'm far along. Very far. I can't breathe properly, thinking about what this means.

*There's a **Thing** inside you. A parasite,* Nia says.

Then I pass out, feeling the crack of my skull against the sink as I go down.

Crap Things about the Unit, Number One:
You don't want to go back.
Except sometimes, it's all you want to do

I was twelve the first time I got admitted to a unit. After a while all the admissions kind of blur into one, but I do remember lying in my room on bed rest, on a mattress that hurt my hips and knees, and the sound of someone crying so hard I couldn't focus on my book. *The Lion, the Witch and the Wardrobe* – the last book I ever took into a unit from home, back in the days when I still read books I actually liked.

The crying went on and on, the sound floating through my door, which was propped open so I didn't get up to any of the little tricks you get to know on a unit. Tricks to try and stop them shoving all that weight on to you. Half of them hadn't even occurred to me then, truthfully.

Looking back, I was so innocent, a deer with eyes so wide open they hurt. The things you pick up when you're on a unit. The people you pick up. Your constant companions, your best enemies. People you never want to see again, can't bear to leave behind.

Like Nia, when I think about it.

Chapter 3

Felicity doesn't speak for a full two minutes after I break the happy news. I know – I count.

Finally, she rearranges her face, takes a deep breath and says, 'Well. That must have been a shock for you.'

'You think?'

'And how far … ?'

'About twenty weeks, I think. More or less,' I say. 'I'm not all that up on how you count pregnancy.' My face twists round the last word.

Felicity pauses. She's trying so hard not to look shocked, I nearly laugh. But even I know this isn't funny.

'Twenty weeks? So it was after … ?' Felicity says.

And I know we're both thinking about what happened to Molly a little over twenty weeks ago and that I'm not going to talk about it. I'm not going to tell her how the day they buried Molly hollowed me out inside. I've been hungry a lot in my life, but I've never felt as empty as that. I guess Felicity knew anyway, but I wasn't about to say that stuff out loud. It's one of our many unspoken Rules of Engagement. Along with No Tissues and No Jumping In With 'Insightful' Questions. I hate those.

My face feels tight and rigid, chunks of the inside of my mouth clamped between my teeth. We stare at each other. The clock ticks our session down: forty-five minutes to go, twenty-five, fifteen … Felicity tries to get me to talk, banging on about Options and College and My Future, which she manages to say like she actually thinks I might have one, but I'm not having it. Not today.

With five minutes left, I say, 'Well, I guess I need to get myself to the doctor's. Get an appointment to … you know …'

Felicity leans forward in her seat. 'No?'

'Oh, for fu–' I catch myself.

She knows perfectly well; she's just trying to get A Reaction. To get me to Feel Emotions and talk about Behaviours and Actions and Consequences.

'To get rid of it,' I say. But my voice does a weird circus trick on me, and instead of coming out *couldn't care less*, it wobbles with so much care I shock myself. To make up for it, I slam the door on the way out and take the extra long way back to the Yewlings, counting each step in my head as I go.

I wait nearly a week before I get up the nerve to call the doctor's surgery, which is a mistake because it turns out you can't just show up and book yourself in for an abortion the same day. The doctor, a plumpish woman with the definite beginnings of a beard, types notes for a seriously long time, two-finger style, as I explain I just need to get it all sorted. Preferably today.

'When was your last period?'

I stare at the ceiling, trying to remember if I had one at the unit before I left, then realise how stupid this is – it's not like there's more than one date of conception to choose from.

'I think I'm about twenty weeks,' I say.

The two-finger typing stops.

Eventually, she begins tapping again and then prints off a slip of paper and speaks in a brisk voice. 'You need to have a scan urgently.'

'What for?'

She gets this look then, half exasperated but also pitying, and speaks more slowly. 'We need to be sure how many weeks you are before we can think about next steps.'

I wonder who this 'we' is she's talking about, but she's

picking up the phone and talking to someone on the other end, saying it's urgent. Then she hangs up and hands me the piece of paper.

'Take this up to the hospital,' she says. 'There's a cancellation at four so they can squeeze you in.'

I take it with a shaking hand.

Outside, I read the letter, but all it does is expand that panicky feeling in my chest until my throat is closing over and my heart is doing quadruple time. I have to hang on to a lamp post until it slows. Hospitals aren't my one hundred per cent favourite places to be. A & E, children's wards – the nurses there just love anorexics. Adolescent units are … more complicated.

Nia sits at the top of the lamp post.

Stupid cow, she hisses.

Also: *Look what you've done*.

And: *That **Thing** inside you is going to make you fat. Disgusting.*

It's too much. I push myself off and start to walk as fast as I can, pulling my phone out as I go. I consider calling Mum for a nanosecond, Laurel for slightly longer. And realise something with a jolt that makes me stop walking.

I want Molly.

She would've known what to do. Her face flashes before me, but I shut it down. I'm not going there.

I haven't got a clue what I'm going to do until four. That's years away.

I walk even faster, on up the hill along yet another spoke away from the shops, the Yewlings, Dewhurst House and towards college. Which means things must be desperate.

If I'm lucky, I'll make it in time for maths.

Edward, my A level maths teacher, looks over his glasses as I slink to the back of the room. 'Nice of you to join us today,' he says.

There's a small rustle of titters and people turning to stare at me, but he's already talking again, putting up equations on the smart board.

I look about for a pen and realise I've forgotten my bag. The boy next to me – no idea what his name is – rips some paper from his pad and shoves it at me along with a leaky biro.

'Thanks,' I mutter, and avert my eyes when I realise he looks like he wants to chat.

I get on with the work instead and feel things settle and calm a little inside. Maths is one of the few things I've always kept up with, even when I haven't been in school. I guess numbers are my thing, for better or worse. But I've missed enough classes that A level isn't exactly understandable. Still, today it gives me something to do that isn't listening to Nia, or thinking about the Thing.

At the end of the class, I shoot out before Edward or leaky biro owner can stop me. I briefly consider going to physics, but first I need a cigarette to calm me down. I scoot over to the unofficial smoking shelter across the road from the main gates. We're not technically allowed to smoke at college, but loads of people do. Right now, getting caught smoking wouldn't exactly be the biggest of my worries.

I stand away from the small huddle of other students, my back turned, and roll a cigarette. The wind cuts into my bare hands, making them clumsy and numb, the tips of my fingers already turning completely white. I know from experience I won't be able to feel them for a good ten minutes when I get back inside.

I keep my head down, still fumbling with the paper and the pouch of baccy.

I hear someone say, 'You coming out later?'

'No. My mum's on a mission, wants me home in time for dinner.'

A flash of jealousy, like my lighter flaring, then going out. No one's insisting I get home in time, though this does have the added bonus of no dinner, unless I manage to haul my sorry butt to the shops first. I hit the lighter's flint again, the metal rasping, but it sputters and dies.

'Here.' A flame flickers in front of my face. Behind it is a girl I didn't even recognise the first few times I saw her in college, on account of her complete ugly duckling style transformation into someone impossibly cool.

It's Sal.

I take a long, awkward drag, then say, 'Thanks' on the out breath, pushing smoke into the air.

Sal is the last person I want to see, particularly today. And I definitely don't want to see that familiar concerned look echoing back at me from Year Six, when I wouldn't eat any cake at her party.

I know exactly what's coming next.

'So … how's … stuff?' she says.

'Oh yeah, doing good, thanks. It's nice to see you. I've been meaning to say hi.'

Sal does a small half-shrug and lights her cigarette.

Sure I have.

We both think it. We both know there are too many years between that birthday cake and now. It's one of the reasons I've been keeping my head down at college once I realised it was her.

I take another drag and this wave of sickness crashes through me from nowhere. I can see in Sal's eyes that I've gone pale. That look of worry mixed with the tiniest amount of irritation, like she's remembering all those times she sat next to me at lunch, trying to make me laugh, waving Hula Hoops rings I wouldn't eat on each finger. She got it down pretty quick. But I still remember the Sal from before. The one I used to argue with about who'd be the red Power Ranger (the red one controlled the Megazord and was therefore the best, never mind it was always a he and not a she).

If things had gone differently, maybe Sal would've been a person I'd have asked to come with me for this scan. I bite down on the inside of my cheek, then make myself smile. 'I need to go. But it was great to see you,' I say.

I get the distinct impression she's shaking her head as I leg it.

The hospital is full of echoes. I take the stairs to the fifth floor and hand the letter from the doctor's to the receptionist. She squints at it and then gestures to the rows of chairs. I take a seat as far away as possible from the sea of bumps accompanied by men with ridiculous expressions of pride and worry on their faces. I try not to make eye contact with anyone, focus on counting the seconds in my head. I'm past two thousand by the time my name is called.

I follow the woman into a little room with a bed and what I assume is the scanner attached to a screen next to it.

'Not waiting for anyone?' she says in a way that I think is meant to be kind.

'No.'

'Right then. If you could lift up your top.'

I turn my head to look at the wall as she puts tissue round the top of my jeans, squirts gel all over my stomach and presses a wand thing into it quite hard, considering.

After a second, she says, 'Ah, here we are.'

I whip my head towards her, but her eyes are focused on the screen.

I want to say, '*Are you sure? There's really something in there?*' But she's already talking about measurements.

Suddenly she smiles and turns the screen towards me. 'There's the heartbeat, see?'

'I don't want to see it!' My voice comes out way louder than I meant it to. I shift my eyes back to the edge of the room.

The sonographer goes kind of still for a minute, then clatters away at a keyboard underneath her screen. I think she says some more stuff – I catch the words 'twenty-three weeks' – but the second she gets the scanner off me, I'm up and pulling my top down over my jeans, not bothering to let her rub the gel off.

I don't take the pictures she tries to hand me.

Chapter 4

'Hedda? I'm Mary. The specialist midwife? We spoke on the phone?'

She's early.

I have a packet of noodles clutched to my chest which I shift so I can shake the hand she's offering. She has a cavernous bag at her feet and I wonder what she's got in there. Better not be scales.

'Can I come in?'

I've been staring at the bag, I realise, and I shuffle back, open my arms. 'Be my guest.'

I see her look around the more or less empty flat, but subtly. I try to ignore the heavy bass coming through the wall adjacent to the bathroom. I remember the first evening here, trying to sleep through the sound of loud music and later the shouting in the hallway, huddled tight under a stupidly thin duvet, my coat slung over the top of it, too keyed up to sleep. Seems incredible to think that was six months ago. It's the longest I've been out of hospital since I was twelve; usually I'd make it three, four months then wind up straight back in. Even three days out seemed too long that first night at the Yewlings. I didn't know how to be on my own at the best of times, never mind suddenly being in my own flat where apparently things like keeping the electricity on and – hollow laugh – buying food were supposed to be my responsibility. I'd nearly called Mum then and there, to beg her to change her mind. She probably would have, given that they were burying Molly the next day, but I couldn't make myself call. Too shocked, for one thing.

Mary turns warm eyes on me. I scan her face and can't find any hint of that fake professional look of pretending not to judge. She must see all sorts, in her line of work. And she's fast, I'll give her that. I only had the scan two days ago. Two days where I've basically done nothing but stare at the internet which, despite being the biggest source of information ever known to man/woman/whatever is not actually helping much when it comes to working out what the hell I do now. Babies don't happen in my world.

'You want a cup of tea?' I say.

'Yes please. White and one.'

I flick the kettle on, turn round to see she has a big pack of notes with a sheet of stickers. I make the tea and sit at an angle to her, arms crossed over my – as of yet – more or less non-existent bump.

'Lovely, thanks,' Mary says. She looks for somewhere to put the mug and ends up resting it on the floor. 'So, shall we have a little look through?' She scans the notes. 'Could you confirm your date of birth?'

We go through some general questions: address, height, weight (I lie, obviously).

And then she asks the kicker: 'Is the father involved at all?'

A quick flash of fumbling fingers, my jeans round my ankles, a rough cold wall. The G & Ts, the first and last alcohol I've ever had, sloshing in my stomach like acid. Over the memories, like the credits from some surreal film, scrolls Molly's List. The one she wrote for me before she died.

I turn my face quickly away. 'No.'

Mary steeples her fingers together and considers me. They're wrinkled at the back, hands of a woman older than I'd first pegged her. Her hair is dyed in a red shade that clashes with her burgundy nails. She's carrying a few extra pounds around the middle.

'And you've considered all your options?' she says. 'You've had counselling?'

I try not to think about the session with Felicity I missed yesterday, or the message she left me on my phone. Internet research counts as counselling, right?

'Uh-huh,' I say. 'I know what I want to do. I don't want it.'

Mary's voice is gentle. 'Hedda, your scan put you at –'

'Twenty-three weeks.'

'Yes. That's –'

'Late. I know.'

Mary's hands come apart with a sucking sound. 'Yes. But an abortion isn't impossible. Given your history, it might well be the safest option.'

'So what do we do now?'

'Well, I should warn you that it'll be a surgical procedure.'

'I know. I looked it up.' I don't mention the pictures I saw of tiny babies, their arms the size of a finger. 'I wish I could … but I can't. I can't have this thing inside me. I said I didn't want it and I don't. What the hell would I do with a baby? It's ridiculous.' I'm trying to sound definite, but the words are coming out wrong.

Mary's fighting it, but the judgement is there now – I read it in the faintest stiffening around her eyes.

'OK. Let me make some phone calls,' she says. She shuffles my notes together and stands up.

I walk her to the door.

I can feel Nia behind me, bony hands resting on my shoulders. I want to lean back into their hardness.

'This is the right thing to do,' I say.

But somehow I'm in front of the door and I can't seem to make my hand reach out for the handle. I think, suddenly, of Molly and the promise I made her: that I'd keep out of hospital. I think of Nia, watching all these months as I've kept my word, like a bird of prey who I take out and fly round the room every once in a while – because Nia isn't something you just let go.

'Are you OK? You're very white,' Mary says.

'Yes. I'm fine.'

I go to open the door, miss the handle and lean on it heavily. Then I look at her.

'No. Not really,' I say.

We go back to the sofa. Mary waits for me to speak.

Impossible thoughts swirl around my head – and over them, Nia whispers. I shut my eyes and try to focus.

'What if … ?'

'Yes?'

'What if I went through with it? The pregnancy?' I say. It's not like I haven't considered it. I'm not completely selfish. Perhaps.

'That's an option.' Mary is choosing her words with care.

'Would it be OK? You know, with Nia – I mean, the ED. Have I damaged it?'

'The baby?'

'The foetus. But, yeah.' I rush on. 'There's people out there, right? Who'd give it a good life?'

'You're considering adoption?'

I nod.

Mary looks at my notes again. 'And you want to know if … ?'

'If the – you know …' I gesture at my middle section. I can't actually say the word 'baby'. 'Will it be all right?' There's an edge to my voice. My head is full of chatter that swings round and round like a fairground ride, trying to work out possibilities, what to do. I lean back and push a hand against my chest to feel the faint, rapid pulse of my heart.

'Well, the scan did show that baby is a little on the small side, if you're sure about the timing.'

'I'm sure.' There was only that once.

'Otherwise it was all fine. Surprisingly so, I'd say.'

Mary carries on looking through my notes while this sinks in.

Finally, she says, 'Adoption is certainly an option. But you need to consider this carefully. I know it's late on for a termination, but in your circumstances, with your history …

Everything seems to be fine now, but you look terribly thin to me. Generally the baby takes what it needs from its mother, but that's not possible if there's nothing to take.'

'I know that.'

'Do you? Because if you continue with this pregnancy and don't get adequate nutrition, you're going to put your own health and this baby's health at very high risk.' She begins to reel off a load of complications.

After a while I hold up my hand. 'I understand. I do. You said the scan showed that everything is developing OK.'

'It is, for now. But if you decide you're serious about carrying this baby to term, then you need to think hard.' She stops and gives me a very direct stare, her head level. It's a bit like someone has thrown a bucket of cold water over me. 'If you want to continue with the pregnancy, you can't mess around. It's not a game and it's not only your life you'd be playing with. If you have this baby then you have to eat.'

Crap Things about the Unit, Number Two: The Rules

There's a lot of Rules on a unit. Times you're supposed to be up, times you have to eat, go to Group or School or Therapy. Your days were laid out in front of you so you never really needed to think about what you might want to do, what you liked. Although it was easy to say what you didn't: getting weighed, obviously. Exercise rationed. Being pushed about in a wheelchair.

There were Rules about being in each other's rooms to try and stop us egging each other on – not that it made much difference.

Before Molly, I didn't really care much about the other patients, except in an 'am-I-thinner-than-her?' sort of way. I suppose I was A Bad Influence. I suppose that once I'd learned every trick going and then some, I passed it all on. Maybe it's something I should feel guilty about – who knows?

Thing about the Rules on a unit was, we broke them over and over. If you wanted to, you could see it as a game. Who could get one over on the staff. Diddling the scales. Trying to get away with it, to win. Us against them. I was good at it. Except there wasn't much of a prize in the end.

Chapter 5

Mary's gone. I make myself a cup of tea and put an entire teaspoon of sugar into it and a bit of milk, then sip tiny scalding mouthfuls while I think about everything she's said. Am I completely out of my mind, thinking I could carry a baby? Everything seems a bit fuzzy and distant – even more than normal.

I do a couple of tight circuits of the flat, searching for something to hold on to. I spot my rucksack from the day of the pregnancy tests and pull out the book I grabbed from the library. *The Life-changing Magic of Tidying.* Huh. I flick through. Apparently tidying will dramatically transform my life, which might be worth a go if I had much in the flat to tidy away in the first place. I think about the chaos of Molly's room at Dewhurst; the staff were always having a go at her to pick her crap up off the floor. Felicity even went in with a bin bag one time, which caused one of the longer unit stand-offs I'd seen for a while. I almost smile, thinking back, then snap the book shut and chuck it in my rucksack.

Something else pops into my head from about a year ago, just before I met Molly. I'd managed to trip and fall down the stairs at college. Well, maybe I fainted, but I wasn't about to admit that. I'd only been out of the unit since just after GCSEs finished so I was seeing Felicity every week as an outpatient, like I am now. She came to visit me on the inpatient bit of the unit the night my status got downgraded yet again. Or upgraded, depending on your perspective. She had this really pinched, tight look on her face. We did that eye-lock thing, and for once, I was the one who looked away. Then Felicity said, 'You know, there's a term for what you're becoming. Career anorexic.'

I didn't care back then. Maybe I even thought it was some sort of achievement. But now? Now, I don't know.

I put my hands on my stomach and try to imagine what's in there.

The Thing, Nia whispers.

There is a life inside me. In me. Of all people. It shouldn't be possible, but it's happening. There has to be a reason for it. I wonder if Molly can see me, wherever she is now. If so, then maybe this isn't just the worst kind of cosmic joke. Maybe it's fate or something.

There's a baby in there. The thought of it moving around, growing and growing, making me fat, sends me spinning to the toilet. I double over the bowl, but then the weirdest thing happens. At the last moment some force that feels like it's not even coming from me makes me straighten up, swallow warm tea and bile back down and chuck the window open to get some fresh air. Being sick is not going to be good for the baby. The baby I'm only a tiny bit sure I can even carry, and less sure that I should.

I sit on the sagging sofa and gaze for ages at the cracks in the plaster on the wall opposite. This is all some bizarre dream. I can't be pregnant. I'm only seventeen, for God's sake.

Like life's going to pay attention to that.

Maybe I should get the abortion.

I go into the little kitchen area, make some noodles and eat them standing up. Then I go in for some fruit. This is all safe food, stuff I can do. I'm still, more or less, following the meal plan from the unit. Sort of. To tell the truth, there's been one or two modifications, a few things quietly dropped. Living on a tiny budget comes in handy when you realise you can only afford to eat 15p noodles all week.

Now Mary's words come back to me again and I know that noodles are not going to be enough.

I stare and stare at the apple core on the counter, trying to work it all through, and that's when I feel it. A funny little twitch, down low and to one side. I've felt it before actually, but not as strong as this, and I realise now what I didn't then: it's not indigestion, or a muscle spasm. That's a kick. A baby, a real live baby inside me, kicking. It's real.

This time I manage to grab hold of the counter and sort of sink to my knees before I pass out.

I'm only out for a second or two. When I wake I see dingy white tiles overhead, and think I'm back on the unit, until I turn my head and see the door of the washing machine hanging open and realise everything is the wrong way around. Then I remember: I'm out. For the first time ever, no one is watching me – not Mum, not staff. I'm in my own flat, because social services didn't have anywhere else to put me, which is insane when you think about it. But I've been doing it, sort of. Treading water while I try and keep my promise to Molly. Or not.

I'm flat on my back. I realise I'm scanning my body, trying to locate pain from the fall amidst the usual aches and wondering whether I fell on to my stomach.

I lie for a long time on the ripped lino, thinking it all over, and realise I've decided. I'm going to have this baby. It's only a few months. I can eat for that long, until they get it out of me. Career anorexic I may be – write-off, screw-up, whatever – but for a few weeks, maybe I can be something else too.

I count out the weeks in my head, then the days, then the meals. Seventeen weeks, 119 days, 357 meals. I can do it, if I take them one at a time.

I twist the idea over and around and Molly's face comes to me – the way she looked the night in the garden, when she told me she loved the world, even if no one in it but me loved her back. If I can't do it for anything else, maybe I can do it for her.

So this is the deal I'm making: Nia and I call a truce. When the baby is safely here and I've found it some proper parents, then Nia can have me back. All I have to do is eat for seventeen weeks and then everything will be like it was before.

I feel Nia standing at my shoulder. She seems to consider it, and then I feel a tiny internal click, like a pact has been sealed.

Done, Nia whispers. And then she melts away like smoke, floating towards the ceiling, watching.

Inside, I feel the baby kick.

PART TWO
COUNTDOWN

Crap Things about the Unit, Number Three: the 'Food'

I've often wondered why all the words we have for eating are so disgusting: gulp, slurp, gobble, suck, chomp, chew, gorge, trough, masticate (that has got to be the nastiest one), belch, burp. All guttural, onomatopoeic (I had an awesome English teacher in Year Seven. Me and Natalie used to sit right near the front and I'd be whispering *o-e-i-a* in my head so I got the spelling right. Can't remember any of the poems we studied though, or any of the ones I wrote. Which is probably a good thing).

Obviously, being made to eat was always going to suck. But meals on the unit sucked in more ways than I could have imagined. All those calories, the fat, the sugar, the whole grossness of having it shovelled down my throat meal after snack after meal. Tube feeding at night. Sitting at the table forever. Yeah, all food would have sucked. But hospital food sucks in a different way. It's worse than the stuff they make you eat at primary school. All soggy chips, scoops of mash, soups which are completely unidentifiable. Butter oozing out of greasy foil on to toast you could roll up. Everything delivered lukewarm on trays with lids that *sweated*. I mean, if you were actually trying to put someone off eating you couldn't do much worse than forcing them to eat that crap day after day.

Chapter 6

17 WEEKS TO GO

I've been thinking about a book Molly showed me before she died, this weird hippie thing about past lives. I never knew if Molly really believed in all that stuff or if she just liked winding the staff up, especially any she'd pegged down as the bleeding-heart type, with their wispy scarves and positive affirmations. I wish I'd found out.

I remember the book said babies choose their parents. Like, all of us choose them, and the circumstances we're born in, for some reason. Because we have something to learn or whatever. Christ only knows why I would've chosen my parents, although they're not that bad really. They definitely didn't deserve a daughter like me.

Mostly, I don't believe in anything much apart from Nia,

and I think if you decide people choose their parents you have to start going into reincarnation and all that sort of stuff. Plus, why would you choose to be born in a war zone, or to parents who don't want you?

More to the point, what could possibly make a baby choose me?

Mary's coming back again next week. In the meantime I'm supposed to be seeing a nutritionist, but I swear I already know more about food than a roomful of them. I get on the internet and read everything I can about maternal nutrition, and make notes in a book. I look up diet plans and meal plans and carry on scribbling and by the end of the day I've devised my own timetable, based carefully on everything I need to eat to gain the right amount of weight; no more, no less. Then I make a shopping list and price it all up. Make some adjustments and add it up again. Steak is a bit pricier than noodles.

Finally, by the evening, I have my plan. I'll go shopping tomorrow.

I'm about to start getting ready for bed when there's a tap on the door. I ignore it, figuring it's probably someone for the next flat down. But whoever it is doesn't go away and I have a look out of the spyhole, then let out a sigh. It's Laurel.

I open the door. 'What are you doing here? You're supposed to be on the unit.'

'Can I come in?' she says and then moves forward, and I find myself stepping back and letting her through.

She curls up in a tiny ball on my sofa and starts biting at the corner of one nail.

She's wearing a long black skirt that should be tight but I can see her knees scything up through it, her feet tucked under her. Her cheeks are hollow and kind of grey, her collarbones standing out. I can't help the comparisons coming. I feel like an elephant next to her, a hippo.

'You want anything? Black coffee?'

She nods and I make it weak, with a splash of cold water. Her fingers wrapped round the mug are skin over bone, the tendons standing out on the backs of her hands in sharp lines.

I want to ask why she's here, but I already know why.

'They'll be looking for you,' I say.

Laurel sips at her coffee and turns eyes that are out of some Disney cartoon on me. 'Yeah. Sorry, Hed. I couldn't take it any more, you know? They're going to transfer me to Newlard.'

Oh. Newland House, a private unit. I remember another girl getting sent there once. We didn't hear from her for months, then when she was finally allowed to write letters, she sent these long, desperate ones that went on for pages filled with teeny writing – like the more weight she put on, the more she disappeared. They watch you all the time, even on the toilet. No one gets away with it, not there. Laurel started calling it Newlard, which we all laughed at, at the time, but it's a place we're scared of.

'When?'

'I'm supposed to be going next week.' She gives me an anguished look, all eyes and skull, her forehead a huge tight dome under thin hair. 'What am I going to do? I can't –' She starts taking gasping breaths.

'It's OK. It'll be OK,' I say. 'Do you want a paper bag?'

I'm mainly terrified she's going to collapse, have a heart attack or something. She looks so bad. But she also looks ... thin. Thinner than me. By far. I know she thinks it too. It's an unspoken competition that permeates everything. And I hate losing. I try and pat her on the shoulder, awkwardly, and we both know I'm feeling only bone. That sharp bit at the top of your shoulder that ought to be padded but isn't. Not for people like us. I put my hand up to my own shoulder, for comparative purposes, and drop it fast.

Laurel swipes her hand across her face, smearing eyeliner to one temple, then looks at me. 'Maybe they'll change their minds. Or the bed will get taken by someone else. I could always ...' She pauses and pulls her legs up closer, rests her chin on them. 'What about you?'

'What about me? Nothing much to report.'

Oh yeah, nothing other than a bloody baby. That just sort of slipped my mind. I think I feel that little twitching kick and I shift forward, pulling my jumper loose.

Laurel is frowning. 'You look … You don't seem …' She stops and there's a tiny part of me that wants to laugh at the puzzled expression on her face. I imagine telling her, the look of horror, and know I can't.

'I'm fine,' I say.

She cranes her head round, so I glimpse the sharp, clean bones at the nape of her neck. She's only been here once before, not long after I first moved in. She'd run away from Dewhurst that time too. It had felt so weird showing her the place, part of me feeling all grown up and oddly proud, another part feeling stupid, like I was pretending to be an adult. I realise now, the place still looks the same; I haven't exactly been busy decorating.

She gives a sigh. 'I wish I could get a flat.'

I know she means so that she can crack on with her version of Nia with no one to stop her. I want to tell her about the quiet, how empty it gets, but she wouldn't understand. Her mum would never kick her out anyway.

So we sit there in silence and looking at her folded up tight takes me back to the unit, to the circle of us all staring at the floor and each other, even though we weren't supposed to be looking.

Crap Things about the Unit, Number Four: Group Therapy

Ahhh, Group Therapy. Group Silence, mainly. All of us scrunched sideways in our chairs, backsides aching, knees rubbing against the wooden arms while the therapist tried to get us to talk about – or, worse, paint – our feelings. An hour's worth, three times a week.

I got to know the carpet in that wide cold room so well. I can see the flecks in it, pale yellow, like vomit, on a dreary blue, when I close my eyes.

Each day the same. The only things that changed were the residents and our relative sizes. The way we counted each other's bones, trying to work out who was winning that particular week. All the admissions were like that, right up until the last one.

Then Molly exploded on to the unit.

The first time in Group, she sat for about five minutes in the stillness, before jumping up and saying in that loud, posh voice of hers, 'Well, bugger this.'

Ellen, who was facilitating at the time, said something completely wanky, like, 'I'm hearing some anger from you, Molly.'

I happened to meet Molly's eyes at that moment, and we both burst out laughing, the sound of it so strange. It seemed to go on forever, that laugh, flinging itself from wall to wall until it infected everyone.

Even Laurel smiled, and I remember that smile so clearly, the wrinkles creasing her cheeks like an old woman. It was the first time I'd ever seen her do it, and at that point I'd known her at least a couple of months. And something about it made the laughter die in my throat and then tears were in my eyes and Molly looked at me like she really knew everything that was in my head. That look went on a long time, while Ellen blustered and the others fell silent. It seemed like the only thing in the world was Molly's eyes, green and shining.

'You miss her,' Laurel says.

God, how I do.

Chapter 7

16 WEEKS TO GO

I took Laurel back to the unit. They probably would've been knocking on my door before long anyway. We sat for a while and then she looked at me and said, 'Suppose I'd better …' And I said, 'Yeah.' And off we went, in a taxi which I knew they'd pay for at the other end.

I gave Laurel an awkward, arm's-length hug and told her to write to me – she's not allowed her laptop owing to a Pro-Ana website incident – and then kind of skulked in the back of the taxi while she slumped up to the door. It opened before she got there to reveal Felicity looking stern. Felicity said a few bits to Laurel then came over to pay the driver. She didn't look at me while she gave him the money to take me back and I thought I'd got away with it, but then she opened the back door and leaned in.

'You need to come to our sessions. Don't make me send the crisis team round,' she said.

I nodded and she seemed to know better than to push it.

Her eyes flicked to my stomach once, before she said, 'Thanks for bringing her back,' then shut the door quickly.

I was thinking about it all the way home – if that's the right word for the flat. Felicity looked worried, like always, but also a little bit triumphant, like she knew stuff about me.

I was also thinking I should speak to Mum and Dad, but that was all too complicated, so then I started to think about Molly's List.

I haven't looked at it for weeks, but I don't need to. I know everything on there.

Molly's List – Things to Do Before You Die

1. Lose virginity. It cannot be as big a deal as people make out and, seeing as I'm not going to be around to do it for myself, you'll have to do it for me.
2. Travel. Go somewhere. Go to the places no one wants to see. Anti-travel the world. You could start in Torquay – there's lots

of old people there and old people rock. They must be on to something. Get one of those vintage Victorian swimming costumes and go for a dip in the sea.

3. Adopt an animal from one of those rescue places and get a certificate. I'm thinking a baby giraffe – they might look funny, but they can see far (she drew a wobbly picture of a giraffe here).
4. Read more books – classics and all that. Read something you actually like and stop picking books at random. You do deserve to read stuff you want to, you know.
5. Fall in love. It doesn't matter if this is mutually exclusive to number one.
6. Change the world, because I know you can.
7. STAY OUT OF HOSPITAL.

I think about the list and how I've only done numbers one and seven so far, and I don't even remember the first one too well, considering I was pretty drunk at the time – and look how that worked out.

I wonder again what Molly was thinking when she wrote it. Did she really believe everything would be solved with a few words on a scrap of paper? But it's more than that. It's like she was casting a spell for how my life should go. Because the thing is … I'm still here. I'm demonstrably not in hospital, for better or worse, even if I'm not sure I've had anything to do with it. Sometimes I think it's only that sprinkling of words Molly left me, not even two hundred of them, keeping me here.

I'm mulling this over, when something outside my window catches my eye. Some numpty decided to decorate the outsides of the flats with window boxes when they were built. To be fair, some people do plant stuff in them: marigolds, herbs – who knows what kind – and that sort of thing. But I've never bothered. Except now there's a plant in a pot in one corner of mine. The breeze must have caught it, making bright red petals dance across the glass. I go over and almost have to shield my eyes from the mass of flowers in the window box next door, shaking crazily in the wind. I try to count how many there are, but the wind is too strong and the flowers blur into one blast of colour.

Did whoever planted them there run out of room and decide they may as well use my box too? Or is it a present for me? But who the hell would do that? Someone who doesn't mind stretching across a fairly decent-sized gap when they're eight floors up, for a start.

I lean forward a bit more, half my weight on the window handle, and then the window is caught by a gust and swings fully open. I swear, I nearly fall out. The ground seems to jump like a pogo stick and, for a second, I'm suspended, perilously close to tipping point. Then I manage to grab the window sill with my other hand and push myself back so hard I land in a heap on the floor. The window swings back and bangs shut, then out again, each thud in time with my heart, which has slowed right down. I'm used to it pausing for a bit, then speeding up, but it seems strange that in my fear it's fainter, not stronger and faster.

I realise I've got one hand doing little circles over the bump, which gives a tiny twitch, like the baby is saying, '*It's OK, I'm fine in here. But don't do it again, all right?*'

'All right,' I whisper back.

And I realise: I was afraid. I didn't want to fall.

That has to mean something, doesn't it?

A little later, I've made a plateful of chicken, broccoli, carrots – which I've overcooked – and some slightly-too-hard-boiled potatoes. Lots of anorexics are amazing cooks, but then I'm not your average anorexic. And I hate cooking. If I had my way, I'd be a spirit floating about, all mind, and do away with food altogether. Not really an option right now.

I've measured everything out and it contains the right balance of calories, protein, etc. I put it, with one of the awful build-up shakes, on the little fold-out table and sit in front of it, watching it go cold.

This might be harder than I thought.

The portion looks ridiculous. I'm used to big portions, from the unit, but not ones I've voluntarily shoved in front of myself. The chicken glistens greyly, and the broccoli is giving off a smell like stale farts. I never liked broccoli anyway. I cut everything up into little bits and decide I'll tackle it like taking a pill. I manage to get down half of it that way, barely chewing.

This shouldn't be a problem. I've done this so many times before.

I get some salt and add a tiny bit and put away another third. There's now one potato, one mushy floret of broccoli and a chunk of chicken on my plate.

I can do this.

I pick up my fork. Get a piece of chicken to my mouth. Put the fork back down again. The smell of it is making me heave.

I can't do this.

What now?

I start thinking about abortions and birth defects and what Mary said. I could leave the rest, but I haven't had enough, according to my numbers. I think about crying, but what good did that ever do anyone, to paraphrase Dad?

Then there's a tap at the door.

Saved by the knock. Probably Laurel again. She's going to be in so much trouble.

I shove the plate away.

I'm already saying, 'Seriously?' as I open the door.

But it isn't Laurel standing there. It's a boy I've never seen before in my life.

He looks a bit awkward and I realise that 'seriously' came out pretty loud.

'Sorry to bother you. I've just moved in next door and I thought I'd introduce myself.'

I stare at him. People do not knock on doors and introduce themselves around here. I glance over his shoulder down the deserted hallway and begin to close the door, but I don't quite shut it.

'And also ask if I can borrow a bit of milk? I tried the other neighbours, but, ah …' He raises wide hands palm out. He must be over six foot, broad-shouldered but skinny, with round geeky glasses.

Does he think I'm going to invite him in or something? I give him my best stare.

'I'm Robin,' he says, and holds out his hand like he's planning to shake mine, eyes up the size of the gap I'm peering through, then wipes his hand on his trousers instead.

I think about slamming the door or telling him to get lost, but I suddenly realise he must be the flower owner and, for some stupid reason, it makes me hesitate.

'Hedda,' I say back, then make my face frosty, so he doesn't come out with some comment about what an 'unusual' name I have, when really we'd both be thinking the word is more like 'stupid'.

To his credit, he doesn't blink.

'I just need a cup of tea. Can't drink it black,' he says, and there's an edge in his voice you only get when you're on your own and desperate for someone to talk to. He doesn't look like the usual type you get round here.

'Have you got a cup?' I say.

'Ummm,' he says.

We look at each other.

'I'll go and get one,' he says.

I shut the door and put the chain on, then go to the fridge, and a moment later he's back. I peer at him through the gap in the door and realise two things. First, he's much younger than I thought – at a guess I'd put him at nineteen maybe. Second, I don't think his cup is going to fit through the gap. He sees me looking and follows my train of thought.

'I'm totally nice, I promise,' he says.

'That's what they all say.'

Yep, all of the approximately three men I've had conversations with recently, including the bald bloke in the corner shop who calls me 'love' and looks at my (until recently) non-existent boobs.

Robin sets the cup down and backs up until he's a few paces away.

'You could sort of slosh it in?' he says.

'OK.' I take the chain off the door and crouch to pour milk into his cup.

I realise he's staring at the pen lines I measured out on the bottle. I don't actually know how much he needs, so I pour about half a pint in, in the end. When I straighten up, two things happen: I wince as my back twangs from where I fell backwards from the window, and then I have to hold on to the door frame because I came up stupidly fast and the dots are doing their funky chicken across my vision.

I tip my head forward and wait, and when everything clears and I look up, he's taken a couple of paces towards me and is hovering with an expression that suggests he's getting ready to make a grab for me if I go down. Which is sort of sweet. As long as he's not a psycho or something.

'There you go,' I say and, though my voice is firm, I can't find it in me to keep the hard edge to it.

'Thanks,' he says. I wait for him to say something else, check if I'm OK or prolong the conversation, but he only adds, 'I'll pay you back.'

I'm about to say 'no need', when I realise he's disappearing back into his flat.

I have a strong urge to call out, 'Wait!' I want to ask him

about the flowers. I want to grab hold of him and say, 'How old are you? Are you on your own? Why are you on your own? Are you lonely? Did you notice I'm pregnant? Do I look thin to you? How thin, exactly? Because, you know, I don't usually look like this …'

But I don't. I might have spent my formative years in the care of the NHS's finest psychiatric institutions, but I'm not a total loony yet.

At least, I don't think I am. How the hell would I know anyway?

Perhaps I could knock on his door, but I already know I can't. I sit back down and push the last chunk of chicken and slimy green broccoli on to my fork and force it down, sloshing a load of water after, like a chaser. Then I dump the plate in the sink and spend an age washing it up, drying and putting it away. It helps to shut out the Nia voice, which would normally be telling me things like *Fat, gross, greedy pig*. It's only partly successful. I can feel her there, brushing the back of my neck, our truce the most fragile of bubbles. Breakable.

Baby, I counter, and the little thing inside me gives a half-hearted jerk, then a larger one, like it's turning a slow somersault inside.

I'm twenty-four weeks pregnant today.

I guess it's time I told the parents.

Crap Things about the Unit, Number Five: Family Therapy

I don't even know how to start with the crappiness of this one. We had years of it, on and off. My parents tried to start with, and maybe even I did too, but by the time I'd hit my last admission it had all settled into a familiar pattern: Mum and Dad sitting there like two mannequins, so tired, so sick of trying to work out what was wrong with me. And Tammy, my thirteen-year-old sister, dragged along to the last few sessions under protest, furiously silent, her eyes too old for her body, just like her brain was – is. Me wishing I could disappear, preferably for good. Because I never knew what was wrong with me, not really.

And the Silence.

The Silence.

Silence.

But I guess I had something to do with that. Silence is the best weapon, I always say.

Chapter 8

15 WEEKS TO GO

'Hedda! This is a … surprise. Come in.' Mum opens the door wider and steps back to let me through, then casts a glance up over her shoulder, towards the stairs.

I've deliberately picked a time when Tammy is in school and Dad should be at work, but perhaps someone is home ill, or there's a teacher-training day or something.

'Just you home, is it?' I say, and I see Mum stiffen, try not to wince. I think I dumb down my accent to annoy her. It's childish, yeah. Sue me. It's also kind of funny. Plus, I need anything I can to put me on the front foot here, because it's not going to be pretty when I give her the news.

'Oh yes, Tamara won't be home until late. She has

orchestra. She's doing a cello solo. Bach.' Mum's cheeks take on an extra pink flush of pride underneath the layers of organic day cream, foundation and blusher. 'So you probably won't be able to see her today,' she adds, and there is a tiny hardening around her eyes (blue eyeshadow and eyeliner – not the best combo for her skin, truth be told).

'That's OK, it's you I wanted to talk to,' I say.

'Oh?' Mum's tone of polite interest also holds a little flutter of fear.

There's such a big space between us. Was it always there? I try to remember what it was like when I was little, before Nia started, but I can't, not really. Nia makes everything blurry. Maybe that's the point.

I follow Mum into the dining room, which has a different carpet, I see. It has that new carpet smell and hoover lines all over it. Mum owns a battalion of Hoovers: upright for main rooms, little Henry or Henrietta or whatever for the stairs, and a dustbusting handheld thingy for whipping away crumbs after meals.

I sit down at the table and run my fingers over the familiar wooden surface. It's the one thing in the house that never gets upgraded. When I look at it, I see the place where we'd have birthday teas and cake, friends from school gathered round to sing *Happy Birthday*, back before Nia. But overlaying those memories, like the slides you get in a microscope, are the years of sitting here for hours, mashing food down, while Mum sat with her arms folded, telling me I couldn't get up until I'd finished. And the times that followed, when I realised I could get up without finishing, so I just did. That last morning, before I fell down the stairs at college, when I never even bothered to sit opposite Tammy, in her usual place behind the cornflakes box, and pretend to eat. I remember how I told Mum I'd grab something at college, and the way she nodded and sank into one of the chairs; how she hadn't done her make-up that morning, like she was too tired to bother. Me walking out, smug and triumphant because I'd got away with missing breakfast again. It's all here, at this table, and I can't work out if the heaviness in my chest is homesickness or just memories reaching back towards me.

Mum is bustling about making coffee. She hands a cup to me, black, and I'm sort of touched, until I remember I probably shouldn't be drinking caffeine.

'So … how are you?' she says, and I can see she's bracing herself.

She darts a glance over me, trying to work out how much I weigh. I can't tell from her expression what the conclusion is, apart from that she doesn't look more worried than normal – and that worries me in turn. How big do I look through her eyes?

I lean back, my head resting on the top of one of the stupid high-backed dining-room chairs. They look like they should be in a sixty-foot banqueting hall or something, not a five-bed semi in Illester.

'Ah, good, thanks. I'm good. I'm pregnant, actually.'

Well, that's one way to do it. I didn't mean to blurt it out, but suddenly I realised I couldn't do the small-talk thing. Mum's expression is almost funny, like her brain is going way too fast, then spinning around on itself and finally stopping altogether.

'What?' she says eventually, and I know I've really shocked her this time because she always insists on 'pardon', like the wannabe middle-class person she is.

Come off it, Hedda.

I straighten my face. This isn't funny.

'I'm twenty-five weeks pregnant,' I say, making sure my voice is low and slower than usual.

A great flush suffuses Mum's face, reaching past her pencilled eyebrows and all the way into her highlights.

'You. Are. Joking.' Each word takes her a long time to get out.

'Nuh-uh,' I say. Then I spread my arms out, cock my head to one side and say, 'Surprise, Grandma!'

Mum's face goes redder still, and even I know I've gone too far this time.

Eventually, she pushes a hand against each cheek and says, 'I suppose it's too late to … ?'

'Yes, it's too late, and anyway, I don't want to,' I say, tipping my chin up.

Mum looks to the ceiling for a moment, then speaks, her voice bitter. 'Want. Yes, that's an appropriate word, coming from you. What you want. It is always what you want, or don't want, isn't it? I don't suppose there's a father involved at all?'

'One-night stand.' I give a defiant shrug. 'No idea what his name was.' I squeeze my hands together under the table as I speak, pushing fingertips down hard in the spaces between the tendons, straining to hang on to my 'I don't give a crap' face, until Mum closes her eyes.

'This … this is … I knew you were selfish before, but even I never thought …' She puts her head into her hands and I wonder whether she's crying.

I reach one hand towards her and let it fall on to the table. 'Come on, Mum,' I say, but then don't know what else to add.

She snaps her head back up. 'Do you have any idea – any idea at all – what you've done? How on earth do you think you can look after a baby? Just look at you!' She circles my wrist with her fingers, then lets it drop.

I make my face a mask.

Mum's eyes narrow. 'You could damage it, you know. What right do you have to do that to an innocent child?'

'I won't. I'm eating. The scans say it's fine. I have a meal plan,' I say, and I can hear my voice, high and defensive.

'And what about afterwards? You're going to raise a baby on your own in that grotty flat? You're nothing but a child yourself!'

I think about saying the grotty flat wasn't entirely my choice, seeing as she refused to have me home six months ago, owing to my Corrupting Influence on Tammy – sorry, Tamara – and all that. And that me being a 'child' never stopped her kicking me out. But I don't want a fight.

'I don't know. I thought … I'd get it adopted,' I say. She starts to say something but I cut over her. 'I can eat for it … I am eating for it. It will be fine.'

This seems to enrage her so much, she's lost the power of speech.

I sense that now may be the time to make my escape. I go to stand, but before I can, she jumps up herself and begins tearing through a cupboard. A moment later she slaps down a bar of chocolate on the table. I almost slam my chair back, like it's a giant tarantula, but aware of Mum watching me, I keep still.

'You're eating, are you? For the baby,' she says. 'Well, fine. Show me.'

She rips open the wrapper, breaks off four squares and pushes them towards me. 'Go ahead.'

We both stare. The squares seem to morph into something huge and ugly, taking up way more of the tablecloth than they actually do. I break one off and hold it between finger and thumb. Its texture is smooth, impossible. I bring it to my mouth and look Mum right in the eyes as I push it between my lips.

I don't let myself feel the way it begins to ooze in my mouth. It's in my teeth, under my tongue. I swallow a few times, to get it down, suddenly smacked in the gut with memories of gorging on Christmas chocolate, my stomach bulging, food pushing up past my chest.

I'm breathing hard, heart pounding. Another square is in my hand, but I can't do it. Nia won't let me. She punches through the truce wall, her shrieks like the strongest of winds howling around my head. I drop the chocolate, but it's already started to melt. How long was I holding it for, under Mum's gaze? It's coating my fingers, tacky and brown. I can't get it off.

I run for the bathroom and sluice my hand over and over, then, without meaning to, retch, noisily. Chocolate-streaked spit splats into the sink. I stay in there for a while.

When I emerge, Mum is on the other side of the door. She looks so sad.

'Hedda, please –'

'Don't,' I say.

I go for the front door and Mum's voice follows me out on to the street.

'You can't be selfish about this.'

I turn. 'I know that! It's not just my life any more, I get it. OK?'

Mum slumps against the door frame as I leave. 'It was never just your life you were affecting.'

So that went well.

I'm trying to get angry, to tell myself it's useless – of course she wouldn't understand, wouldn't be supportive. What did I expect? But I'm crying as I stumble back up the stairs to my flat. Not even silent tears. I fumble about with the keys but my eyes won't stop streaming, and I keep swiping at them with the back of my hand and making stupid little yelping noises as I try and keep the sobs in. Then I drop the keys and swear and suddenly I'm so tired, more exhausted than I can ever remember feeling – although that can't be true, surely? And the keys seem a million miles away, lying on the floor, the shiny heart keyring Molly gave me face down. There's a big scratch in the back of it that's going in and out of focus. The next thing, a large brown fist closes around them and I wipe my eyes again before looking up into Robin's face.

His look is a little concerned, a lot wary. He reaches across me and pushes the keys into the lock, then opens my door for me.

'Here you go. I suppose it's pointless to ask if you're all right?' he says.

I have no idea why I start laughing, but I do. Well, sob-laughing, the nasty heaving kind. I have to put my hands against the wall, I'm shaking so much.

Robin looks more than wary now – he looks positively alarmed, casting glances up and down the corridor. Eventually, he turns back to me and says, 'Come on.'

He pushes my door open a little more and steers me with a very light touch on the shoulder to the sofa, then pours a glass of water and hands it to me. 'You'd better drink this.'

I take it, spill some on the way to my mouth and wipe my chin with my sleeve.

The laughing has stopped now, thank God, but in its place is a deep mortification.

'Tissues?' he asks.

'Bathroom,' I manage to get out.

He comes back with a bog roll and drops it into my lap.

I give my nose a good blow, then take a few deep breaths and wonder for about the millionth time how in the world I've got myself into this situation.

'Right then,' he says, as though we've just had a long conversation. 'I'll be off.'

I blink a couple of times and it isn't until he's almost out of my flat that I manage to say, 'Hang on! I mean … do you want a cup of tea or something?'

'No, thanks. You take it steady.'

'Thank you,' I call after him.

I replay the conversation with Mum several times over dinner (more chicken). I'm with her on most points really. It's true – I am selfish. I don't know whether the selfish part is Nia or me or if that's even a distinction worth making. I feel the urge to cry welling up yet again, which is ridiculous. I don't do crying, haven't for ages. It's a talent of mine, to switch everything off – at least, it usually is. Maybe all the tears are some sort of pregnancy-related weirdness.

After I've forced my dinner down, I feel little rhythmic twitches coming above my hip bone: hiccups. Perhaps the baby likes chicken. Someone has to, surely. Then I start to wonder if the flavour crosses into the amniotic fluid and if the baby literally can taste it, which sets off a whole train of thoughts centred on bits of chicken fat congealing inside me, sticking there and never quite coming out. I think about my stomach getting bigger and bigger, blowing up, the rest of me following suit, and it fills me with horror.

Suddenly, I want this baby gone. I want Nia back. I want a world of white. Safe, silent, clean.

But it's too late now.

I take a while to calm down, but once I do, I give Mary the midwife a call.

'I want to know more about adoption,' I say.

Crap Things about the Unit, Number Six: the Other Patients

OK, so this one is sort of tricky. It's hard to explain what it was like, the relationships you develop with the people in there with you. The way you need them and sort of hate them. The way you really love them. The drama and intensity of it all as a handful of society's truly messed-up squeeze themselves into this artificial space and bond, like in that film *One Flew over the Cuckoo's Nest*, but on teenage hormones. How we were all so innocent. Sad, yeah, but innocent too. And then, all of a sudden, we weren't any more.

Chapter 9

12 WEEKS TO GO

I'm at the doctor's, waiting for my appointment with midwife Mary and a social worker I've not met before. I'm twenty-eight weeks pregnant today and it's definitely starting to show. I spend half my day sideways in front of the mirror, trying to suck it all in and make my stomach concave, like it should be, but it doesn't work. So, I put on the baggiest clothes I can find and try not to think about the chart in the kitchen where I mark off each meal.

252 to go. The number makes me go hot inside and I have to count my breaths to calm myself down. Tonight I'm planning the same thing I've had every night. It feels safer that way. Although I'm really, really starting to hate chicken. More than usual.

Mary put me right at the end of clinic hours so we'd have more time, but the waiting room still has at least three other pregnant women, all clutching their set of notes. I've remembered mine, as I'm trying to be non-selfish and adult and all that, but I've taken them out of their silly little folder and squashed them down in a ruck-sack. With my hoodie pulled over my stomach, I don't really look like I belong with the others. I hope.

I flick through a magazine, the type that puts big red circles around cellulite snapped from a mile away on the front cover. Next to a story about some B-list celeb's 'worrying' weight loss is an ad featuring a woman in a bikini with clean sliced hip bones and washboard abs pushing a buggy. I consider tearing the picture out, to rip into a million shreds or fold away for thinspiration, I'm not sure which.

To distract myself, I listen as two of the others strike up a conversation. The usual stuff I assume pregnant women talk about.

'When are you due?'

'February sixth.'

'Ah, not long to go.'

'Hope so. Can't wait. I'm having the largest glass of wine imaginable. In fact, I've told my partner he can bring a cool bag to the birthing centre.'

My ears prick up at that.

The wine lover is somewhere in her mid to late thirties at a guess, with a roundish face that has that outdoors look to it and acres of curls. The other woman almost reels back in shock, her mouth pinched tight, one hand clutched protectively over her, frankly, hippo-like bump.

'But what about the breastfeeding? Alcohol crosses over into breast milk, you know.' Her voice changes from judgemental to booming. 'Mica! Put that down!' She clicks her tongue. 'Heaven knows where it's been.'

I follow her gaze to where a toddler with a snotty nose is chewing on a board book. I have to admit, I'm sort of with judgy woman on this; it doesn't look hugely clean.

'Mica!'

Now the toddler is staring into the middle distance, licking the book. A bit of snot is inching down his lip. Judgy woman gives a huge, exaggerated huff and heaves into a standing position.

'Mica, what did I tell you?' she says, pulling the book away with a jerk.

Mica's little bogey face starts to crumple in on itself and a high-pitched whine forms at the back of his throat. Something tells me this is only the warm-up. He sucks in a big breath through his nose and snot blasts out in a scream. I practically have to duck. Eww.

Just then, there's a beep and judgy woman glances at the screen and picks up her enormous baby bag in one arm and the kicking toddler in the other, sitting them on either side of her bump, and marches down the corridor, ignoring the wails and thrashing. You've kind of got to admire it.

I lean back and let out my breath in a tiny sigh.

'Well. That's as good a contraceptive as I ever saw. Bit late for us though, I suppose,' says the curly-haired woman.

I look round, then realise she's speaking to me. My first thought is pure panic. *Do I look pregnant?*

OMGOMGOMG. I look pregnant. Or fat.

Or both.

She spots my mortified look and says, 'Oh gosh, sorry. I just assumed, since this is an antenatal clinic ...'

I manage to locate my tongue. 'No, that's OK. I am, you know ...' I do a gesture around my stomach area, then wonder if I should do the pregnant woman belly-rub thing, for emphasis. I feel like I'm on the stage, wondering what my lines should be.

'Thank God. That would've been a bit mortifying. Quinn – that's my partner by the way – always says you should never ask a woman when she's due, unless she's literally having contractions in front of you. I sometimes think he should have been the woman, not me. He'd be better at this pregnancy lark anyway. It's awful, isn't it?'

I make a strangled noise that comes out a bit like 'mm-huh'.

'Precisely.' She smiles a really nice, wide grin. 'I'm Lois – I know, I know. But what can you do?'

'Hedda,' I say, and she sits back, impressed.

'Like the play?'

I nod. My turn to be impressed now.

'Saw a production of that a few years back, at the Fringe, I think. It was atrocious.'

I grin this time. 'I've never seen it.'

'Wise choice. So, let's do the boring questions, shall we? Looks like we'll be here some time. When are you due? Boy or girl or surprise? Feeling OK? Relative merits of travel systems versus prams? Makes and models?'

I don't know how to answer. I'm wrong-footed by how nice she is; she's not giving me that sideways look I had off the receptionist, it seems like she simply wants to chat.

'I think I'm due in May sometime,' I say. 'And yes, it was a surprise.' I realise the second I've said it that it wasn't what she was asking, but her face softens in sympathy.

'A spring baby will be lovely,' she says, then rifles through her notes and pretends not to notice my sudden tears that well up out of nowhere.

Stupid pregnancy hormones. Again.

A door opens along the corridor and we hear poor Mica wailing as he's swept through by judgy woman, who gives Lois a nod and me a swift once-over before disappearing through the double doors.

A moment later, the beep goes and Lois stands up.

'That's me then. And the bump.' She gives her stomach a rueful sort of pat, then looks me dead in the eye. 'Do you think we're allowed to kill all those people who insist pregnancy is some sort of magical time?'

I get a sudden sense she's nearly as adrift as me. Then she slips a piece of paper into my hand and gives me that lovely wide smile again.

When she's gone, I open it to see she's scrawled her name and mobile number in what looks like eyeliner. I pop it in with my notes at the bottom of my bag.

When it's finally my turn, I realise I'm both nervous and hungry.

It's not always easy to tell, after all these years, but the vaguely regular meals seem to be setting my body up to expect more, which is a bit of a worry, if I'm going in for the understatement of the year.

I knock on the door, like Mum taught me, even though the midwife just pressed whatever button they press to summon you in, so I'm guessing she's expecting me.

Inside is Mary and a woman in her early twenties who I assume is the social worker. She's wearing social worker uniform, in any case: jeans, tunic top, boots, slightly harried look. My old one left a few weeks ago – not that she did much. She was pretty much just there to make sure I had a roof over my head and benefits set up, seeing as I'm not eighteen yet, and she had a habit of looking at her watch every time I opened my mouth.

Sitting next to new social worker lady is also … Felicity.

I sense an ambush.

'Oh. Hello,' I say.

'Hello, Hedda,' Felicity says.

We eye each other.

'Aren't you supposed to notify me or something before calling a case conference?' I say to Felicity, then glance sideways at the social worker, who gives me a direct look back.

'Would you like to sit down?' she says. 'I'm Joanna. I did send a letter to notify you that Felicity would be attending.' She rifles through some pages, no doubt trying to produce a copy. I have no expectation she will, but to my surprise, she finds the piece of paper and hands it over. I scan the words explaining that she'll be attending my appointment, has liaised with Dewhurst House (aka Junior Loonies) and feels it'll be beneficial if my key worker also attends and to contact her if I have any concerns etc., etc. …

'You've got the flat number wrong,' I say.

'Have I? Oh dear. I am sorry.' She pushes all the messy papers back into a large leather holder. 'But we're all here now, so would you object … ?' Joanna leaves it hanging, but I'm not looking at her any more.

I'm staring at Felicity, who has already looked me up and down. Her eyebrows twitch up ever so slightly.

'No. That's fine.' I turn on my best smile, which fools probably no one.

Mary clears her throat. 'So we thought perhaps we'd have a chat first and then we can do your usual appointment afterwards.'

'Fine by me. There's not a lot to say, is there? I just need you to tell me the process, what I need to sign.' I keep my expression business-like, upbeat. No room for doubts here.

'I'm not sure –' Mary says.

Just as Felicity says, 'Yes, let's go through it.'

There's a pause, and we all look at Joanna, who, I realise, has been taking everything in with sharp eyes. It's like a game of tennis, my eyes shooting from one face to another. All these people shuffling bits of paper, here because of me. For a while. Once, it might have made me feel powerful. Now? It just makes me tired.

'All right,' Joanna says.

She starts talking and I let the words wash over me. She goes through options like Mum and Dad having the baby – I give a short laugh at this – or foster care for me and the baby together, but I shake my head.

'I'm not interested in all that stuff. Why prolong anything? I just want it all sorted as fast as possible.'

Joanna finally gets on to adoption. It seems it's not as straightforward as I thought.

'Legally speaking, you can't give up the baby for adoption in the first six weeks,' she says.

I feel my spine straighten like someone's yanked me up by my hair. Six weeks! What the hell am I supposed to do with it for six whole weeks? What about college? I mean, it's not like I was going much – and truthfully, I've more or less stopped altogether in the last couple of weeks – but it'd be nice to have the option.

Joanna sees my expression. 'But the baby can be placed with the prospective adopter or foster parents directly after the birth.'

I sink back down, but only by a centimetre, because it's starting to dawn on me that I'm actually going to have to go through with the birth. I wonder if they could just put me to sleep for it and wake me up when it's all over and the baby's gone.

'OK,' I say. 'That sounds fine.'

'Hedda, I think you need to do some work on this,' Felicity says.

I restrain myself from rolling my eyes. I am not going over this adoption thing with Felicity. Far as I'm concerned, it's a done deal.

'I'll come to my next session, I promise,' I say, and I can hear the sulky note that's crept into my voice, like I'm twelve or something.

Mary wants to get on with the actual antenatal part of the appointment. As Joanna and Felicity leave, I sense her watching them with a faint air of disapproval. It lingers as she takes my blood pressure and weighs me.

I stand on the scales backwards out of habit.

'Good,' she says, and it takes a lot of willpower not to turn round and eyeball the numbers. *They're only numbers*, I try to tell myself. *And it's only for a few more weeks.*

As if there's any such thing as 'only numbers', Nia would say.

I get a sudden pang, like an echo coming from an empty room, and shake my head, try to focus on what Mary is saying.

'Could you hop up for me, luvvie?' she says, and I realise there's a lot more things she wants to say before I do, but she's only getting out a contraption she calls a doppler.

'We'll have a little listen,' she says as she presses it to my bump.

'Hang on,' I say, panic spiking through me because I'm remembering the scan and the woman trying to show me the Thing inside me, when the room suddenly fills with a sound like galloping horses. 'What the fu–' I break off.

'Your baby's heartbeat,' Mary says.

I can feel my own heart begin to race, until the room is filled with the two sounds, one interior, one exterior.

I should be saying 'stop it' or 'turn it off' or 'I don't want to hear it'.

Instead I hear myself say, 'Is it supposed to be so fast?' and my voice wobbles.

'It's fine. Everything is fine. We'll send you for a growth scan, and you need to go and see the obstetrician, but it all seems to be coming along nicely.'

'I … Just … Wow …' I get out.

That's a heartbeat. My baby's heartbeat. I mean, the baby's heartbeat.

All the way home, that galloping sounds in my head, over and over, steady and strong. Out of habit, I walk the long way round, to add another mile on to my journey. It's good to be out in the fresh air, away from the damp crawling up the walls of the flat.

I stop outside Mothercare and stare through the window. On impulse, I wander in and flick through a few rows of baby clothes. Everything is soft and cute and tiny. The lights are so bright they sting my eyes. I loiter by the prams, remembering Lois's quip about travel systems and buggies. I swear, some of them look like they're intended for wartime, with huge wheels and a million pieces that can click on and go this way and that. I lift the corner of one, experimentally, and can barely get it off the ground.

'Can I help? Are you looking for anything in particular? That one has an umbrella fold – handy if you have a small boot.'

I seriously have no response to this.

The salesgirl looks barely older than me. Could, in fact, be my age. I might even have gone to secondary school with her, on the few scattered weeks I was there. I haven't exactly kept in touch with anyone from school, unless we're counting the awkwardness at the smoking shelter with Sal. They did try. I have a box full of letters written out in gel pens and covered with silly doodles from Sal and Natalie, back when we were a trio in primary school. Natalie hung on longer than Sal in the end, if we're discounting that cigarette at college the other week. I haven't seen Sal since. Looks like I've given up smoking anyway – every time I've tried one, I feel sick as anything. Guess the baby's good for something – my own little nicotine patch. I imagine Molly laughing, saying, 'Well, I'm delighted you're quitting, but you could've chosen a less drastic course of action, you know.' My mouth gives a twitch.

The salesgirl's smile is looking a bit forced now, but it seems impossible to stop the marching thoughts. Once again, my hand hovers near my bump. Is it getting obvious?

'Did you want to try it out?' the girl says. I think she's speaking slower than she usually might to a customer.

I drop my hand and back away. 'No … no thanks.'

I leg it, out past the rows of toys and maternity clothes, the couples browsing with new possibilities in their eyes. This isn't my place. This could never be my place. I shove my head down and hurry for home.

Not long after I get in, there's a tap at my door. I recognise Robin's knock and this time I don't put the chain on before I open it.

'Hello!' I say. Too bright, overcompensating for the crying incident the other day.

He holds out a letter to me. An opened letter. 'This came for you –'

I snatch it and surprise myself with how loud my voice comes out. 'Had a good nosy, did you?' I pull the letter to me and glare at him.

He takes a quiet breath. 'What I meant to say was, I began opening it before I looked at it properly. I was waiting for … I stopped when I realised it wasn't for me.'

I look again at the letter and realise it's only half open. I feel my face get warm. 'Oh. Oh right, yeah. Well, thanks for that,' I say, knowing how lame I sound.

'You're welcome,' he says, and his voice isn't exactly cold, but it nearly is. He goes back into his flat.

I'm about to shut the door, but all of a sudden I feel like I have to talk to someone. Not therapy talk, or family talk, or unit talk with Laurel or whoever, but just with someone my age. Someone normal.

I hesitate for a while outside his door, then tap on it softly. It takes a minute for him to open up, and when he does he stands there, eyebrows raised.

'Hi-I'm-sorry-can-I-come-in?' I say in one big rush.

Smooth, I am.

If he's taken aback he doesn't show it. He holds my eyes, like he's reading what's going on in my head, then stands back and gestures for me to enter.

His flat is like mine and completely different. The layout is the same, but there's a smell of fresh paint, providing at least temporary cover for the mould and damp. I reckon he's painted it himself; there's quite a few splashes of blue on the ceiling where he's gone over the lines and a couple on a brightly striped rug on the floor. Most of the walls are covered in posters of films and stuff. No telly, but rows of books and DVDs and a laptop in the corner. I can see a stack of saucepans in the kitchen bit, two of them still wrapped in plastic. Actually, all his stuff looks brand new, like he stopped off at Ikea just before he moved in.

'Want a drink?' he says.

I have a look at his books and DVDs, my head turned to one side so I can read the titles while he boils the kettle. He has a lot of *Star Wars* stuff.

'You a big fan then?' I say.

He pokes his head out to where I have hold of a light-sabre that looks like it could be a prop from one of the actual films. Something tells me it cost a mint.

'Yeah. Well, the originals, not the prequels.' He says 'prequels' the same way you might say 'dog crap'.

'Haven't they done new ones?' I'm quite pleased I've dredged this up. I vaguely remember hearing some heated debate at college about female leads and someone called Rey, who I realised was a girl after it morphed into a discussion about feminism or something. I didn't exactly have anything to add. It happens like that sometimes, this gap between what other seventeen-year-olds talk about and the stuff I grew up with in Dewhurst, which was more along the lines of who was suicidal that day, or how it was so unfair because someone else had a lower target weight than me.

'Oh yeah, they have. I've heard great things, young padawan,' he says in this weird voice that I think is supposed to be Yoda or something.

'You haven't seen them?' Weird, given the amount of *Star Wars* crap he has knocking about.

He pauses, coffee spoon in the air, and says, 'Not the latest, no. I had, um, some stuff going on.'

Oh. Stuff. Well, that makes two of us then.

'I haven't seen it either. Can't say I'm too fussed,' I say.

He turns back to the cups. I stare at that lightsabre. We had A Boy on the unit during my last admission. They were sort of like the lesser spotted woodpecker of unit life and he left soon after I got there, but he did leave behind a *Star Wars* DVD that Molly made us watch when she arrived. I was still getting to know her then, but she wasn't bothered by my silence and sulks. That night, she yanked me up and made me do a pretend lightsabre duel with her until she'd got me laughing. I told myself afterwards that it had probably burned off a fair few extra calories, so that made it OK.

'Do you want to come and do your own milk? It's semi-skimmed,' Robin says.

He must have remembered the lines measuring my milk out from before. I'm about to go and do it, when something stops me.

'That's OK,' I say. But I can't resist adding, 'Just a splash will do. No sugar, thanks.' I put the lightsabre carefully back on top of the cupboard and wonder who exactly has one lying about. Does he duel with himself when he's on his own in here? And why *is* he on his own in here?

Robin comes in a moment later with tea with just a splash and hands it over. I take a scalding sip, and there's a funny feeling inside me, like the tiny click of a cog loosening. Coming up fast behind is a familiar crackle, like an electric shock, that comes with handing over control to someone else. I look for somewhere to put the tea, but I don't want to risk spilling it on the rug.

'I'm sorry again, about the letter. It was good of you to bring it over,' I say.

'No problem.'

'It's just ... Well, the thing is, it was about an appointment. At the antenatal clinic,' I say, then throw out my best stare.

'I thought so, the other day when you looked like you were about to faint,' he says. 'You had that look about you.'

'What, are you a doctor or something?' I say, only half teasing, but I've obviously asked the wrong question because his face closes down.

I scan his photos without being too obvious what I'm doing. There's a couple of girls in one, and another of a little boy with a cheeky smile which I assume is Robin. I can see the edge of his window-box flowers from where I'm sitting.

'Aren't you going to ask about the father?' I say.

'That's not really any of my business, is it?'

'S'pose not. There isn't one, anyway. Not that it matters. I'm putting it up for adoption, so I can get back to my life,' I say, sticking out my chin and trying to sound more definite than I feel. I have no idea why I'm saying all this to him. To shock him? To put him off me? Because even though we've barely exchanged twenty words, there's something about him I like.

Felicity thinks I play games to test people. Maybe I do. I like to be sure, that's all. And most of the time, what I'm sure of is that people will let you down so it's best to give them a push in that direction sooner rather than later. People are pretty predictable.

Robin has been staring at me while I'm thinking this. Not in a bad way, but in a curious, slightly detached way, like he's studying me.

'So, getting back to your life, huh? My grammy is always saying life is this rare, precious gift. That's why she loves orchids so much – they might be almost impossible to grow sometimes, but it's our job to try and make them flower anyway. Like life, I guess.' He pauses, rubs at his head all embarrassed, then looks back at me. 'What are you planning to do with yours then, after?'

I think about this, can't decide if I like it or if it's just more positive-thinking BS, like in the cuckoo's nest – I mean the unit. It rings different somehow. I only have one plan for after: Nia. But I can hardly tell him that.

'Oh, you know ...' I say, smiling.

But he doesn't return it. He looks serious.

'I'll make it up when I get there,' I say. Not sure what possessed me to say that. 'What about you?'

A shadow seems to pass over his face. 'I'm making it up too,' he says.

'Fair enough.'

We reach for our drinks at the same time.

'Um ... How long have you lived here?' he asks.

'Few months.'

'You're pretty young to be living on your own,' he says.

'Look who's talking.'

He nods a bit, as if to say, 'Point taken'. 'Do you like it here?'

I laugh, then stop when I realise he really wants to know. 'Didn't exactly have much choice. My mum didn't want me back home this time, after … Well, you can't blame her really.'

'Can't you?'

I think about this. 'It's funny. My mum kicked me out a few months ago – well, said I couldn't come back home, which is the same thing really. I suppose it wasn't exactly a surprise. I mean, I've been pushing her all these years, and I guess sooner or later she was going to give up. Actually, I don't know why I said it's funny. Unless it's cos the joke's on me.'

'Why? It's not like it's totally your fault you're in … this situation. Unless it was an Immaculate Conception,' Robin says, then drops his eyes and rubs the back of his neck.

I pause for a moment, then say, 'It's not … I'm an Anorexic, you see.'

He seems to think about this for a second, but he doesn't look shocked, or make one of those horrible half sympathetic, half curious faces. 'My little sister's friend had that for a while. She's all right now though.'

'Good for her,' I mutter. I lift up my chin. 'Anyway, I'm not one at this precise moment. I'm having a little holiday on account of this.' I waft my hand at my stomach.

'Huh,' he says.

'Huh? What does that mean? Like I said, I'm not keeping it or anything. I'm just ... babysitting.' I start to smile, but Robin frowns. 'I wouldn't know what to do with it, would I?' I add.

Robin is silent, his eyes seeming to stare right through the wall over my shoulder, like he's remembering something he'd rather not. Well, we've all been there, I guess.

'So what about you? What's your story?' I say.

Forget my usual policy of ask nothing, give away even less – I actually want to know how come he's living here by himself, whether he's scared too. Maybe I need to fill the silence the truce seems to have left. But it's more than that. He seems ... kind. And I guess it's sort of OK to have someone to talk to who has nothing to do with, you know, Nia, units. Or whatever. Probably it's the stupid baby hormones making me go soft and blurry round the edges.

I definitely catch it this time; a raw pain that twists at his mouth.

'I suppose ...' He brings his attention back from whatever place it's been and looks at me properly. 'Well, similar to yours really. Difference of opinion with my parents. Not really reconcilable. I left before they threw me out, but then ...' He puffs up his cheeks like a hamster then lets the air out like he's getting rid of something. 'Never mind. I'll tell you another time.'

I raise an eyebrow. 'Must've been some difference for you to wind up here.'

'Yeah. If you want to know the truth, I can't go back, for reasons I won't bore you with, but this was the only place I could afford. Just about. They're not exactly paying well at Aldi.'

'You're working at Aldi?' I start to laugh again.

'What's wrong with that? You get a staff discount,' he says, and he's half smiling and half hurt.

'Nothing, nothing,' I say, but I'm properly smiling now and so is he.

We kind of grin at each other for a bit and then I realise it's probably time to bring this little whatever-it-is to an end. I don't even know the guy and I'm still not entirely sure why I decided to barge into his flat and then share a load of majorly personal information about myself. I like him though.

I stand up. 'Thanks for the tea.'

'Any time. I mean that.'

'Oh, and thanks for the flowers,' I say at the door.

Robin inclines his head and smiles.

Crap Things about the Unit, Number Seven: How Terrifying It Was

I don't think I want to explain this one.

Chapter 10

11 WEEKS TO GO

I like to find out stuff. It's a curse of mine. The internet should be banned for people like me.

The day after my talk with Robin, I'm out doing circuits of the estate, just to clear my head, though I keep tabs on the number of steps. I spent far too long looking at stories about adoption. I read about girls like me, who got pregnant by accident and had their babies adopted. Some of them seem all right, good even, say they made the right choice. But there are others too. Ones who feel like something huge was ripped away from them and now they're left with nothing but a great, aching hole, made up of guilt and longing and all the things they've missed and will never find again. Even the older ones who got back in contact with their kids, once the kids were old enough, are sort of messed up. But maybe I'm just reading the wrong stories.

I tried switching to stories written by children who were adopted, but that wasn't much better. They stuck in my mind, like porridge scrapings on the side of a bowl, gluey and rough. I've sat in front of a few cold bowls of porridge in my time. On one memorable day, dinner showed up when I was still making my way through the morning's snack. Fun times.

Now I've read them though, I can't pull them back out of my head. I really want one of those things that can wipe out memories, like in this film Molly showed me once, *Eternal Sunshine* something-something – I can't remember the full title. Clearly I only have a good memory for the crappy stuff.

I do another circuit of the estate. It's almost time to start walking up to the clinic for my appointment with Felicity – I'm actually going, so things must be dire – when I see her coming up the road on the opposite side. I call her the Walking Woman.

I almost cross over, to say hello or something, but chicken out at the last minute. Doesn't stop me wondering, as always, about who she is.

This is what I think about her:

I see her circling the roads on the estate. Maybe in her seventies, but I don't know. Dandelion hair. Slacks that hang, well, slackly, on sticks. Or thick tights bunched under a straight skirt. She hunches forward, back humped, walking with her chin leading, like a chicken pecking, stiff-legged. Sometimes she has carrier bags dangling from her minuscule arms. I imagine them containing tinned tomatoes and spam and laxatives.

She's there in all weathers, just walking.

I noticed her not long after I moved to the Yewlings and, since I have, she's everywhere. Her eyes are focused on something inside, intent, determined. Impossible to break through.

But I know who she is. She's Nia. Perhaps she's been Nia forever. The thought horrifies me, even as I marvel at those legs which are too small to hold her up and admire her determination.

One day, I think the Walking Woman will die, right there on the side of the road. Her heart will falter and stop. Nothing else will break her.

I see her, in dreams, always walking.

Sometimes I think she might be me.

* * *

So, yeah. Kind of gloomy thoughts, I suppose. I'm almost at the unit now anyway, so I try and tear my brain away from the Walking Woman and focus on what I'm going to say to Felicity. She's running late, as usual, but I don't mind. If I'm lucky it means less time for me.

I put my head down as I go past the inpatient part of the unit. There are a couple of girls outside smoking, their fingers all bone. I don't know them, and the thought sends my heart fluttering. I'm moving away from unit life, out here in the cold, looking in.

I itch for a fag suddenly, but I'm not giving in to that. This baby's got enough to contend with without being addicted to nicotine from birth into the bargain.

I let Felicity weigh me. I've put on, she tells me, sounding surprised. I fight conflicting urges to smile smugly and say, 'See?' and to wrench the chart out of her hand so I can get a look at the number. I'm obviously keeping an eye on things, but the unit scales are the 'proper' scales.

Felicity finishes writing in the notes and swivels to face me. 'So … how are you?'

'OK,' I say, and I know from the way it comes out that this is going to be one of those sessions.

Felicity senses it too; her face tightens around the lips and she fights her eyebrows back up into neutral position.

A couple of minutes go by.

'You know what, screw it,' I say. 'I'm not OK. I think … I think I've messed up. Like, more than normal, I mean.'

Felicity makes an encouraging noise and tries not to look as surprised as I feel that I'm breaking the Rules and actually talking rather than my usual tricks of staring into the distance as she waits with varying degrees of patience or talking about stupid things, deflecting all her careful questions and insights. And sometimes – OK, maybe more than sometimes – I shout. Hurl whatever I can think of that might insult her. Try to make her hate me.

I never said anything about being a good person.

Today, though, I'm giving it straight and for some reason I can't seem to stop.

'I've been reading all these stories about adoption and I guess it's like … the shock's worn off, right? And now I'm starting to realise that … that …' Bloody hell, I'm welling up here.

This must be the first time Felicity has had to use the ever-present box of tissues with me. She hands them over slowly, like I'm a bird she's trying not to scare away.

I blow my nose and continue in a flatter voice, trying to keep it all controlled, but I have this unbearable urge to talk for once, to get the thoughts out of my head. 'I realised I've done something … what's that word? Irrevocable. Not just for me, but for … you know.' I nod down at my bump, which is now starting to put some strain on the hoodie. 'Like, there's someone else affected by all this now and I feel … I guess I feel guilty.'

'Mmm …' A Felicity Silence ensues.

I'm not saying any more.

Except, somehow, I am.

'I went and saw Mum, told her the news. And she was furious. She called me selfish. And she said something about –' I break off and try to remember what Mum said.

Felicity leans forward in her chair.

'That was it – something about it never being just me that this affected. And I know that's true. I knew it before – I really did. But now I guess I'm feeling it.'

Felicity opens her mouth and there's this light in her eyes I haven't seen before. It's a mixture of excitement and hope and, for a second, I feel like bony fingers are digging into my heart, because she thinks we're having some sort of Breakthrough or at least A Moment.

I've said too much.

I give a forced laugh. 'Must be those pregnancy hormones. Or maybe the baby is like in that film – what was its name? – where because the baby can feel stuff, so can I, you know? Like a personal fuzzy-feeling factory. I'm not saying I'm worried. Once it's out …' Now I really do need to shut up.

Felicity stares at me, then sits back suddenly. 'Normal service will be resumed, I suppose?' I've never heard her sound so icy.

'Something like that.' It's supposed to come out defiant, but I'm flushing.

'Mmm.'

More silence. This time, I'm the one who's uncomfortable. Felicity watches me watch the clock tick down the last few minutes of our session, getting myself back under control.

When it's time to go, I give as bright a smile as I can muster and say, 'See you next week!'

I stand up and walk out before she can say anything more, but somehow it doesn't feel like the victory it usually does.

And on the way home, Molly is at my shoulder, keeping me company.

Crap Things about the Unit, Number Eight: Your Best Friend Dying in Front of You

Molly. After the first day in Group when she swore and we laughed, we spent pretty much all the free time we had together, which in hospital is quite a lot. Meals and school and Group take up only so many hours in the day, even for those of us who know how to spin out a bowl of soup.

Molly was bulimic. The worst kind. I might have learned quite a few food disposal tricks from her, looking back.

The thing is, though, hospital wasn't always crappy. It's never as straightforward as that. Molly was bulimic and messed up, sure, but she also had the most brilliant laugh I've ever heard and could do amazing impressions of people. Mainly the staff – the consultants loved that. I'm lying – they didn't, obviously – but we all did.

And she could play the saxophone, like she should have been a professional jazz player, and she had a ridiculously flamboyant fashion sense, all layers and even hats. I know that makes her sound deeply weird, but it worked on Molly. She was just herself, gave exactly no craps what anyone thought. You wouldn't have known anything was wrong with her unless you knew where to look. Her make-up was always perfect, and if she was pale – well, we all were. Her pale was the interesting rather than the yellowy grey variety.

Molly made the list for me not that long before she died. Sometimes I wonder whether she knew what was coming. She was strange like that, even if she did take the mick out of the hippie staff – the ones who liked to waft crystals and mindfulness about along with their positive affirmations. I don't really believe in spirits or whatever, but I swear this is true – she'd make stuff happen. In the evenings, when we played board games (seriously, we did – Scrabble being a particular favourite), if there was a dice she'd whisper the number she wanted out loud before she rolled and nine times out of ten she got what she wanted.

Maybe it was coincidence. Probably it was. Or that thing where you only notice the stuff that proves your theory – confirmation bias, according to Google. But I'm not convinced. She had an air about her, like she wasn't quite in this world, is all I'm saying. Plus she always, always kicked my butt at Snakes and Ladders.

Anyway, we'd been talking one night, standing together looking out of the window at the moon, and she'd come up with the idea of a list. And I didn't realise what she was trying to say.

She had a heart attack and died in the bathroom with the rest of us watching as the nurses tried to revive her.

I found the list under my pillow later the same day.

Chapter 11

10 WEEKS TO GO

When I said Molly was at my shoulder the other day, I didn't mean literally, of course. I don't really believe in ghosts or any of that stuff. But I do sometimes get a sense of her, a faint presence, like she's not really gone – she's still here, watching over me. I wonder what she would have said about the baby, but I think I kind of know. She would have laughed her head off, that's for sure.

She also seems to have an interest in Robin, for some reason, or at least I sense her somewhere in the air when I see him. Maybe she thinks I should get to know him. We've bumped into each other in the hallway a couple of times and once I almost invited him in, but he looked like he was off out somewhere. He has a nice smile, I think, but he's so quiet. I never hear anything coming from his flat, not like the sketchy bloke the other side who was playing music until the early hours again last night.

I've been out today, just walking. Originally, I thought I might go to college, but my feet veered away and I kept going until I ended up not far from Dewhurst House. I stayed round the corner though, the unit just out of sight. I imagined the staff inside preparing snack, the smooth gloss of the table, each knot of grainy wood encased in a clear plastic shell.

I take a slightly different and shorter route home, avoiding the town centre and cutting up a bike path that stretches past rows of well-kept terraces set back in one of the nicer parts of town. They have long back gardens and a Victorian air about them, with gables and bay windows. When I was little I wanted a bay window, with a window seat and curtains, so I could read books in my own little nook. I liked all the ballet series the best. Sometimes I wonder if Nia started because I wanted to be like one of those dancers. Poetry on legs, floating. An artist, not a normal person. Maybe that's why I don't trust books any more, at least the ones I used to like. Or maybe it's all just another big skinny excuse.

I keep looking at the houses as I pass, and notice one has a cute little home-made stall out the front with a sign that looks like it's been done by a young child. *Vejetables 20p*, it reads in felt tip over a table stacked with twisted carrots and muddy potatoes.

I stop and look in my purse. I've got just under a quid in change so I grab a bunch of carrots and three potatoes and put the money in the butterfly money box.

There's a box of eggs too, but I don't know how much they are. I wonder if they've got chickens in their back garden.

A woman comes out of the house and smiles at me.

'Do you want to take these too?' she says, pointing at the eggs. 'We have more than we know what to do with.'

'I'm out of change,' I say with an apologetic smile.

I swing my rucksack on. The straps are digging in a bit and I shift, trying to get it comfy. The bag pulls at my hoodie, stretching it tight over my stomach.

'When are you due?' the woman asks.

'May sixteenth,' I say.

'Oh, lovely. Boy or girl?'

'Girl,' I find myself saying, though I don't have any positive confirmation of this. At the last growth scan the sonographer asked if I wanted to know and I said yes, but the baby wasn't cooperating. Still, I think she's a she. I know she's a she, somehow.

The woman smiles. 'Girls are the best. A handful, mind, once they get to school. The cliques! You forget what it's like at that age.'

I wonder what she'd say if I mentioned I'll never see the baby go to school, or have to deal with ironing uniforms and wonky spelling. Apart from my own spelling, that is. I content myself with a polite smile.

'Have you thought of any names?' the woman asks.

'Not yet.' The new parents will probably change it anyway. But the woman's face is so expectant, I say, 'I thought maybe Molly.' I can almost hear Molly at my shoulder laughing and saying, '*No way! Why would you want to saddle a poor child with that name?*'

'That's a beautiful name,' the woman says.

A shout floats out from the house.

'That's one of mine,' the woman says. 'Take care.' She turns to go, then moves back and hands me the box of eggs. 'No charge. I'll slip another pound in, in case Kayleigh notices. She can't write wonderfully yet, but she can most certainly count. They're freshly laid today. You look like you need feeding up.'

I take the eggs, though it's been an age since I've had one and they are not on the meal plan.

'Thanks,' I say.

I carry them carefully all the way home – there's

no room for them in the rucksack – and set them on the floor while I look for my key, which I finally locate after emptying most of the contents of the rucksack on the floor.

'Need a hand with that?' Robin has appeared from nowhere up the corridor and I jump back, nearly squashing the eggs in the process. Which would solve one dilemma, because I'm not sure I can eat them.

He stoops to pick up the bunch of carrots while I get the door open, then goes back before I can stop him for the rest of my stuff.

'Where do you want these?' He's holding the eggs.

'Anywhere's fine,' I say. 'Some woman just gave them to me. Turns out there's perks to being pregnant after all. I don't know what to do with them.'

'Omelette?' Robin says after a long pause. I must look blank because he adds, 'You do know how to cook one, don't you?'

'Why, do you?'

'Well, Google does. How hard can it be, anyway?' He gets out his phone.

I really don't know where to start with that. How do I explain exactly how hard eggs are, in my world?

Robin scrolls through a few pages, then puts the phone down.

'Right, here we go,' he says, giving me this confident look. He's totally faking it. He actually starts rolling his sleeves up. It's sweet. 'Where's your frying pan?'

'I don't have one,' I say. It's not like I'm going to be frying anything any time soon.

'That's all right, I've got one.' He consults his phone again. 'Butter? Herbs?'

I shake my head. 'I've got salt.' I nod to the side where a big bag of table salt that split when I opened it is sitting in one of the two bowls I own.

'Wait there.'

Robin goes out with his phone and comes back carrying an armful of stuff which I eye warily. It looks like an awful lot of ingredients for an omelette. Plus it's not on the meal plan.

'I got all this from work,' he says. 'I didn't really know what to do with it, but now I do. It's time for Operation Omelette.'

He stands to attention and out of nowhere a tiny laugh escapes through my lips and floats off towards Nia on the ceiling. Nia is not impressed.

'You should sit down. Should you be walking about with that giant rucksack anyway?'

'Sorry, what year are we in? Cos for a second I thought it was 1950,' I say, but I do sit down.

I hate to admit it, but I am tired. Maybe I walked too far today, and that's a sentence I never thought I'd think.

Robin mutters to himself, bending his head over his phone. I close my eyes and open them again when I hear the sound of an egg hitting the floor, closely followed by a hiss and the smell of burning butter.

'Damn,' Robin says.

'Need a hand?'

'No, you rest,' he says, doing his best to channel Mr Confident, although he looks a tad wild-eyed.

There's that tiny smile fighting to get out again, so I shut my eyes and let him get on with it.

Before I know it, Robin is waking me with a gentle press of his hand on my shoulder.

'Dinner is served,' he says. 'Oh, and you snore.'

'I so do not!'

He gives me a smirk, then says, 'Voilà!' and sweeps his hand towards the table, which has two plates on it. He looks very, very pleased with himself.

I sit in front of an omelette made with what appears to be twenty eggs. And red and green stuff. Robin's omelette looks a little singed, but all in all I have to admit with a sinking heart that it's probably edible.

'What's in it?' I say, narrowing my eyes at the plate, like it might jump up and peck me.

'Eggs, butter, tomatoes, basil, cheese. My blood, sweat and tears. OK, I made up the last part.' He shoves a big forkful into his mouth and chews. 'Lovely, if I do say so myself.'

I stare at my plate. I'm telling myself it doesn't matter if it isn't in the meal plan, that this was a nice thing for Robin to do, and anyway Nia and I are On A Break (we watched a lot of ancient *Friends* reruns on the unit; Laurel was a bit obsessed though we all knew it was because of the way Monica kept getting skinnier and skinnier), but none of this is helping me to actually move my hands. My heartbeat has sped up and the baby seems to sense it because she starts partying, kicking the hell out of my stomach just above my hip bone. It really hurts.

'Oof,' I say. I put my hand there and feel a tiny, sharp lump. I think it might be a foot. The room swoops for a moment.

'Are you OK?' Robin gets up and comes over.

'Yeah,' I get out. 'It's kicking, is all.'

I've taken off the hoodie and my vest top is stretched tight over my bump. He looks down and we both see the bump move.

'Ohmigod,' I say. It's like the scene out of *Alien*. Any minute now something is going to burst out of a hole in my side and scuttle off. I can almost see Nia, like dark smoke on the ceiling, recoil.

Then Robin says, 'Can I?' and – before I can say, 'Can you what?' – he places a hand really gently on my stomach.

The baby goes still.

I go still.

Then it moves again and he grins.

'Wow! I felt that. You've got a strong one in there, I reckon.'

'Yeah,' I say faintly.

Robin goes back to his seat and picks up his fork again. The baby twists inside me, like she's telling me to hurry up and eat already and it's this thought, that perhaps what the baby really, really needs right now is eggs and tomato and basil and whatever else it was, that makes me pick up my own fork and push a tiny mouthful past my lips.

It's really nice. No, that's a lie. It's amazing. I take another bite and suddenly this hunger takes over me and I start to shovel it in. The plateful is gone in three minutes flat and I take a long drink.

Robin finishes his up, but – wisely, I think – doesn't comment on how fast I got through mine.

What's going on?

I remember Molly, when she was on the rampage, grabbing food and forcing it down without pausing to chew or even breathe, the panicked look on her face and the relief when she'd finished and got rid of it. My stomach feels hard and swollen, uncomfortable.

Did I just *binge*? Was that what it was? I've never done it before. Been sick, sure, but never because of a binge. And I was always really proud of that. Secretly, when the others talked about it in tortured whispers, I'd stay smugly quiet, secure in my control. Unwavering. Nia was never like that for me, until now.

Felicity's face pops into my head and I know what she'd say: that eating a normal plate of food does not equal bingeing. Still, the strongest urge to run to the bathroom and get rid of it all washes over me, but then something else happens: another urge fights back. For a while, two impulses battle in my head, Nia and … who? Nia's been part of me for so long; we've always wanted the same things. So who is arguing back? Who's been arguing back all these weeks? My head feels like it's going to burst, and in desperation I look at Robin, who reaches one hand across the table, as if to take hold of mine, then thinks better of it.

'Talk to me,' I say. 'I need a distraction.'

'About what?'

'I don't know. Anything. Please, just anything.' I whisper the last part.

So he talks. He tells me about his job at Aldi, how he's applying for everything going that might vaguely pay the bills and doesn't involve endless shelf-stacking. About how he's fed up with ready meals and toast and how he's going to learn to cook. Gradually, the panicky feelings begin to die down and I can focus on what he says.

He stops and looks more closely at me. 'You back with me now?'

I nod. 'I'm sorry. I'm not really used to … I usually stick to the meal plan.'

'I saw,' he says, and I follow his gaze to the kitchenette, where a colour-coded chart is pinned to the wall, an open notebook underneath it listing everything I eat and drink, calorie content, weight in the morning, mid-morning, after lunch, after dinner, at bedtime.

Suddenly, I take in the flat through his eyes. The absence of anything on the walls, the bare floors. The lack of soul. And I feel shame in every single part of my body, right down to my toes.

It's not a comfortable feeling – understatement of the year – and I shift about, as though I can shake it off if I move fast enough.

'How come you planted the flowers?' I say, because it's better to say something than sit here feeling like this.

'My grammy loves gardening. My parents were out working a lot when I was little and Grammy – she's my dad's mum – she used to look after me and my sister. She'd make us do the weeding, water the plants, pot them up, that sort of thing.'

'I didn't know you had a sister. Older or younger?'

'Younger. She's finishing her GCSEs.'

I remember there were two little girls in the pictures on his wall.

'Just the one sister?' I say.

'What about you? Any brothers or sisters?' he says quickly.

I remember what he said about leaving before his parents could kick him out. I guess he doesn't want to talk about it, which is fine by me. I should know better than most about having stuff you'd rather not say out loud.

Instead, I think about Tammy, and an image comes to me, hazy like it's reaching through layers of dirty glass: Mum, holding this tiny bundle, smiling down at it; and weaker still, this twisted feeling, all wrong and bitter and shameful.

Today seems to be the day for feelings, like I'm on a fair-ground ride except there's no one to press a button and make it stop. Traces of omelette and tomato still linger in my nostrils and at the back of my tongue and again I fight the urge to run and dispose of it.

'Yes, one little sister. Tammy. Or Tamara, as Mum insists we call her.'

'What's she like?'

'Gifted and Talented,' I say, my voice short.

'Ah.'

'Well, I guess after me, Mum and Dad deserved a better version.' I try and laugh, but it's not my most successful attempt.

'Wow. That's harsh.'

I pull off a shrug. 'It's true. I'm not exactly winning Daughter of the Year any time soon.'

'But Tammy is?'

'I s'pose so. I haven't seen her for a while. Mum is worried I might be A Corrupting Influence.'

'She told you that?'

'Good as.' I sigh. 'The thing about Tammy is, she was always the golden one. I think she just came out right, you know? When she started school …' I stop to remember. 'Tammy started Infants a few years after me and right from the beginning she was just amazing. She could already read and write and she was good at everything. Literally everything. She was put straight into a Year One class – I remember Mum going on and on about how Gifted she was even before she got put in the official Gifted and Talented scheme thing. She always found it so easy to make friends; there would always be party-bag stuff, you know, like those crappy plastic maze games, all over the house from all the birthdays she'd been to.' Unlike me, I don't add, seeing as I don't want to seem like a complete sad case. I had friends, obviously – well, Sal and Natalie – but not like Tammy. I look up at Robin and add the kicker. '*And* she was Mary in the nativity play and sang a solo. I remember watching her in the audience. There's still a framed picture of her up on stage in her little blue scarf.'

Robin is smiling. 'What were you?'

'A sheep, obviously.'

He starts to laugh and I manage to smile too, but then my grin fades.

'Anyway, the awesomeness continues and Mum doesn't want me upsetting her. Let's just say they weren't too happy they had to cart Tammy in for Family Therapy at the unit last time I was an inpatient. I told Felicity – she's my key worker – it was a bad idea.'

'Was it?'

'You could say that. Anyway, they're all probably better off without me.'

'You really think that?' he says.

'I don't know. Sometimes.'

He dips his chin, closes his eyes for longer than a blink should be. When he looks back up, I'm caught by the expression in his brown eyes, warm and glittering with something I don't understand.

'And what about the baby?' he says. 'Do you think it's going to be better off without you too?' He's giving me this intense stare, not like he's judging my choices, but like he really needs to know the answer.

I find I have to look away. 'Bloody hell. That's ... pretty personal. But ... yeah, I think that. It needs proper parents, people who are OK, who can look after it.'

'How do you know you can't?'

I've had enough now. I jump up and start clearing the plates, then bang them about in the sink. Robin stands next to me and dries, but doesn't ask me any more questions. I tell him about the woman with the eggs and her slightly mercenary daughter, which makes him laugh, and he tells me some stories about when his sister was little and sneaked downstairs one night and got caught eating sugar directly from the bag. Somewhere in it all, the over-full feeling begins to fade and, by the time I say goodnight to Robin, I realise two things: I had fun and I no longer feel like throwing up.

Crap Things about the Unit, Number Nine: Crochet Madness

The crochet thing was Molly's idea.

'We've got to do something otherwise it really is going to be the cuckoo's nest in here,' she said.

Did I mention I stole the *One Flew over the Cuckoo's Nest* thing from Molly (who got it from someone else, I expect)? She wouldn't have minded me using it – she was generous like that.

Anyway, Molly decided that, seeing as half the unit was on bed rest and/or being tube-fed or only let out in wheelchairs, perhaps the rest of us ought to do something other than trying to burn off calories and smuggling anorexia memoirs in and out of each other's rooms when we thought no one was looking. So she taught everyone how to crochet.

We were all rubbish, naturally. But Molly's stuff was just beautiful. She made this gorgeous pink poncho and when she saw how much I liked it she gave it to me and made another for herself and then anyone else who wanted one and soon most of us were going round in crochet ponchos, like a uniform or something. I still have that poncho in a box somewhere under my bed.

Actually, I liked crochet. I sort of thought I might crochet something for the baby to wear when it goes to its new parents.

Chapter 12

8 WEEKS TO GO

Something weird starts to happen after Omelette Gate. When Robin said he wanted to learn to cook, he meant it. And I'm starting to realise that when Robin has a project, he really goes for it. He begins showing up with all this stuff he's got from work that he 'accidentally' has too much of, asking me to help him with a new recipe. It's like he's appointed himself as some sort of Head Chef-Coach. I'm not stupid; I know what he's doing. What I don't get is why.

A lot of the time, I want him to go away. There are days I won't answer my door, but I watch him through the spyhole. He waits for ages in his dorky uniform, always looking hopeful, until I tiptoe back to my meal plan.

Sometimes though, I let him in.

He does most of the cooking to start with, but after one too many 'helpful' comments from me, he decides I have to be his sous-chef. He picks up this handheld food-chopping gadget from Aldi which you have to whack really hard and we take it in turns to pulverise an onion. I quite like that session, until the guy next door hammers on the wall and then we chop a bit quieter.

There are one or two disasters – soufflé turned out to be a challenge way, way too far – but most of it is more or less fit for human consumption. Some of it's even nice.

As the cooking sessions go on, I realise I'm starting to save up little things to tell him, stuff I get off the net or from the random books I grab from the to-be-shelved section in the library. Like the fact that elephants are pregnant for 680 days.

'And I think I have it rough,' I say. Then I add, 'Apparently it's because they need to be super brainy when they're born so they can use their trunk properly and stuff.'

Robin smiles, but I interrupt him before he can speak, 'And did you know polar bears have to put on four hundred pounds when they're pregnant? Four hundred! Maybe it's not so bad being a person after all ...' I trail off and he gives me this funny half-pat on the shoulder and an even funnier look.

* * *

One day, he cooks some chicken and rice and serves me out a half-portion which is mainly salad. I eat a few leaves, ignoring the dressing on the table. Robin waves a massive forkful in the air.

'Go on, try it. I made a *marinade*.' He says this like he's just turned lead into gold.

I put a piece on my fork, have second thoughts and cut it in half, then rest the fork on my plate.

'What's in it?' I say.

'Tomatoes, some spices.'

'Really?' I look at the chicken again and my heart goes quicker. I wish it would beat like a normal person's. The baby boots me one in the ribs.

'That's all, cross my heart,' he says.

He starts eating again and I slide the chicken off my fork and slip it under a piece of lettuce. Robin doesn't notice.

I jump up and clear the plates when he's finished, and my leftovers go straight in the bin under the sink before he can clock how much I've had.

Nia gives a tiny, triumphant nod from her corner of the room, but she doesn't say anything.

'Do you fancy going somewhere sometime?' Robin says from right behind me. He's light on his feet, I'll give him that.

I push the cupboard door shut on the bin and turn in one movement.

Robin's eyes flick to the empty plate in my hand.

'Like where?' I say.

'Cinema? Bowling? I don't know. Thought you might want to get out of the flat,' he says.

I smile before I can help it, then switch it off fast. I don't want him getting any ideas. 'That might be nice,' I say. 'Sometime. You should get off – I'll do the washing-up. And thanks for dinner.'

When Robin goes, I weigh myself and check my meal plan. There's a nagging feeling inside, like when you're in school and you know you haven't done your homework. I try and push it away but it floats in the air, while Nia hovers somewhere behind, like a boxer squaring up to an invisible opponent.

I realise I don't like tricking Robin. It makes me feel small, somehow.

Never mind that, I say to myself. *Things are going* OK. Sure, the bump has become unavoidable and I can hardly bear to look at it in the mirror, but I'm doing it, just about, this thing no one thought I could. Only a few more weeks now.

I reach round to pinch my bum and the backs of my thighs, then, to be sure, get out a tape measure. Only my stomach is allowed to get bigger. The numbers wrap around me like steadying hands, telling me it's OK. And I do like seeing Robin, even Robin bearing food. I like the way his eyes crinkle up when he smiles, for one thing. And he's funny too.

I'm not happy, exactly, but things seem a little lighter. Though that could be down to spring being on its way and things being, you know, actually lighter.

I exist like this for two weeks. I go to a session with Felicity and manage to talk about my experiment with the Dark Side, aka Cooking With Robin. I even try to make some sort of Princess Leia analogy – I think Robin must be rubbing off on me.

But she frowns and says, 'Still planning to resume normal service after the birth, I take it?'

'Well, I'm halfway now. Only eight weeks to go. That's …' I stop to do a calculation in my head. 'One hundred and sixty-eight meals.'

Felicity gives me A Look. 'Mmm.'

'What?' I say.

'It sounds to me like you're playing games, Hedda. Are you still counting everything?'

'Yeah. So? Why not?'

'Because you know that you use numbers as a crutch. They're your safety net. A habit. One you need to break.'

'Everyone does it. Everyone counts stuff.'

'We're not talking about everyone.'

Felicity clearly wants it every way, and call it pregnancy hormones and general knackeredness or me being me, but I sit up straighter and glare.

'Oh come on. Let's take you, for example.' I ignore her warning look, her mouth that's about to open and issue the word 'boundaries', and keep going. 'You've got two teenagers, right? I bet you're counting down the days until they move out – either cos you want them gone or you can't bear for them to leave. Or maybe both.'

Felicity flinches, and I think, *Bullseye*.

'And your two weeks in the sun – I bet you know how many weeks you've got left until you fly out to – hang on, let me guess – Kos?'

'Hedda, this is not –'

'And you definitely count down the minutes until the end of our sessions, don't you?'

Felicity's cheeks go ever so slightly pink and I sit back. But it doesn't make me feel any better. The reverse, actually.

I sigh and speak more softly. 'Anyway, I thought you'd be happy I'm eating. I mean, I didn't expect you to get out the balloons and party poppers, but still ...'

She sighs too. 'I am happy you're eating. But I'm

concerned about what will happen after the birth. Has the situation become … firmer?'

This question is because I may have sort of missed an appointment, or two, with Joanna the Social Worker.

I don't answer, but when I get in from my session with Felicity there's a message on my phone.

'Hello, Hedda. It's Joanna. I'm a little concerned I haven't heard from you. I'm phoning to let you know I've identified a prospective match for the baby. We can proceed, if all goes well, to arrange for the baby to be placed with them immediately after the birth. They're a lovely couple. Please call me back. If I don't hear from you, I'll pop over next week.'

But I don't want to speak to Joanna about it yet. I need to research … what? I don't know. It's just that suddenly I have this urge to get all the facts lined up in rows, to understand the weight of them.

I go online and spend an hour watching, fascinated, the video diary of an Ana woman who also happens to be pregnant. Even though she's about eight months gone, she's still really, really thin. In the video posted a few weeks after the baby is born she's lost all the baby weight and looks like a model. Cheekbones I'd give a lot for.

That night, I lie in bed and listen to my breaths coming short and panicky, the baby wriggling like a fish over and over in my stomach so I can't sleep. I pinch my thighs, my upper arms. If I stay busy enough, I can keep her quiet in the day, but in my dreams, Nia screams at me: *Fat, fat, fat.*

I spend the morning getting on and off the scales and the number gives me a cold, sick feeling. I try and try to remember this is for the baby, not me, but Nia is having none of it. I turn the long mirror in my bedroom to face the wall and cover the one in the bathroom with a towel. I shower as fast as I can and try not to look down, but at night I can't avoid it. I'm getting big.

After the scales incident, I walk the long way to town and go to the charity shop. I close my nose against the musty old-lady smell and grab some leggings and more long baggy T-shirts. I don't try them on. Mirrors make my heart clench so hard I worry it might stop altogether.

I put the clothes on the counter to pay and wait for the inevitable question.

'When are you due?' The woman behind the counter smiles as she hands me my change.

'May,' I say. Then I add before she can get in first, 'Not long to go!'

A woman with a huge bag of toys clicks her tongue as I turn to go. She glares at my bump and pushes past, so the hard plastic edge of one toy scrapes along my side. I shrink back, one hand going instinctively to my stomach, too surprised to call her out. I hear her mumble something about 'scroungers' as I walk out of the shop, and have to work hard to hold my head steady.

On the way home, I catch sight of myself in a shop window. I'm expanding, out of control, like all those elastic bands I've wrapped myself so tightly in are pinging off in all directions and I'm leaking out, fat and greedy. Even my tummy button has popped out and it feels so weird and soft compared to the rest of me. I can barely touch it.

At my obstetrician appointment I get weighed and I sneak a look at the number, which is edging towards a figure that features in my nightmares.

It's for the baby. I can still go back in a few weeks' time.

Nia is unconvinced. I feel her sitting on my shoulder, like a bird of prey, as I step off the scales.

'You've gone a little pale. Feeling OK?' the obstetrician asks.

I don't tell her how afraid I am.

The baby though – she's happy. And she is a she.

I have a growth scan during my appointment. I lie there watching the baby dancing about inside and her heartbeat flashing in the dark.

The sonographer says, 'I'm almost certain it's a girl,

though these things are never one hundred per cent guaranteed.'

And I think, *I knew it, I knew it, I knew it.*

A baby girl.

But whose baby girl?

A few weeks ago it all seemed so simple, but I'm not so sure any more.

One day when I get home from a day wandering aimlessly round town, someone's waiting for me in the hallway. It isn't Robin. It's someone I wasn't sure I'd even see again.

Dad, with Mum more or less hiding behind him.

I stand there looking at them for a ridiculously long time, before opening up the door and saying, 'Er, hi. Come in?'

Dad comes in first, still in his suit from work. He does something in insurance in the City, has done since I can remember, which involves stupidly long hours, a ninety-minute commute each way, lots of time working weekends and trips abroad. If I counted all the time we've spent in one room together since I was born it probably wouldn't add up to much.

'Hello, darling,' he says and kisses me on the cheek. 'You're looking really well.'

This is code for 'You've put on weight'.

I suck in my breath like he's socked me in the gut.

Mum shoots him a venomous look, then turns to me and I realise she's super tired under all her make-up. Nervous too, if her hands twitching at her oversized necklace are anything to go by. Then I remember what happened the last time I saw her.

'Tea or coffee?' I say in a voice that's pretty flinty.

'Coffee please,' Dad says.

Just as Mum says, 'Pot of tea?'

'One coffee and one tea coming right up. I don't have a pot. Or a cafetière.' I don't apologise for this.

While the kettle boils, I watch Mum and Dad take in the flat. Only Dad has seen it once before, when I first moved in. I daren't look at Mum's face, because I know what she'll think of the place. Dad's bushy eyebrows are frowning and he narrows his eyes at the mould speckling the top corners. I think he mutters something like 'Damn disgrace' as I stir in his sugar, but Mum shushes him.

'You could do something to brighten the place up a bit. Some proper curtains,' she says and motions towards the old sheets I've pinned up over the windows.

'No money,' I say and push a cup of tea into her hand.

They give each other a look and I try and work out what it means.

Dad clears his throat. 'We wanted to talk to you, about this baby business. You see, your mother thought …' he glances at Mum, 'we thought … well. Mum tells me you're thinking about adoption. And we're not sure we agree with that. We're still your family and –'

'Are you?' I say.

'Yes, we are, whether you like it or not.' Dad rarely raises his voice so that shuts me up.

Mum, I notice, isn't looking at me or him, but at some invisible spot high up on the wall. I get the impression she's holding her breath. Her hands are stiff by her sides.

Dad plants his feet further apart and leans forward in his I Mean Business position. 'We think you ought to consider letting your mother … us … raise the baby.'

I can't speak for a second, and Dad pushes on. 'It's our grandchild and it's not right for it to go to strangers.'

'She,' I say.

'Pardon?'

'She. The baby's a she. And I'm curious. Is this something you've both decided, or just you, Mum?'

Dad hesitates, then when Mum gives him a look, he says, 'It's our decision. Both of us.'

I sit back on the little fold-up chair; there's not enough room for us all on the sofa. 'See, I don't think so.'

'It's ridiculous to think of you here alone in this flat

with a baby,' Mum says in a burst. 'You need to –' She clamps her lips back together.

'We want you to come home, darling. You and the baby,' Dad says.

'What about Tammy? Aren't you worried about how this affects her?' I don't try particularly hard to keep the sarcasm out of my voice.

'Tamara will understand,' Dad says.

Out of the corner of my eye, I see Mum shift.

A sudden pain shoots through me, right in the chest, and I let out a little noise.

'What is it? Hedda?' Mum says and she comes over to me. I see the worry in her eyes, and it makes the pain worse.

'It's nothing. Some heartburn,' I say. I stand up. 'Thank you. For coming, and for what you said. I'll … think about it.'

They know me well enough not to argue.

But on the way out, Dad pushes a cheque into my hands. 'Call me any time if you need anything,' he says.

When they're gone, I unfold it. It's for £500. Perhaps I could get a buggy after all.

Crap Things about the Unit, Number Ten: Family Therapy, Mark Two

I'm cheating. This one was already on the list. But now I keep thinking about one session in particular, the last one we had before Mum decided it was all too much for poor Tammy, just before I got out the last time. Looking back, I think that's when Mum made her decision. Tammy or me. And we know who she chose: the daughter who wasn't a lost cause.

Felicity had been harping on yet again, trying to get us all to open up about Feelings and Family Dynamics and The Function My Anorexia Performed, and how that needed to change when I got home, when I really didn't see the point. As far as I was concerned, crap happened, and I was the way I was because, well, just because. That's all.

That day, I'd barely made it into the room because only a week before it had been the night of the List, when Molly and I looked at the moon and had one of those conversations that happens on a unit, that comes out of nowhere.

'I can't wait to get out of here,' Molly said.

'Mmm, yeah.'

She turned and looked me full in the face. 'You sound so sincere.'

I'd never heard her like that, not when talking to me.

'What do you mean?'

Molly looked back at the moon, which was huge and low in the sky, no clouds to obscure our view. 'You know, sometimes I think you like it in here.'

'No I don't!'

'Oh, not the eating bit. Just ... it's different in here, isn't it? No school, no worries about exams and what to do with our lives. All the people fussing around after us, telling us to eat, taking us on day trips.'

'What, like the aquarium?'

Molly laughed. The aquarium had been the brainchild of one of the support workers. It had all gone quite well until Charlotte, an anorexic originally from Newcastle – they send you all over the country to wherever there's a bed so she hadn't seen her family for weeks – suddenly decided the turtles reminded her of her little brother and she was homesick, and she pitched a complete fit. We got some stares from the other visitors as she wailed, leaning back in her wheelchair, us surrounding her in our ponchos and the staff flapping about.

'Yeah, that was a bundle of laughs,' I said.

Molly bit down the side of one nail, really short. It must have hurt but she didn't show it. She'd cut holes in the wrists of her sleeves to poke her thumbs through, but I knew what they were hiding: rows of cuts crossing each other like scores on a chopping board.

'Seriously, you know what I think? I think you're in here because you're scared.'

'Whatever,' I said, starting to laugh, but then stopping when I saw she was serious. 'What, are you, like, Felicity now or something?'

'It's not a game, Hedda!' Molly said and her pale face flushed a deep red. 'You could die, you know. You will, soon probably, if you don't sort yourself out.'

'So what?'

'So what?! You're worth more than that! That's what. Just look at you.'

I have to admit, I wasn't looking my best. I was actually near the unit's target weight, but I'd come down with a chest infection I couldn't seem to shift and all the coughing had left me exhausted.

Molly went on. 'You're far nicer than you let on, Hed. Don't you want to get out of here and do something?'

'Like what?'

'I don't know! Anything. What do you want to do?'

I opened my mouth to reply, and then realised I didn't know.

'It's not too late for you. You can have an amazing life filled with ... with ... oh, I don't know, all kinds of wonderful things. Are you really going to spend the rest of it in places like this?'

'Well, what about you?'

'We're not talking about me.' Her voice was flat, a locked safe. There was no way I was ever getting in, not on any terms but hers. I loved her anyway – I couldn't help it. 'Don't you want to know who you are? Or who you might turn out to be?' she said.

Trouble was, I didn't have a clue who I was, apart from Nia.

'Come on, there must be something. One thing you want to do,' she said. 'Have you ever wanted to travel? See the Pyramids or something?'

'Hadn't really thought about it,' I said, and I knew then from the hurt look she turned on me that it was a mistake using the I-don't-give-a-damn voice I normally reserved for my sessions with Felicity.

'Well, start thinking,' Molly said. She turned to me and gave me a hug.

I put my arms up and hugged her back and we clung on like that for a while, me knowing she was feeling my spine and the back of my ribcage.

'I'll start you off,' she said. 'I'll make a list. That way, you'll have to do stuff when I'm not here any more.'

Molly said things like that quite a lot, so I didn't pay as much attention as I should have. I didn't know I'd be watching her heart stop in the bathroom the next day.

So, at that Family Therapy session, with Molly dead, I was upset, I suppose. OK, I was raging. And I know it wasn't Mum's fault, but somehow what happened was Felicity asked some question and Mum gave some crappy non-answer, and I looked her right in the eye and said, 'Why did you call me Hedda?'

'I beg your pardon?' Mum said, notching up her accent to

something approaching the Queen's, which was her go-to defensive manoeuvre.

'You heard. I'm serious, I want to know. You could've called me Kate or Helen or Jane, or any boring name at all, but you didn't. You stuck me with Hedda and I want to know why.'

Dad wriggled in his suit – he was itching to head off and get his train to work, I could tell – and said, 'Well, we've told you before. Your mother and I met at a student play –'

'Yeah, I know that. You bumped into her at the bar in the interval and the rest is history, blah-di-blah. Though, by the way, ditching your girlfriend to go off with Mum was really classy. If you want my opinion.' No one did, obviously.

Dad was pretending he was somewhere far away.

Mum was white.

I carried on anyway. 'And I know the play was *Hedda Gabler*. But seriously, did you even watch the fucking thing?'

'Hedda.' Felicity's voice held a warning.

Tammy sat quiet, her eyes fixed on the carpet, a thumb plugged into her mouth like she was three or something.

Me though? I was on a roll. 'Cos I've read it. Hedda hates her life. She hates being married. She shoots herself in the head at the end. And I'm wondering why would a mum choose that name for her daughter? Unless maybe you think *you're* Hedda.'

'That's –' Mum began.

'I think you're like her. I think you hate not having a career and spending all your time polishing the stupid display cabinet and filling up the freezer. I think you hate it all, just as much as I do, except –'

I broke off there, because Mum was already on her feet. She didn't look at me, but at Felicity. 'These sessions are not doing my daughter any good. I think it's pointless to continue.' By 'my daughter', Mum was definitely not referring to me. 'Come on, Tamara.'

And the next moment they were heading out of the room, Tammy giving me a triumphant little smirk around her thumb.

Dad looked a bit shell-shocked, but after a few blustering words he followed them out.

'Well, that was fun,' I said in as sarcastic a voice as I could muster.

Usually, Felicity would've called me out on that, told me I was using humour as a defence mechanism or something, and I would've argued back. But after Molly's death, I don't think either of us had the heart for it.

Instead she looked at me and said, 'Hmmm.'

But there was none of the usual thoughtfulness or annoyance or whatever in Felicity's voice. She just sounded sad.

Chapter 13

6 WEEKS TO GO

'Do you want to chop this onion?' Robin says.

We're cooking again, this time a curry made from scratch, an open *Cooking for Dummies* type book on the counter. Robin has bought himself an actual mortar and pestle. I didn't know real people use those, thought it was something only chefs on telly do. He's giving something a good whack and I glance at the wall, worried about the neighbours.

It smells really good.

Nia hisses a warning in my ear.

I start chopping, but after a while Robin looks over and says, 'Bit finer.'

'You want to do it?' I say, gesturing a little too close to his chest with the knife.

He backs away and pretends to cower in the corner. 'On second thoughts, those are perfect, thank you.'

My eyes are starting to water from the onions so I go through to the living area and open a window. The flowers are still going strong in the window box, all reds and oranges. Even mine. Robin's told me when to water them – in the evening so the sun doesn't frazzle them – and, unbelievably, I haven't killed them yet.

'I love these, you know,' I call back to where he's stirring at the stove.

'The flowers? Me too. My grammy's always saying you've got to have colour about.'

I think about what Mum said, about the curtains.

'I don't really know how to decorate,' I say later, at the rickety little table.

Robin sits back in his chair and says, 'I could help you paint if you like?'

I remember the splashes of paint on his ceiling.

'Really?' I say. 'Maybe not blue though.'

I'm still eating. I've managed about a third, which is fair going, I guess. In what direction, I'm not sure. Nia seems to have grown wings again and is circling my head. I take one more mouthful, and know that's all I can do. Anyway, I think my mouth needs about six pints of water to cool it down.

The baby is moshing inside, like she can't wait to get out. More fool her.

I press my hand down on my stomach, hard. *Stop that*, I think. *It's your bloody fault anyway.* Cos blaming a baby for my own stupidity is obviously a sane option.

'Sure, why not? I'd like to help,' Robin says.

When I realise what he's going on about, I say, 'OK. Thanks.' Even though I suspect it's going to take more than a splash of paint to make this place look like anything other than a dump.

'You're not going to eat any more?' Robin says.

I shake my head. The food feels like it's wedged at the back of my throat. I shift about, but leaning forward makes it worse.

'DVD?' Robin says. 'I think it's about time you watched the first one.'

This is because I might have let slip that the DVD we watched in the unit that time was *The Empire Strikes Back* and I've never actually seen the others.

An hour later, I finally stop tapping my feet and settle back to watch.

When the film finishes, Robin turns to me. 'Well?'

'Ah …'

His face falls. 'You didn't like it?'

'No, no, I did. It was very … spacey.'

'Spacey? That's it?'

'Who was the old guy again?'

'Obi-Wan. Hang on – you weren't paying attention, were you?'

'Sorry … I was a bit distracted.'

Robin shakes his head, but he's smiling.

We go into town the following day and choose paint, curtains and a rug from a big discount shop. I insist on white paint because it's the cheapest, but Robin makes me buy a bright sunflower print too.

We spend the rest of the morning splashing paint on the walls. It speckles our hair and our shoulders. Then Robin gets out the new drill he bought and gives a serial-killer chuckle as he presses the button to make it go, wiggling his eyebrows so I can't help it and start to laugh.

Several attempts and approximately fourteen 'trial' holes later, the curtains and picture are up, if slightly wonky. The whole place seems cleaner, less depressing. The sun is out and it glances off the freshly white walls. I give the window a wipe, half an eye on the curtain pole in case it crashes down on top of my head, but it stays put.

If you look out past the park and the estate you can see the edges of trees and hills in the distance, sharp and green in the sunlight. I put my hands to my eyes and make a little frame, so I can pretend I'm actually living out in the countryside, not several floors up in a tower block.

Robin rolls the rug out, which is a bright blue with tiny cream squares in it. My back is starting to ache and there's a nagging, grinding pain low down in my pelvis when I walk, but I'm used to things hurting. I still put my hand to my back though.

'Here. Do you mind?' Robin stands behind me and pushes his thumbs into the small of my back.

I yelp, because it hurts, but he says, 'Relax,' and continues pushing and circling with his hands.

Slowly, the pain eases off and I turn and give him a grateful smile. We stare at each other.

'Why are you being so nice to me?' I say. I don't ask it suspiciously or sarcastically. I just really want to know.

'Because you need help and I like you, and I can,' Robin says back.

'I don't need anyone feeling sorry for me,' I say.

'Who said I did?'

But his face tells me different, and just like that, the good feelings melt away. I hear echoes of Felicity's voice, remember the expression on her face when she said I was becoming a career anorexic. Maybe I do push people away from me, stop them getting close.

I think about the notebook where I've been keeping a list of all the crap things about the unit, shoved in a cabinet by my bed. When I started writing it, in those silent, scary weeks I was first here, I didn't think I'd make it. I thought my own list would help me remember. Help me keep my promise to Molly to stay out, or something. I don't know. But the more I write, the more I wonder. Was hospital all bad? Not always, no. Not always.

When Robin leaves, I look at the Ana videos again and weigh myself. Then I read more adoption stories on the net and try and think about what I'm going to do and realise I really don't know. But the insistent movement of the baby is a constant reminder I can't put things off forever.

I pick up the phone and dial Joanna's number.

We meet the following day in a Starbucks in town. It was my idea to meet somewhere neutral, away from Joanna's office or my flat. Luckily the place is pretty quiet as it's a weekday.

Joanna's tunic and jeans combo is still intact.

She buys a cup of herbal tea and I try hard to keep the smirk from showing on my face. Why do social workers always drink herbal tea? It smells pretty nice though and I decide I'll have one too, which is a mistake because it does not taste the way it smells. I push it to one side.

'So ...' Joanna says. She has a big bag with her but hasn't pulled out any notes, thank goodness.

'So,' I say.

Joanna waits and the silence stretches on forever.

I don't know how to start so, in the end, I say, 'I don't know how to start.'

Joanna nods.

This is excruciating. Worse than Felicity sessions.

'I think I might have changed my mind,' I blurt out.

Joanna puts down her cup carefully. 'Go on,' she says.

'Maybe ... maybe ... I don't know. I don't feel sure of anything any more,' I say. 'My parents came to visit me the other week. They were talking about adopting the baby themselves. My dad said it was his idea too, but then he's not the one who's going to be looking after it, is he? They said I should come home.'

'That could be an option. What do you think?' Joanna says.

'I think it wouldn't work. Mum doesn't really want me there. And I can't see how a baby is going to make things easier between us.'

'I can't make the decision for you, Hedda. But you need to know that my paramount concern is for the welfare of the baby. Keeping it is a potential option, but I would need to know that you're capable of parenting well. Do you think that you can?'

'Honestly? I don't know. What does good parenting mean anyway? What does it look like?' I'm talking more to myself than her.

There's a pause.

Joanna breathes on her cup of tea and waits.

'Maybe I should meet this couple,' I say. 'It might help me make up my mind.'

'That may not be the best option at this stage,' she says.

'Why not?' My voice comes out with an edge of panic.

'Does that worry you?'

'Well, yeah. I need to know more about … I need to be in –' I stop. Control. I was about to say 'in control'. Ever since I found out about the baby, everything has been out of control. And I want it back.

We finish up our meeting with nothing decided, except that raw panic seems to be growing as fast as the baby is. I feel further away from a decision than I ever have, and I'm running out of time.

I have my first antenatal class to go to after I meet with Joanna. I'm not exactly looking forward to it. I have a suspicion it'll be full of proud bumps and dads-to-be all giving me that look that says I shouldn't be there. That unlike theirs, my bump is a massive screw-up.

My life seems to be one round of appointments. Guess it is a career of sorts.

I sit in the room with the other pregnant women, the only one there without a partner, and think about all the people involved in my life: social worker, therapist, midwife, obstetrician. Mum and Dad. Robin. Laurel and Molly. But circling them all like a fortress is Nia. For all that there's actual people in my life, Nia is the only one in this room with me right now, even if I've got no one to blame for that but myself.

Two rows down from me is a girl about my age, sitting with a woman I assume is her mum. Guess I'm not the only screw-up after all. They put their heads together and laugh over something on the girl's phone.

The baby pushes against my ribs, and I lean to one side, bracing my hand on the empty seat next to me.

The antenatal class is possibly one of the most terrifying things I've experienced. The midwife passes round tools they might use for an 'assisted delivery' and the forceps look like something they used in the Dark Ages. For torture. One woman goes white. Her partner helps her from the room.

Another asks about natural birth. I stare at her like she's mad, but everyone else is nodding intently. One of them is taking notes, like squeezing a humongous baby out of an impossible space is an exam and she's determined to get an A*.

The woman who nearly passed out waddles back in and I stare at her. I mean, I'm assuming the rest of the people in here (if we discount the girl with her mum) actually planned this. You've gotta wonder why they're looking so shell-shocked now.

I tune out during the breastfeeding talk; there's no way I'm doing that.

On the way out, there's another group coming in, all trying to manoeuvre their shiny new buggies around each other and causing a pile-up. One woman sits cross-legged on the floor, pulls her top down to reveal a massive, veiny boob and shoves her baby on to it. It's like a car crash you can't stop watching.

'Hello again!' It takes me a second to place the woman with curly hair, because she looks like she's aged about ten years, but then I remember Lois from the doctor's waiting room. I'd meant to text her but didn't really know what to say. She's holding a tiny scrunched-up baby in one arm like she's been doing it forever.

'This is Ethan,' she says and her face softens and seems at once even older and kind of luminous as she looks down at him.

'He's lovely,' I say, although this is not, precisely, the truth. He's sort of squished together, with his legs folded up and a bright red face.

Before I can say anything, another woman, with perfectly straightened hair, manicured nails and an ugly-as-hell baby, has said hello to Lois.

Lois smiles back, but it looks forced to me.

'Is he good for you? Sleeping much yet?' the woman says.

Lois makes a non-committal noise.

The woman goes on. 'Chloe did ten to seven last night, didn't you, darling?' She smiles at her baldy baby.

Lois hangs on to her own smile, barely, and I see the tiniest of smug looks flick over the other woman's face. She hasn't bothered to even glance in my direction.

'I really need the loo. Could you hold him for me?' Lois says in my ear and, before I can think of an excuse, she shoves Ethan into my arms and disappears.

I freeze. Ethan wriggles, and I tighten my grip, trying to work out what to do. He opens up his eyes and they're really bright, like he knows stuff. He definitely knows I'm not his mum because his little face squashes up and he opens his mouth to reveal very pink gums – and yells.

Oh no.

'Shh-shh,' I say and try and rock him a bit, but that

seems to annoy him even more. He's wriggling now, arms flung to the side. I'm convinced I'm about to drop him.

'Oh dear, what's all this fuss now?' Lois reappears, scoops Ethan up and holds him high on her shoulder, patting him on the back. He quietens down.

'Sorry,' I say. 'I'm not really that good with … I never held one before. A baby, I mean.'

I've flushed a deep red, but I'm also itching to get out of there, to run far away. One of those *Star Wars* spaceship thingies would be nice.

Why did I think I could look after a baby? I can't even hold one properly.

The women all start to file into the new class.

Lois gives me a half-wave and says, 'Good luck! See you on the other side.' Then she drops her voice and comes right up to me. 'I know it's a pain when people give you advice, but if you want some from me: take the epidural.'

After the antenatal class, having a gigantic needle shoved in your back doesn't sound all that bad to me, if it means you don't have to feel anything afterwards.

'I was planning to,' I say faintly as she disappears.

Shame you don't get an epidural for life.

Unless you count Nia, I suppose.

Crap Things about the Unit, Number Eleven: Leaving

In hospital, you pretty much live on a day-to-day basis. You spend your time moaning about your portion being too big, your target weight too high. Gossiping about how annoying the staff are, or which one fancies which. You go to Group and school. You see your shrink once a week and gripe about Family Therapy. You pull tricks to rig the system and pretend your weight is higher than it is. It's a whole world, one you know.

And then you hit your target weight and it's time to leave and suddenly there's a different world out there and you're supposed to be in it and have plans and stuff, when really all you can think about is how to get safe again. How to go back, to where there are clear rules. Sucky rules, sure, rules you bitch about, but rules you've also, weirdly, come to love.

Maybe Molly was right. Perhaps I did like it there.

Sometimes.

Chapter 14

4 WEEKS TO GO

I don't see Robin for a couple of days after the antenatal class. I lock myself in my flat and sort of just let the terror take over. I don't eat much. One night I dream I'm bingeing on a giant chocolate figure, like the snowmen you get in a Christmas stocking, except I realise with a sickening feeling that it's a baby. But even though I try and try, I can't stop eating it. In the corner, Molly watches, her face completely white, the way it was that day in the bathroom.

'You have to choose,' she says.

I wake up shaking and sweating, with a horrible squeezing pain down one side, and can't get back to sleep. I've read about this, Braxton Hicks contractions, and it reminds me the birth is getting stupidly close.

All of a sudden, I'm really tired and bizarrely I want Mum. I want her to come and say it's all right like she did when I was little. I want her to look after me, tell me what to do.

I get dressed and start walking, even though it's only six in the morning, and don't stop until I get home. To Mum and Dad and Tammy's house, that is.

I knock on the door. It takes a while for it to open and then it's not Mum standing there, but Tammy in fluffy slippers and a dressing gown. Her usually perfect shiny hair is sticking out a bit and she has three spots on her chin. This, perversely, cheers me up.

'Oh, it's you. Hello,' she says and peers at me through her fringe, which I suspect she's had cut to hide the sprinkling of acne I see peeping out from underneath it.

'Can I come in?'

We go and sit in the living room.

'Do you want me to get Mum?' Tammy says and her voice is polite, like I'm a snake that's about to bite.

She can't stop looking at my bump, especially when the baby rolls over and one side of it goes up. Which hurts. I never really thought about pregnant stomachs before, and it's still a shock to feel how hard and tight my skin is. Plus, the baby does not stop moving, ever. And I can't lie on my front because it's physically impossible, or my back because then I feel like the bump is flattening my lungs, so I have to sleep on my side, like a beached whale. The baby pushes hard against my hand on my bump, like she's trying to chuck me off. Or planning to exit directly through the skin. She feels strong enough. For the millionth time, I try not to think about the birth or what might come after.

'Do you want to feel it?' I say to Tammy.

She comes over with a shy look, and hesitates.

'It's OK,' I say. 'Put your hand there.'

Tammy presses one hand to my bump and the baby kicks it. Tammy jumps about a mile and then laughs. She puts her hand back and leans down so her mouth is up close.

'Hello! I'm your Aunt Tammy!' she says.

I well up. Tammy realises I've gone quiet and looks up at me through those long lashes of hers, questioning. A moment later, whatever spell the baby cast over us is broken by Mum coming into the living room.

'Hedda!' she says. It's hard to tell whether she's pleased to see me or not.

Tammy gets up and goes off to the kitchen.

'What are you doing here?' Mum says.

'I don't really know,' I say. 'I just wanted to see you, I suppose.'

Something in Mum's face softens. She looks at the bump.

'You want a feel too?' I say.

Mum presses a hand there and her eyes go really distant. There's a trace of a smile on her face.

I want a time machine or something. I want the past five years never to have happened, to take it all back.

'I remember when I was pregnant with you, you were such a little wriggler,' Mum says. 'I can still feel your feet right up here under my ribs.'

'Yeah, I feel like I'm getting crushed sometimes,' I say.

'Children do that to you,' Mum says, and I go cold again.

'Have you come to a decision yet?' she says. 'You can't have long left to go.'

I thought I'd decided on the way here, but now I'm actually in the room with her, I don't think I can say it. I can't ask if I can come back.

Tammy calls out from the kitchen, 'Anyone want toast?'

'I've already eaten,' I call back. The lies come back so smoothly, I almost don't register this one.

Mum looks at me harder. 'You seem different.'

'Yeah, carrying a whole human kind of does that to you,' I can't help saying, but we both know that isn't what she means.

We give each other a long look and I wonder what she felt when she was carrying me. What her hopes and dreams were for me, for herself. It's possibly the closest we've been in a long time, even though we're not saying anything. Mum's eyes have a bright sheen to them, a look that seems to reach through time and stir memories, hazy and indistinct because they're layered over with all the things that came later.

Tammy comes in with some peanut butter on toast and is about to start eating when Mum recovers herself and says, 'Tamara, crumbs!'

It's like someone's flicked a switch and the moment is gone. I feel myself shut down.

I heave myself up to follow Tammy into the dining room and that's when it happens: a strong squeezing sensation in my back, like the worst kind of cramp, and then my waters break, all over Mum's new carpet.

PART THREE
COUNT UP

Chapter 15

Anorexia hurts. Starving yourself ain't pretty. When your weight gets low enough, everything aches, all the time. You get so cold, like your bones are pure winter. Your hair falls out and your skin dries into a million little cracks. You grow hair on your back. Your joints feel rusted. It gets so your brain is iced over. Even cushions are too hard to sit on, it hurts that much.

Giving birth hurts more.

I scream through a contraction, suck in gas and air through the mouthpiece, but it is doing zero for the pain. It dies away after an eternity and I pant, 'Where the fuck is my epidural?'

Mum doesn't even tell me off for swearing, which means things must be bad.

The midwife makes soothing noises. 'Not long now.

The anaesthetist is on his way –'

I scream again as another contraction comes. I was wrong – those forcep things aren't the torture. This is. They're like the sea, waves of contractions, coming without any pauses now. I'm up on my knees, gripping the sides of the bed, my eyes blank with terror. It's all happening too fast, I'm not ready, and I try and say this, but I can't seem to get out proper words.

'Take a drink, sweetie,' Mum says and pushes a straw into my mouth.

I gulp water, then more gas and air as another contraction comes and I think I might lose my mind with the pain; maybe I'm already dead. I'm pulling at the gown they've put me in, grabbing at my hair, totally out of control.

Suddenly, I feel an unbearable urge, like I've taken about a hundred laxatives, except it's not in my bum.

'I think I'm pushing!' I gasp.

Mum is somewhere near my head. I can hear her voice from far away, soothing, scared.

She rubs my back, but I shrug my shoulders violently. 'Don't touch me!'

She moves her hand, but when I turn my head sideways she's still there. I squeeze my eyes shut as another huge contraction comes and I feel the worst kind of grinding sensation in my pelvis. I throw my head back and howl, like I'm an animal.

I lose count of how long I push. Time belongs to another planet. There's nothing but me and the pain and the only thread holding me to any sort of sanity is Mum's voice, telling me it's OK, that I'm doing really well.

But I'm not doing well. I'm so tired now. It feels like I've been in this room forever. The midwife turns me on my side and I cry between pushes, sucking on the gas and air.

I hear Mum say from far away, 'Can't you give her something?'

'It's too late for the epidural,' replies the midwife.

'Just. Knock. Me. Out,' I grind through my teeth. Then I open my mouth and this sound comes out, a low animal roar, louder than any noise I've ever made in my life, and then I feel the worst burning sensation down below.

'That's it – the head is out. Now I need you to stop pushing for a moment. That's it. Just pant for me. Well done. Good girl,' the midwife says.

'I can't do it, I can't do it, I can't do it,' I sob.

'Yes you can. Here, feel this.' She pulls my hand down between my legs and there's this astonishing thing there, all hot and squishy.

Oh my God, I think, but then another contraction comes.

'Push!' the midwife says.

And I do, everything popping, Mum's face, wet with tears, above me.

'Come on, Hedda,' she says.

I look into Mum's eyes and I push and I push, screaming out, and then suddenly there's a rush and release and the pain goes. I slump back on the pillows.

The midwife is holding something tiny and grey and I just register this, and the fact that I somehow seem to be wearing no clothes, and then she puts it on to my chest. The baby is very warm and she fits right on my ribcage, like she was always meant to be there.

But she isn't crying.

'She's not crying. Why isn't she crying? Is she OK?' I say. I crane my head back, trying to get a proper look at her.

The midwife rubs the baby's back with a towel and after a moment that lasts forever, the baby turns her head to one side, takes a big breath and opens her eyes.

There's the softest click inside.

'Hello,' I say.

She looks at me. Her eyes are full of secrets, like she's been on some long journey. There's a strange hush in the room, like some ancient magic has infused it.

The midwife asks if I want to cut the umbilical cord, but I shake my head. I can't move my arms from the position they've found by themselves, cradling the baby automatically. I think Mum does it.

Then the midwife says something about the placenta, and some more contractions come, but I barely notice them because me and the baby are still looking at each other.

When the midwife takes her away to weigh her, the space left behind feels cold. I begin to shiver all over. Once she's been weighed and checked over, they put her back on me. She's small – five pounds, eleven ounces – but fine considering she came so early.

'Do you want to try breastfeeding?' the midwife says.

To my surprise, I agree.

The baby doesn't seem so good at it though. She sort of sticks her tongue out and slides on and off. It's a bit of a shock, truthfully.

'She'll get the hang of it,' the midwife says.

'I'm so proud of you,' Mum says, and she leans over and kisses me on the cheek, the feeling of it so familiar and distant at the same time, like an echo.

Mum cuddles the baby while the midwife helps me to the en suite and puts me in a shower to clean me off. Then she tucks me up in bed and puts the baby back on my chest.

This time, she cries. Her mouth opens and shuts like a little fish.

I try again and again to feed her, but nothing is coming.

* * *

A while after, Dad and Tammy arrive. I'm on the ward now, surrounded by crying babies and the long beeps of call bells. I'm exhausted. The baby is in a little tub by the side of my bed. She still hasn't had a proper feed.

I've had half a slice of toast and a cup of tea, which Mum has insisted on putting two sugars in. I drink it to keep her happy, but the window at the far end of the ward is open and through it, a long way away, I think I hear Nia rustling through a sky that is packed with layers of white clouds. *We had a deal*, she seems to say.

I turn my head from the clouds to look again at the baby.

'She's a little cracker,' Dad says and he looks all proud.

'Can I touch her?' Tammy says, and I nod.

Tammy reaches for the baby's hand and the baby opens her eyes and closes her tiny fist around Tammy's finger.

'Does she have a name?' Tammy says.

'Not yet,' I say.

I don't know if I'm meant to name this baby or not.

I sleep through dinner, conveniently, but have a small bowl of cereal Mum's rustled up from the ward. She watches me like a hawk as I eat it. It's almost like old times.

The baby sleeps on. I suppose being born is pretty tiring.

Just before visiting hours are up, Robin arrives. When I got Mum to call him I could see her dying to ask if he was the father, but I didn't have the energy for that conversation.

'Hi,' Robin says when he gets to my side. He's shown up with flowers, a small bunch of white roses. 'My grammy told me they're for new beginnings.'

'Trust you to know that,' I say with a smile.

Mum puts them in a vase and I'm about to ask if he'll water my window box when he leans over the cot and there's this look in his eyes, like he's been smacked in the stomach.

'She's beautiful,' he says and then he smiles and I start wondering if I imagined the look or if it's the drugs talking.

It's a bit awkward introducing him to Mum and Dad, seeing as they've never met him before, but he soon has Dad engrossed in a discussion about cricket, of all things. At least Mum realised straight away that Robin can't be the father, given the baby's so pale, so I don't have to have some sort of whispered conversation with her about it.

I turn back to the baby.

'I really think she needs a name,' Mum says.

'What about Rose?' Tammy says, looking at the flowers.

I sound it in my head. It seems to fit.

'Rose,' I say.

* * *

In the middle of the night, Rose's cries wake me up. I struggle to latch her on to my boob, but she still won't feed and the midwife is concerned. I'm in tears with exhaustion and shock and a million other feelings, but most of all, I just want to sleep. Rose keeps crying, and I get a flash of ugly irritation.

'Shall I take her away for a bit and give her a bottle?' the midwife says. 'You need to rest.'

I know when to admit defeat. I nod.

I lie back, relieved, while the midwife scoops Rose up and the crying recedes.

I sleep for a little while, but then wake up, wondering where I am.

Then I remember.

Rose.

And Nia.

Rose.

Nia.

Nia.

A familiar presence fills the ward, floating on the ceiling, watching me. Calm now, like she knows her time has almost come.

I feel her, a shape-shifter shimmering into something solid.

She's back.

Chapter 16

DAY 2

The following morning, a midwife brings Rose back. I cuddle her for a bit, and if my arms are too full for breakfast, well, I'll get something later.

Nia flaps her wings in approval.

'We'll be looking to discharge you later on today,' the midwife says.

'You're sure?' I ask.

What I want to do is clutch at her and say, '*Really? You're really letting me walk out of here with her?*' And also: '*Don't let me walk out of here with her. I don't know what I'm doing.*'

Rose is so small. I never knew small could feel bad before, but it does.

Mum went out shopping and bought a few bits and

pieces – some tiny baby vests and babygrows, nappies, blankets. Because, of course, I don't have any of that stuff and it seems the maternity unit expect you to bring your own nappies. Also, your own pads. No one tells you how much you bleed after you give birth. It's earthy and gross and makes my stomach heave.

Rose goes back to sleep and I watch her for a while. Then my curtains are pulled back, and Joanna is standing there in yet another patterned tunic top, holding a big file.

She peers into the tub. 'So, this is Rose,' she says.

'Yep.'

Joanna sits in the chair at the side of my bed. 'And how are you getting on?'

'OK, I think, considering. She's having some problems feeding.'

Joanna flicks through the file, and then looks at me.

I scoop Rose out of the tub and put my mouth down so it meets the soft hair on her head. Her fontanelle, the little bit where her skull hasn't closed over yet, pulses steadily. I'm reminded of *Alien* again. This creature in my arms, she doesn't seem real, doesn't feel like she was inside me.

'We need to discuss your plans,' Joanna says.

'I'm keeping her,' I say to the top of Rose's head.

It was a foregone conclusion the second the midwife put her on me. She's mine.

Joanna takes a long breath. 'And where –'

'I'm going home with Mum,' I say. I might know Rose is mine, but that doesn't mean I'm sure I can look after her on my own. And Mum has been pretty insistent. It's nice to let her take charge for once. For now, anyway.

'Permanently?'

'I don't know yet, OK?' I give Joanna a long look, a look that asks a question and gets a provisional answer.

'We'll need to monitor things very closely,' is all she says and I know I'm on the tightest of probations. That if Joanna had her way, Rose would already be leaving, going to proper parents. But for now, she simply arranges to visit me in a few days for a check-up.

The clouds have cleared and there's sharp, yellow light glinting off the rows of cars in the car park. Dad had to buy a new car seat and he spends ages fiddling with straps and frowning while I stand and hold Rose and try not to sway. I'm smarting from the stare a couple of old ladies gave us in the lift on the way down, and I also ache pretty badly in places you really don't want to ache. When she checked me over after the birth, the midwife said it all looked 'in excellent shape', but it doesn't seem like that to me. It feels like I got kicked by a horse.

Mum senses I'm tired and says sharply, 'Peter! Hurry up, for heaven's sake.' Then: 'I'll take her.' Her voice is possessive, but I really feel like I might faint at any moment – the old dot to dot swarms my vision – and so I pass Rose to her. Mum takes her and I get into the car extremely carefully, desperate to sit down, but unable to find a comfy position. Mum half turns away and whispers something to Rose, which I don't catch because she nudges the door shut with her hip. I watch them both through the glass.

The drive back is not much fun. Dad's doing about fifteen miles an hour, but he still seems to hit every road bump wrong and I grit my teeth against the pain. I feel like asking Mum, '*Why did no one tell me about this?*', but I can imagine the long-suffering sigh, her eyes rolling to the ceiling as she says, '*Well, what on earth did you expect, for heaven's sake?*'

What did I expect, exactly?

I don't know.

I didn't expect the way I felt when I was giving birth, how the pain took over every molecule so I wasn't even there.

I didn't expect that when I look at Rose, for long moments nothing else exists, nothing matters except her.

Not even Nia.

* * *

I insist on carrying Rose through the front door myself, but I can sense Mum hovering, her arms itching to hold her. We put the car seat on the living-room floor, Rose fast asleep, and I wonder, *What now?*

'You should try and get some sleep when she does. I told your father to make up the spare room,' Mum says.

This room was, in fact, my room until a few months ago, but in the meantime Mum's clearly bought up half of Laura Ashley. Floral wallpaper covers the marks left behind by posters of kittens and ballet dancers from before Nia started. I never put up new posters after the first time I got out, a bit before my thirteenth birthday. After that, this room began to feel more like a holding pen anyway. Temporary. When I spot the matching floral curtains, comforter and cushions on the armchair Mum's installed in the corner, I start to have second thoughts about Rose's name. Perhaps I was still high on the drugs when I agreed to it. In the back of my mind, I quite fancied a unisex name, or something with an edge to it, solid and sharp. Less feminine. Then I look at her skin, soft as a petal, and think about the fact that roses are pretty tough too, what with all the thorns. Anyway, Rose is Rose now. It's too late to go back.

To keep Mum happy, I lie down on the bed and drift into a half-sleep, but I'm sucked out of a dream by high-pitched cries coming from downstairs. I really, really don't want to wake up, but the cries sound frantic and some instinct makes me lurch out of bed and stagger downstairs.

Mum and Dad are holding a hissed conversation in the kitchen.

'You need to test it on the back of your hand,' Mum says. 'Come on, for goodness' sake.'

I peer round Mum and see Dad holding a bottle of formula. He passes it to Mum, who's rocking Rose in her arms. Rose is screaming her head off.

'Why didn't you wake me?' I go to take Rose and, for a moment, there's resistance, then Mum lets her go.

I walk into the living room and Mum follows, holding the bottle.

'Why don't you let me feed her?' she says. 'You need to rest.'

Dad hovers behind her with a tea towel in his hand.

'No thanks,' I say in as firm a voice as I can muster.

I pull down my top. Dad coughs and starts inspecting the door frame. I turn back to Rose and try to guide her on, but she's so hungry and frantic, she thrashes around, managing to smack herself in the face with one flailing fist. This shocks her so much she stops crying for a moment. Stops breathing, it seems. This probably lasts about ten seconds, but in that time I can hear the slow *thud-thud-pause* of my heartbeat. Then Rose opens her mouth the widest I've seen it yet and lets rip.

I jiggle her about, try to shush her, but she keeps on screaming, high-pitched yells which seem to come out even on the in breath.

What now?

Mum is waving the bottle about. 'I really think –'

'Give me a minute!' I shout, which startles Rose. The crying feels like it's been going on forever. I can feel panic rising, hot and choking, and guilt for scaring Rose.

Nia watches from the corner, amused.

Mum thrusts the bottle into my hand, but I drop it on the floor. She goes red and I can see the interior struggle as she battles between needing to get a cloth and clean the carpet immediately and wanting to stay and make me give the baby a bottle.

She opens her mouth, but I say loudly, 'I can do it! Just leave me alone for a minute, will you?'

Dad has melted away, muttering about tea, and Mum leaves to get a cloth. I do a couple of circuits with Rose and sing the only nursery rhyme I can remember in her ear, 'Twinkle, Twinkle, Little Star', but I can't think of all the words, so then I hum, but she's having none of it.

I rock her, but that makes her cry more.

'Sh-sh-sh ... please, just ... shh!' The last one comes out much louder than I intended and of course it's at that moment that Mum comes back into the room.

'That's enough,' Mum says firmly, and she reaches down and pulls Rose up and out of my arms.

A moment later, she's plugged the bottle into Rose's mouth and the room quietens until all you can hear is Rose chugging the bottle down at a million miles an hour.

Mum looks up at me and her voice is cold. 'I will not let you starve this child.'

She turns back to Rose, leaving me open-mouthed and breathless.

I go to the bottom of the back garden, to get away from the smell of Dad cooking one of his 'specials', which involves vomit-inducing fried eggs, chips, beans and ham. Apparently, it was my favourite when I was little, not that I have any recollection of this. And also to get away from the sound of Rose's grunts as she began necking the rest of the bottle.

I stare up into the sky for ages, but when I go back inside I can't even remember if it was sunny or not outside, only that Nia was watching me from the branches of a tree, like she's waiting.

Mum is kneeling by a shiny pink changing mat in the living room doing Rose's nappy. Another first outside of hospital I've failed to do myself. She snaps the poppers closed on Rose's babygrow and puts her down in a Moses basket I didn't even notice before in the corner.

'There, all done,' she says.

Rose is sleeping peacefully. I stand over the basket and watch the light shining down on her smooth cheek, her tiny clenched fists disappearing into the sleeves of the babygrow. She doesn't look much like me. She doesn't look much like she belongs to anyone, except herself, like she's on loan.

'I wonder if she knows what she's let herself in for, picking me,' I mutter.

'Pardon?' Mum says.

'Nothing.'

Chapter 17

DAY 4

Rose was born four days, a lifetime, ago.

Everything seems to blur into an endless cycle: cry, feed, change, cry, feed, change.

On day four, I wake up feeling like the flowers in the wallpaper have gone 3D and are reaching out to strangle me. Rose is next to my bed in her Moses basket, asleep after a long night where I tried and tried to get her to settle.

Nothing is going right. I can't even feed her myself. After that first bottle, she screams if I try and breastfeed her, so formula it is.

I'm crying before she even wakes.

I haven't showered since I got back from hospital. Dad

braved my flat to get me some things, though I'd have rather he hadn't gone in there, seen my charts and meal plans. I heard him updating Mum in a hushed voice that stopped when I walked into the kitchen with Rose.

Mum is in a cooking frenzy, the smell of it curling under my door and making my stomach twist. I'm eating some of it. Sort of. The healthy stuff anyway.

At night when Rose wakes, I'm desperate for sleep, but when she drifts off again I can't follow her there. I keep one hand dangling in the Moses basket, like if I move too far away from her she might stop breathing. Or disappear, like a mirage. So I scroll on my phone, reading about how to get babies to sleep. Not much agreement there. And, once or twice, I have a look at the Ana woman's videos, see how fast she lost after the birth. One night, trying to navigate to another page, the phone slips out of my grasp and smacks Rose on the hand. She wakes, yells, and when I've finally got her back to sleep, I lie there for the longest time, shaking.

'Mnargh.' A little bleat tells me Rose is stirring, winding up to crying.

I sit in bed, carefully, as everything is still painful, and realise the whole front of me is wet. It takes an age to work out the sharp, stale smell is milk. I run to the bathroom and throw up, silently, then chuck the T-shirt in the bin and get back into bed.

Mum knocks on my door a while later.

Rose has gone back to sleep, and I'm crying.

Mum stands over me, and then says, 'Baby blues.'

'What?'

'It's the baby blues. Everyone gets them. You'll feel better in a day or two, but for now, you should have a shower. The midwife is coming at ten.'

I let her carry Rose downstairs and take a shower, flinching away when it hits my chest, which is sore and swollen. For the first time in ages, I can see the bottom of my stomach. It's hideous. Baggy, like a balloon that's started to shrink, scored with livid red stretch marks. I look further down and see my thighs, and have to hold on to the wall to stop myself falling.

Fat bitch, Nia says from the top of the shower curtain.

I jump and nearly slip over, then turn quickly to face the other way and concentrate on letting the hot water sting my chest.

I drag myself out of the shower and dress in the loosest clothes I can find, but they make me look even bigger. A pair of pre-pregnancy jeans are in the bottom of the bag Dad's brought, but I can't get the button done up. I bite my lip, but it's no good: I can't stop crying.

'Hedda! Mary is here,' Mum calls up the stairs.

I don't even bother to wipe the tears away as Mary says,

'Congratulations.' She weighs Rose and says she's put on weight and is doing well. Mary gives me a once-over too, and presses pretty hard on my stomach to make sure everything is going down like it should. Apparently, it is. Not fast enough for me though. The tears are still coming, the drops chasing each other down my cheeks and falling off my chin.

'It's your hormones,' Mary says.

This does not make me feel better.

An hour after Mary goes, it's Joanna's turn. I've made a supreme effort and have managed to stop crying, brush my hair and put some make-up on, but I'm pretty sure I still look like death.

'How are you doing?' Joanna says.

'Fine.'

Joanna makes a note. 'And what are your plans?'

I look at her, blank.

'Will you be staying here?' she prompts.

'Yes, they will,' Mum says. As I say, 'I guess so.'

We both stop and look at each other.

'For now,' I say.

Mum's neck goes pink.

Joanna asks a load more questions, says she's liaising with Mary and then asks Mum if she can have a word.

They retreat to the kitchen and I have to work really hard not to throw a glass against the wall. Rose is asleep on my lap, and her mouth curves up into a little smile. I watch, entranced, until I remember reading that it probably means she's just done a wee.

Mum looks more flushed when they come back, but Joanna simply arranges to visit the next week.

Mum won't say what they talked about.

In her sleep, Rose smiles again.

DAY 6

Once there was a girl on the unit who basically stopped sleeping. They tried giving her pills, but even they wouldn't knock her out. We could hear her at all hours, pacing, arguing with the night staff, refusing to get back into bed. After a few days of this, she flipped out and the last I saw of her she was being taken off to a secure unit.

I think of this girl at three in the morning, when Rose wakes for the fourth time that night. There's a continuous buzzing in my ears. I make her up a bottle, pretend I can't hear her slurps and grunts. I put her back in her basket, but she yells and squirms, pulling her legs up to her chest and kicking them back down. I try patting her with my hand, struggling to keep my eyes from closing, but that's not working either.

I hear Mum get up and hover outside my door, then hold a hissed conversation with Tammy, who's complaining that she's been woken up. Again.

'Can't she just make her sleep?' Tammy says in a sleepy whine.

To my surprise, Mum gives a strange sort of laugh, then says, 'Babies don't work like that.'

'Well, can't you take her?'

'No, I can't. And you need to be more supportive of your sister.'

'But –'

'I mean it,' Mum hisses louder. 'Now go back to bed.'

Eventually, I bring Rose into bed and feed her again, trying to knock her out with milk.

Gradually, she stops crying. Then her mouth slips gently off the bottle with a soft *plop* and she's fast asleep. The curtains are a little open and moonlight slants through the gap, falling on her curved cheek. I trace it with my eyes, move to her eyelashes and tiny lips, then up into her hairline. She looks so fresh and new and I can't bear the thought of her getting older, realising what a crappy place the world is most of the time. But looking at this impossible, tiny person in my arms, I wonder – maybe it doesn't have to be like that for her.

I start to make wild promises in my head. Promises I'll keep her safe, won't let anything bad happen to her.

But I don't say them out loud.

How can I make promises that will only be broken?

DAY 7

'What do you think you're doing?'

It takes me a while to open my eyes and focus on Mum, who's standing over me like an avenging angel.

Rose is still nestled in the crook of my arm, sleeping soundly.

'You could have rolled on to her,' Mum says in a hard, loud voice. Which wakes Rose up, of course.

'I fell asleep,' I say to the gap in the curtains.

'You could have killed her!'

'But I didn't. She's fine.'

I'm too tired to properly argue, but Mum's not done.

She follows me down to the kitchen and wipes the already clean surface with hard sweeps as I boil the kettle and fish around in the steriliser for a bottle. The ones from last night are lined up in a row next to the sink, waiting to be washed.

'Why are you feeding her again? You're becoming

obsessed.' She narrows her eyes at me. 'And I saw you at dinner last night – you only ate your vegetables.'

'I'm feeding her because she's a newborn baby, Mum. They need feeding, you know. And my weight is fine.'

'What that baby needs is to be on a schedule,' Mum says. 'She needs to know who's boss. You're over-feeding her.'

I ignore her and squint at the powder in the little measuring spoon. 'I thought you were worried I was starving her.'

Mum sucks in her cheeks then lets out a puff of air towards the ceiling.

'I'll give Rose her bottle while you have some break-fast,' she says.

'No thanks. I'll get something in a bit,' I say.

Mum's lips pinch tight together, but I grab the bottle and carry Rose back upstairs to feed her.

DAY 8

At the breakfast table, Tammy yawns theatrically and I catch Mum glaring at her. Rose is in her bouncy chair, watching as I eat an egg-white omelette with tomatoes. It makes me think of Robin. He's texted a couple of times, but mostly I'm too knackered to remember to reply. The lack of sleep is making my ears hum and my head has that fuzzed-over feeling.

I can't remember how many calories are in an egg white. Or a tomato, come to think of it. My fork stops and my fingers itch to get my phone out and check, but Mum is watching me, so I say nothing and keep eating, past the point of fullness. I've noticed it comes sooner than it did before Rose was born. I have an almost unbearable urge to check how much I weigh, but it's no use; if there's any scales in this house, they're well hidden.

Needless to say, Dad has already left for work.

Tammy yawns again, stretching her arms up to the ceiling. 'I might miss music and come home straight after school tonight, Mum,' she says.

Mum whips round. 'No, you will not. Your Grade Eight is coming up.'

'But I'm really tired,' Tammy whines.

I feel Mum's glare glance off the back of my head.

DAY 10

Mary visits again and discharges me and Rose to the care of the health visitor, which seems like a milestone of sorts. Before she goes, she presses the back of my hand.

'Good luck,' she says.

I want to tell her how grateful I am – for her calmness, her lack of judgement – but, like usual, I can't find the words, so instead I try and put what I'm feeling into a smile.

It's a sunny day, all blue-washed sky and fresh grass. Sunshine makes the clouds sharp edged, like the ones in the jigsaws we used to do on the unit. Molly never had the patience, but I'd be there for hours, slotting all those blank pieces together until I found the one that fitted.

I lay Rose on a blanket in the shade under a tree in the back garden, the same one Nia stared at me from. Nia doesn't seem to be there now, or at least not if I concentrate on watching Rose looking at the patterns made by the leaves. I think about taking her out somewhere, for a walk maybe, but I don't have a buggy yet.

I wait until Dad gets home at about ten that evening and hang around while he eats a reheated plate of risotto. Mum is in the living room, with Rose.

'Dad? Do you think we could go shopping for a buggy?'

He drinks some wine. 'Of course. I'm a bit stacked out this week though. Could your mother take you?'

I grimace, but say nothing.

Dad puts down his fork. 'She's trying hard. This hasn't been easy for her, you know. You could try to meet her halfway.'

I feel my lips go into a pout. 'Like how?' I say. 'She just wants to criticise everything I do.'

'She wants what's best for you. And for Rose.' He picks up his fork again and takes a mouthful. 'Let her go shopping with you.'

'All right,' I say, because, let's face it, I don't exactly have a choice.

We start arguing before we've even left the house. Rose is strapped into her car seat, which I'm insisting I carry even though I can feel my sore stomach protesting. Since the birth, my core, those muscles that are supposed to hold you tight, have turned jelly-like, as though I'm about to fall out of myself, front first.

Mum keeps getting in my way. She puts a hat on Rose even though it's in the high twenties outside, and tucks a blanket around Rose's bare toes – she kicks socks off and I think she prefers them uncovered anyway.

More drama when we try and get the car seat into the car. By the time we've worked out how to thread the seat belt around, Rose has begun to cry.

'Maybe I should get her out and feed her,' I say.

'Leave her there,' Mum snaps. 'She'll go off to sleep when we get going.'

'But –'

Mum goes to the side of the car and opens my door. I know if I try and get Rose out Mum will sulk for the rest of the day, so I sigh and say, 'Fine.' I get in.

Rose's crying seems to go on and on, and I'm at the point of screaming, '*Stop the car!*' when she thankfully falls asleep.

She sleeps in her car seat all the way round Mothercare while we look at buggy after buggy. The same salesgirl is there as before, but she keeps talking to Mum, not me. They finally settle on one.

Mum turns to me. 'This fine with you?'

I bite back my sarcastic response and nod, my eyes fixed on Rose.

Mum turns back to the salesgirl. 'Now, about a cot …'

I open my mouth to protest, but think better of it and let Mum have her way. She buys all sorts: changing bag, a cot and bedding, clothes, a sleeping-bag thing. I start to wonder if the salesgirl is on commission. I nearly faint when I see the amount at the till, but Mum hands over a card without comment. We pile the boot with all the stuff, but Rose's eyes open and she starts winding up to cry. I know for sure she won't go back to sleep again on the way home.

'I need to feed her,' I say.

Mum huffs.

'It's been four hours,' I say. 'The book says she needs two to three ounces of milk every four hours.'

I get out the ready-mixed formula and measure it on the bonnet of the car. My hand shakes and I spill some, then wipe it away with my sleeve before Mum notices.

When Rose is done, I realise she needs a nappy change. I get out the fold-up changing mat from the new bag and spread it out on the back seat.

'What are you doing?' Mum says. 'You can't change her there, for heaven's sake.'

'Why not?'

'Because … because it's not decent.'

I feel like screaming, '*Who exactly do you think is going to care?*' But to keep her happy, I traipse back into the shop and find the baby-changing table in the loos. It takes ages because Rose won't keep still and I'm scared she's somehow going to fly off the table and hit the dirty floor.

A woman comes in with a little boy and gives me a harried look, then they disappear into a cubicle. There's some rustling about while he goes to the toilet, then she says, 'Hang on, I need to … No! Don't unlock it!'

'I can see your bum,' he says.

I nearly laugh, but I'm too tired.

When I emerge, Mum says, 'Finally.'

We get Rose strapped in and drive home in silence.

It's my first trip out with the buggy. I pack the gigantic changing bag for every eventuality I can think of, shove my phone in a side pocket and strap Rose in. Mum stands at the bottom of the stairs and watches as I crash the buggy into the doorway twice before I manage to get it out.

'Back soon,' I say.

She makes a movement as if to stop me, then draws her hand up to her mouth like Molly used to do when she was about to bite her nails. Mum checks herself though, and simply says, 'You have your phone?'

'Yes. I won't be too long, just going round the block,' I say.

But I don't just go round the block.

Once I'm out and walking, I don't stop until the smart rows of identikit houses are far behind me. I don't even know where I'm going. I realise it's just me and Rose for the first time. No midwives or social workers, or Mum hovering nearby. We're properly on our own.

'Well. And how are you?' I say to her.

She watches me with serious eyes for a while, then casts an indifferent look at the 'stimulating' black-and-white mobile Mum insisted on attaching to the top of the buggy and a moment later she's asleep.

I stride on, and realise I know where I'm going: the Yewlings. Maybe I want to show Rose where I live, I don't know. When I get to my block of flats I see that the lifts are, as usual, out of order and I'll either have to carry Rose all the way up then come back for the buggy – not likely – or somehow bump the buggy with Rose in it up eight flights of stairs.

I'm thinking about what to do, whether I should go back to Mum's and if I can manage the walk because I'm completely knackered, when there's a voice at my shoulder.

'Hello.'

I whip round, heart going a million thuds an hour, and see Robin.

Something lights up inside. I didn't realise I was missing him until I see his face.

'You scared the life out of me,' I say.

'Nice to see you too.' He peers into the buggy. 'Hello, Rose.'

Rose ignores him; she's still fast asleep.

'So are you back or is this a social call?' he says.

'The second one. But I don't know how to get this up the stairs.'

'No problem.' Robin picks up the back of the buggy. 'I've got all the weight – you just need to steer the front.'

It's hard work though and I'm sweating buckets by the

time we get up to our floor. I spend ages turfing out everything in the changing bag before I turn to him.

'Er, I think there's been a technical hitch,' I say.

'No key?'

I shake my head. 'Seems not.'

'Come on then,' Robin says.

We go into his flat and, sensing the change, Rose wakes up. Robin makes a cup of tea then sits on the other end of the sofa while I feed her. When she's done, I spread a muslin cloth under her head and pop her on the rug, then give Robin a proper once-over. He looks exactly the same as the last time I saw him and it seems crazy that the whole world and everyone in it hasn't changed.

'So ... Er, how are you getting on?' he says.

'All right, I guess.'

He's giving me this look like I'm someone new.

'Mum's driving me insane though,' I say.

'Why?'

And I'm off with a long list of complaints about Mum and the way she's interfering and how annoying it is. I leave out the fact that she's constantly nagging me about how much I'm eating. I suspect Robin might not be sympathetic on that front. Robin listens calmly until I get to the end of my rant.

'Sounds like she's just worried about you,' he says.

I've missed that about him, the way he tries to see things from every point of view. Even though I only want him to see things from mine.

Robin insists on giving me change for the bus back to Mum's and I agree because, truthfully, even I know I've walked too far today. In my head I fast-forward through the days until I've recovered enough from the birth to begin exercising properly again.

He carries the buggy back downstairs and gives me a hug at the entrance.

'See you soon?' he says, and there's a different question in his eyes.

I get on the bus and spend ages trying to fit the buggy into the space provided. I feel like everyone is staring at me, and when I finally sit down, I'm sweaty and red-faced. No one offers to help. Rose isn't bothered; she's asleep again.

I stare out of the window at the tower block fading into the distance. I think how good it was to go out on my own and how much I enjoyed seeing Robin again. By the time I get home, I'm almost smiling.

The fight goes on for what seems like hours.

'Didn't know where you were … not answering your phone … nearly called the police …' Mum goes on and on, as I change Rose and put her down in her basket.

I go into the kitchen and find some noodles, but these are my safe food and Mum knows this.

She glares at them. 'You can't just eat those.'

'Watch me' is on the tip of my tongue.

But she suddenly says, 'Joanna came round.' Her voice is dangerously quiet.

I freeze, noodles in hand. 'What did you say to her?'

'Just that you'd gone out. Which isn't the half of what I should have said. She's coming back tomorrow.'

I don't believe that's all she said, but I'm too exhausted to fight any more. Instead, I make the noodles and eat them up in my room, like old times, except for Rose slumbering peacefully on in her Moses basket.

When I finally fall asleep, I dream I'm in a huge labyrinth and I can't find my way out. I know something is coming, but I can't see or hear it and I don't know which way to run. I hurtle around corners, push through gaps too small to squeeze through, scraping my arms on rough stone. Everything shrinks, squeezing tight.

I wake up and listen to Rose breathe and the sound of my heart and I know I can't stay here. It will be better when it's just the two of us.

We'll work it out together.

Chapter 18

2 WEEKS

'Well, I suppose this is it then.' Dad stands at the door to my flat, shuffling his feet forward and backwards, like he can't quite bring himself to leave. 'I've put some money in your account.'

'Thanks, Dad,' I say.

'And you'll phone us and let us know how you're both getting on?' he says.

'If you want me to,' I say.

'Maybe phone my mobile,' he says.

I nod. Mum isn't speaking to me.

'She'll come around,' he says. 'She's just worried about you and Rose.'

'She doesn't need to be. Rose is putting on weight. We'll be fine,' I say.

Dad does his foot shuffle thing again, then finally goes.

I put the chain on, then turn to Rose in her car seat, the buggy and all the other new stuff piled next to her. Dad said he'd drop the cot off in a couple of days but until then Rose still fits in the Moses basket.

'Well. It's the two of us now,' I say to Rose.

I unstrap her and show her around. 'It's not much, but we'll make it home, right?'

I don't feel self-conscious any more, talking out loud to Rose. It feels like the most normal thing in the world and, anyway, she's a good listener.

It's nice, here in the quiet, just Rose's snuffly breaths and her warm head snuggled under my chin. Her hair is so smooth and I turn my head so my cheek rubs gently on it, like a cat, my arms around her feeling strong.

But after a while, I begin to feel antsy. The flat is smaller than I remembered, the walls too close in a way that reminds me of the labyrinth dream.

'Let's go and see Robin, shall we?' I say to Rose.

I knock on his door and he gives a huge smile when he sees us. 'You're back then?'

'Yep.'

'Well, you're in time for lunch!'

I work hard to keep my face from falling.

We go in and Robin holds Rose. She looks super comfortable in his arms. He holds her the right way too, up high against his chest, not down flat like you think you should hold babies. Took me a while to figure that one out.

'You're a natural,' I say. 'You been getting in some practice?'

It's only a joke, but for a second Robin looks strange, like he's off on some other planet or something. Then he passes Rose back to me slowly, like he doesn't quite want to let her go. Can't blame him – she is gorgeous.

'So, did something happen between you and your mum?' he says.

'Pretty much.' I give him a quick replay of the argument I had with Mum. 'After that, I realised I couldn't do it. She was taking over. I felt like I couldn't breathe in that house. And I suddenly saw I have to do this on my own, my way.'

'How did your mum take it?' Robin says.

'Well, she threatened to report me to social services, for starters. But I'm not worried,' I say.

This is a lie. I'm actually terrified of what Joanna is going to say, but I couldn't stay in that house any more. It's got nothing to do with Mum hovering at every mealtime.

Robin looks sceptical, but luckily for me, Rose wakes up so I change her while Robin begins cooking.

But when he puts the plate on to the table, my stomach twists in on itself.

'I can hold her while you eat if you like?' Robin says, his voice eager.

'That's OK. I need to give her a quick feed,' I say and turn away from the searching look he gives me.

Unlike me, Rose is never one to turn down food. She's filling out already, little dimples appearing over the backs of her hands. It's good chubby. Definitely good chubby. I tuck the blanket over her fist and try and concentrate on what Robin is saying.

'... got another interview next week for some care work. It's a zero hours contract and they'll want me to do nights, but the money isn't bad. Better than Aldi.'

Rose is making my arm go dead. I shift her round and accidentally pull the bottle out of her mouth. She makes a grab for it.

Greedy.

Was that Nia or me?

'Don't look so horrified! It's not the worst idea in the world,' Robin says.

'What? Oh no, I just ... That sounds good.'

I ease the bottle away from Rose and lean her over my

hand to burp her. A moment later the surplus milk shoots out of her mouth into a muslin cloth. The acrid smell of partly digested milk fills my nostrils and my stomach churns.

I breathe through my mouth and say, 'You'd be good at it.' I think he would, actually.

'Come on, pass her over. She wants some cuddles with Uncle Robin, don't you, Rose?' He pulls her up, out of my arms. 'Sit. Eat.' Robin ducks his head over Rose and touches her on the cheek with one finger.

My feet drag as I walk to the table, but when I look down I relax a little. It's poached fish, no sauce, veg and rice. All low-fat stuff. I can do this. I want to, almost, because Robin looks so pleased and expectant.

But when the plate is half empty I push it away.

'That's all you're having?'

'Got a slightly dodgy tummy. Think I'm out of the habit of a cooked lunch. It's all sandwiches, salads and soups at Mum's. I'll grab something later. But thanks – it was lovely,' I say and give a bright smile, the sort that hurts your cheeks if you try and hold on to it too long.

It's amazing, how the lies come, like putting on a favourite pair of jeans. It doesn't even feel that wrong to lie to Robin. It's how it is, that's all.

'Hedda ...'

'I just remembered! I said I'd go to a baby group. We ought to get ready.' I scoop Rose up. 'Thanks again. Maybe see you tomorrow?'

I'm already half out the door.

Robin shakes his head, but says, 'Sure, if you like.'

The baby group was another lie. I'm not going to one of those things. Still, I can't stay put now I've said I'm going out. Only problem is, I've got no way of getting the buggy downstairs unless I ask Robin and then he might want to come with me or something.

I walk down the hallway to check the lift, which for once is actually 'working', but don't fancy it. There's a fairly high chance I'll either get stuck in there with Rose, or with Rose and someone else too. Probably someone I really don't want to be stuck in a lift with. The thought makes me shudder.

I consider my options. It's not far to walk to the library from the bus stop. I could carry her.

I pack some supplies into my rucksack, change Rose's nappy and set off.

It's fine to start with, although it takes an age to carry her down the stairs; I'm worried about falling and grope like an old woman down each step. As I near the bottom of a flight, a slo-mo vision hits me of tripping, Rose falling from my arms and her head cracking dirty concrete. I stop and breathe hard, arms tight around her. But I make it to the bottom without any accidents. My arms are shaking though, and they don't stop until the bus arrives and I've sat down. For a small person, Rose is actually really heavy.

In town, I stand outside the library. A woman lumbers past me with the buggy equivalent of a four-by-four, which she steers with an expert flick of the wrist through the doorway. Just before the door bangs shut, I grab it. It's heavier than I thought, and for a second I think I might drop Rose for real, but I shoulder it open and shimmy through, scraping my butt as I go.

I have this image of myself as one thing, one size, and moments like this are still as much of a shock as they were when I had the bump. I should have fitted through that gap. I'm suddenly, completely sure I can't do this. I'm homesick for Nia. I want to write her a love note or crappy poetry. I want to wrap her through me and hear her roar blotting everything else out. I stand, paralysed by grief, holding tight to Rose, my cheek on her soft head.

She shifts in my arms and opens her eyes wide, as if to say, '*Where are we now then?*', like a puppy. That's the thing about babies. They don't let you stop and think for more than a few minutes at a time. It's kind of comforting actually, learning Rose, working out what she might need. It pushes Nia away, to where I can handle her. Though I wonder sometimes how can someone who came from me be so contented – in the daytime, at least? She may as well have a tail.

The library smells the same as always. I wander up and down rows of books, holding Rose up over one shoulder, debating whether to do my usual trick of choosing one at random, and somehow manage to find myself in the Mind, Body, Spirit section. More specifically the shelf with the ED books. Can't think how that happened. I take a look at the spines. I know most of these on sight, but one sticks out, an anorexia memoir I've never read. I slide it out and bend down on one knee, balancing Rose along the length of my arm, and rest the book on my other knee. Each chapter is headed up with the author's weight, a relentless downward march. I flick through with my free hand, to see how low the numbers go.

'Hello.'

My hand jerks and the book tumbles to the floor.

It's Lois, with Ethan strapped into a buggy. Forget Rose filling out – he's gigantic.

I stand up and shift so I'm in front of the book and smile.

'Hi. How are you?' I say.

'Oh, surviving. You know how it is,' Lois says, and for a moment her face takes on a desperate look. I wonder when was the last time she had a conversation with anyone apart from the bitchy woman at her baby group. The next moment, she smiles brightly. 'Who's this?'

'This is Rose.'

'What a beautiful name. And isn't she a little poppet? I won't ask if she's good. I hate it when people do that. What they really mean is, does she sleep?' Lois says. 'Which is not Ethan's favourite pastime.'

I can sort of tell that by her long roots and the craters under her eyes. She looks fatter than when I last saw her, like she's been living on cake or something.

'Yeah, Rose doesn't do much of that either,' I say, and Lois seems to relax.

Ethan wriggles in his buggy and she leans down to pass him a soggy-looking teddy. I take the opportunity to pick up the anorexia book and slip it on to the shelf behind me, pages out.

Lois straightens up. 'But look at you! Where's all the baby weight gone? There's nothing to you,' she says, and I know – I know she's two parts jealous, only one part concerned. A surge starts at my feet and works its way up through my body, so I'm tingling with it, powerful.

I shrug. 'Oh, you know. Rose keeps me running about,' I say, doing my best impression of a grown-up. 'Anyway, I probably need to get going.'

'Well, nice seeing you,' Lois says, and I can see she's trying not to care.

A little slice of guilt cuts through the powerful feeling, then fades away. I move Rose to the other arm.

'Where's your buggy?' Lois says.

'I carried her.'

'You're joking.'

'Nope.' I start to leave.

'Hang on a minute.' Lois reaches under her buggy and pulls out a stripy baby carrier. It looks expensive. 'Here. I can't get on with it – Ethan screams whenever I try. But Rose might like it.'

She holds it out, but I don't make any move to take it. For starters, I don't have any cash to spare.

'Go on,' Lois says. 'I was going to offer it around my baby group, but I'd far rather you had it. You'd be doing me a favour – I hate to see things go to waste.'

Lois helps me strap Rose in. I like the feel of Rose snug next to me, the padded carrier spreading her weight across my back and shoulders.

'Thanks,' I say.

'Any time. Give me a call if you need anything. We could always grab a coffee sometime if you want to swap sleep-deprivation horror stories!'

'Sure, I'll text,' I say. 'Thanks for the carrier.'

Maybe I will text her. Might be nice to help someone else out for a change. And I like Lois. She can't be that much younger than Felicity, but it doesn't feel that way.

When I'm sure Lois has gone, I double back for the book and tuck it under one arm. I get a sudden sense of Molly, peering over my shoulder, one eyebrow up. Then I notice the children's section, with a picture of a train full of books on the wall. I take Rose over to have a look.

It's a bit tricky leaning down with her strapped to my front, but I kneel and scan the rows of board books. I notice *The Very Hungry Caterpillar*, which I definitely don't pick, then *Spot the Dog*. I take that and then dither in front of one with bunnies and another with aliens, then decide on the aliens because they're cute little red ones and somehow I think Rose might like them. She spent a good ten minutes staring at the sunflower print in our living room the other day anyway, so I've decided she likes bright things.

I check the books out, then decide I'll walk home.

Rose falls asleep as soon as I start walking and doesn't wake until I climb the stairs and unstrap her.

It feels like a tiny triumph, sort of.

Chapter 19

3 WEEKS

I wasn't kidding when I told Lois last week that Rose doesn't sleep much. I wake up feeling like a zombie. I swear last night was the worst one yet. Aren't babies supposed to sleep, like, twenty hours out of the day? Rose seems to get by on less. A lot less. I don't feel as sore as I did when she was first born, but if I take things too quick, I know about it. My stomach muscles are still shot, but I've been doing sit-ups to help with that.

I feed Rose, then read her the alien story before I put her down for a nap. I think she likes me reading to her. She stays super quiet anyway and seems to be looking at the pictures, although I remember she can still only see in black and white. It feels good though, like I've done something right for a change. When she's asleep I cook up some lunch. Nothing too tricky. Then I need to get ready for my session with Felicity. I rifle through the rack of clothes and old chest of drawers in my bedroom for something to wear, which doesn't exactly take long. My old hoodie is in a crumpled heap on the floor, like a discarded friend. It's warm out though. My jeans don't do up properly yet, but they almost do. Another couple of pounds should do the trick. I settle for leggings and a long baggy T-shirt to cover everything up, then I sort Rose out and set off.

As we're leaving, the dodgy guy who lives on the other side of me opens his door. I get a flash of the tattoos crawling up his neck as he gives me and Rose a filthy look.

'You want to keep that baby quiet,' he says and slams the door before I can reply.

I think back uneasily to him banging on the wall when Robin and I made too much noise cooking, and how much Rose cried last night.

The hill up to the unit seems longer than usual. The sun is out and it feels like it's sucking all the moisture from my skin, leaving me panting and exhausted. My legs are jelly-like by the time I make it to the top. I'm worried about Rose overheating and when I sit down in the waiting room, she's hot and pink in the face. I run my finger over her fontanelle, feeling it pulse, worried in case it's sunken in too much. I've read that's a sign of dehydration in babies and I must check her fontanelle a million times a day. She stirs and opens her eyes, but doesn't seem hugely impressed by what she can see, which is mainly chairs and white walls. Or she senses the atmosphere in this place. Whatever it is, her face crumples and she begins to cry. Can't say I blame her.

It takes me a while to calm her down because she's gone from zero to hysterical in the space of two seconds, but eventually I get her to take a bottle. When I look up, Laurel is in a seat opposite me. Her chin is practically on the floor. I consider reaching over and pushing it back up, but wait until she's managed to blink a few times.

'What is that?' she says, eventually.

'Hello to you too. What do you think it is?'

'But … but … when? How? Is it yours?'

'Well, I'd hardly be feeding someone else's baby, would I? And she's a she.'

Milk trickles down the side of Rose's face. I sit her up on my lap, muslin at the ready, and wait for the inevitable sick-up, which comes a minute later.

'Why didn't you tell me?' Laurel looks near tears.

She comes to sit in the seat next to me, and reaches out a tentative finger – which I can't help noticing is significantly plumper than the last time I saw her – and touches Rose on the cheek.

'Well,' I say slowly. 'You were in New–' I catch myself, '–land, and I suppose I thought ... It was a bit of a shock, you know? And then she came early and I guess I'm still trying to get my head around it all.'

'What's her name?'

'Rose.'

'She's beautiful.' Laurel says it on an out breath, all wistful.

I smile in that proud parent way I'm pretty sure I'd have rolled my eyes at a few weeks ago. I can't help it; Rose is so beautiful, I still can't believe she's mine. Even if I'd be a hell of a lot happier if she'd just bloody sleep.

'What about you? How are you doing?' I say carefully.

Laurel shrugs and grimaces, pulls at her top. 'Well, I got out last week. They discharged me back here for out-patients, at least until I'm eighteen.' She twists her face, then adds, 'Couple of months to go.'

'Who's your key worker?'

'Angie.'

'Oh, you're lucky! I still have –'

I break off because Felicity is coming into the room. She smiles hello to us both and then retreats towards her office.

I'm about to follow when Laurel puts a hand on my arm. 'Can I come round sometime?'

A part of me wants to say no, but I recognise that post-discharge look, that panicked 'what do I do now?' made up of freedom and loneliness and fear.

'Um, yeah, definitely,' I say. 'Maybe in a week or two. I'll text you, OK?'

'OK,' she almost whispers. Then, louder: 'Bye, Rose.'

As I make my way to Felicity's office, I'm trying not to think about Joanna, who visited a couple of days ago. The way she scrutinised every bit of the flat, her head twisting towards the sound of banging and shouting from the bloke next door.

'Is there often … disruption?' Joanna said.

'Oh no! He's usually fine. Friendly, you know?' I pasted as bright a smile on as I could, coughed as another crash came from next door. It sounded suspiciously like someone throwing furniture.

Then a huge slam that rattled the walls, and everything went quiet again, except for Joanna's pen going *scratch*, *scratch* on her pad. When she looked up, I knew it wasn't good.

'I have some concerns, Hedda. You don't have much of a support network around you.'

'I'm going to a baby group,' I lied. 'And making friends. I'm going for coffee with someone from the group, Lois. She has a lovely little boy called …' I broke off. I don't know why I couldn't remember the baby's name. I tried and tried to conjure it up, but it was like the space where the name should be had been erased.

Joanna pursed her lips. 'You look exhausted. You can't do this all on your own.'

'But Rose is fine! I took her to get weighed the other day and she's putting on weight. She's right where she should be in the charts.'

Joanna sighed. 'Hedda. It's about more than how much she weighs.'

Then she started on my sessions with Felicity, making me promise to attend each one. She'd be back the following week to do some sort of assessment. I saw her out, holding on to Rose so tight she began to squirm in my arms and cry.

I give my head a shake, trying to dislodge it all, and tap on Felicity's door. When I go in, I see she's not happy.

'Hedda, it's not appropriate to bring Rose to your sessions,' Felicity says.

'Well, what do you want me to do? I don't have anyone to leave her with,' I say.

'What about your mother?'

'We're not exactly speaking at the moment.'

'Mmm.'

I really, really hate Felicity's 'mmm's.

'It's not my fault!' I burst out, which makes everyone jump, me included.

I walk up and down with Rose to settle her back down, looking at the spidery plants on the shelves, which are lined with books that all have ridiculous titles. One in particular catches my eye – something about the 'unmothered child'. This, amusingly, is next to another book all about letting go and building confident kids.

I swing back to face Felicity then point to the books. 'Which one is it then?'

'I don't think I follow …'

'Seems to me you're going to mess up whatever you do, if you're a parent.'

'Is that how you feel, about Rose?'

I shake my head and laugh – a proper one, not sarcastic. 'You can't just leap in with a question like that! I mean, there's Rules here.'

Felicity holds my eye and I blush. We both know there are Rules to our sessions, but I've never actually said anything about them before. It's kind of a rule of mine. Or was, anyway.

'You brought it up,' Felicity says, but she's smiling back at me too.

We talk about Rose. Felicity listens while I list all the awesome things about her, like the way she pulls the most amazing faces, and how soft her feet are.

But when I say, 'I never knew a baby could be so perfect,' Felicity frowns.

'You know, there's no such thing as a perfect child, or a perfect parent,' she says.

'I didn't say *I* was perfect, obviously. It's just … isn't it my job to think she's perfect?'

'I'd say it's your job to see her,' Felicity says, 'flaws and all.'

I consider this for a while. 'I don't think my parents ever saw me, except when I was trying to disappear,' I say.

Felicity leans forward in her chair. 'That's interesting. Can you tell me a bit more about that?'

But I can't, because suddenly I'm crying.

I'm glad Laurel isn't still in the waiting room when I leave with Rose strapped to me. I walk fast, letting my feet thud the hot pavement, feeling the sweat trickle along my hair-line. I start to cross over to the bus stop and force out the thoughts, instead calculating what I've eaten so far today and what else I could, should and will eat, when it happens.

Perhaps I'm tired. Maybe Rose shifts slightly in her sling and pulls me off balance. Or I'm too distracted. But as I lift my foot up on the far side of the road, it catches on the kerb and I'm falling, Rose's tiny skull heading for the road, just like in my nightmares. I shout out and make a desperate lurch to the left. I hit the kerb hard with my elbow, my hand up over the back of Rose's head, but I was walking too fast and my rucksack is full of heavy tins. The momentum pushes me forward and I feel my fingers crunch against the kerb.

The top of Rose's head hits the pavement.

'No!' I struggle with the backpack, trying to get myself up and check if Rose is OK.

There's blood all over my hand and I don't know for a minute if it's coming from me or her. Cold, sick horror floods through me, slowing my heart down. The dots start to swarm and I grind my teeth together and force them away. Rose is screaming her head off.

'Are you all right?' A woman has rushed to my side and attempts to pull Rose up and out of the carrier, which makes her scream even more.

I twist away and manage to get my backpack off, then unclip Rose and lean her forward over my arm. There's a graze on the back of her head. It's small and faint, but it's there.

'I'm so sorry, I'm so sorry,' I whisper to her, but my voice is shaking and she senses my fear because she's really bawling now. I start to cry too.

The woman pats my arm. 'Don't cry, love. She's OK, just had a little bump, is all. I know these sling contraptions are all the rage these days, but I've never understood what's wrong with a pram. See, there, she's settling down now. I reckon you both got a bit of a fright, didn't you?' The woman pats my arm again on my good side.

When I get up I wobble.

The woman sucks in air through her teeth in a thoughtful smack. 'You'd best get that seen to – it might need a stitch,' she says.

I look down and realise blood is dripping from my elbow on to the pavement.

Behind the woman is a queue of people waiting for the bus. A girl, younger than me, smoking and looking bored. Another girl, with a buggy, who's texting and doesn't look my way. I'm thinner than both of them. An older woman with bags of shopping nestled against her ankles who gives me a hard stare and a tut.

'I think you'd best take the number six the other way up to the hospital and get yourself and the little one checked over. Just to be safe,' says the woman who helped me up.

'But don't worry – they're tougher than they look, even at this age.'

The bus pulls up and everyone files on.

The woman gives me a nod and a smile as she gets on.

'Thanks,' I croak out, but the doors are already shutting.

I limp over to the other side of the road, my knee stinging where I banged it on the way down. I sit at the bus stop, because my legs feel strange, like they might not be connected to my body.

I can't stop whispering how sorry I am to Rose, or fussing over the graze on her head. I find a muslin and press it to my elbow. When I've got some of the blood off, which is awkward because I still have Rose in my arms, I see it's not that bad after all. And now Rose has calmed down, she seems fine. I look again at the graze. It's tiny, barely bleeding at all.

If you take her to the hospital, they'll report you.

The voice seems strong, clear. Coming from somewhere in the vicinity of my shoulder.

But what if Rose is hurt?

I pinch my bottom lip between my fingernails, over and over.

She's not. She's fine. But you won't be, if you take her to hospital.

The number six arrives and the doors open.

I stand up, but dots crowd out my vision again and I'm not sure I've even got the right change.

'Well? You getting on or not?' the bus driver says.

Eventually, I take a step back and shake my head.

The bus pulls away, leaving Rose and me standing in a cloud of exhaust fumes.

Chapter 20

4 WEEKS

Rose is fine. She's absolutely fine. The graze on her head fades after a couple of days and I comb her silky down over the tiny red mark it leaves behind. Her cord stump, the place where she was attached to me, has healed over and been replaced by an impossibly neat little belly button.

We don't go out much, but that's because:

A: the lift is busted again and I'm not chancing the sling.

And B: it's been raining all week.

So much for the summer. There are baby things drying all over the flat, hooked on doors and radiators. The place is starting to smell musty, but when I open the windows, the wind gusts rain through and soaks the sleepsuits hanging on the arm of the sofa. At least it's watering the flowers in my window box, because I'm in no state to remember. I'm running out of pretty much everything.

I stare out of the window at the dull drizzle. The sky looks low and heavy, as if all that rain is dragging it down on top of the world like some huge, grey duvet. Despite the rain, the air is close, muggy.

Joanna is due in a couple of days to do a visit and an 'assessment', which she hasn't done before. I'm guessing it's because I'm on my own with Rose now. I get on to Google to figure out what this assessment might mean, but all I can find is a bunch of stories that make my throat squeeze tight with fear.

I manage to give the kitchen area and bathroom a scrub-down with some washing-up liquid, but then that runs out and I know I'm going to have to use the sling again. Or ask for help, one of my least favourite activities. I could ask Dad, I suppose – he's emailed from work a couple of times – but I can't bring myself to make the call. Mum has left a couple of messages on my phone, but I deleted them without listening. I'll have to face her sooner or later, but it may as well be later in my opinion.

Rose pulls up her legs and grunts in a way that means a poo explosion is about to be unleashed. I'm tired. Really, really tired. I change her nappy, again, my arms moving on their own and my head still stuffed full of thoughts. *How did I manage to drop her? Should I have taken her to the hospital? Does this mean I'm a bad* … I shut that thought down.

Rose wriggles and kicks with her legs and manages to smear poo along the edge of the changing mat and on to the patterned rug.

I swear – I just can't stop myself. I wrestle her into her new nappy, ignoring her cries, her little legs bending up like a frog's. I chuck the nappy into a nappy sack, but she kicks one more time and manages to knock it on to the floor, poo side down.

'Great. Just great,' I mutter.

Rose starts to cry.

I clear up the mess as best I can with the dregs of the washing-up liquid, but it only smears the poo in a yellow streak over the rug. I feel a million times older than I ever thought possible. Rose is working herself up into a fury, and it takes every ounce of control to stop myself from shouting at her to shut the hell up and let me think.

I bundle up the half-packet of wet wipes I seem to have used into the flimsy blue nappy sack and shove it in the bin, which stinks of days'-old nappies and food scrapings, wash my hands and scoop Rose up to feed her.

As she settles down and her cries turn to happy little

grunts, a wave of remorse spikes me between the ribs and flows up so my scalp is prickling with it.

How can you be so impatient? Some mother you are.

'I know,' I whisper out loud, to myself, to Rose. To Nia.

Back in the hospital, when they put her on me, I was so sure she was mine, that I should keep her. I never stopped to think what it would all mean: the crying, the lack of sleep, the nappies and formula. Never having a second to myself to think. Rose's need. Sometimes I don't know if I can cope with how much she needs me for everything. I look at the way she searches for me; how she curls tight and safe on my chest and slips into that baby sleep, trusting. It sends this rush of warmth through me, knowing I'm her world.

But then I start with the what ifs? What if this is all a huge mistake? What if I can't look after her? It's all too scary, so I weigh myself again and feel a flare of triumph at the number. Nia pats me on the shoulder, like I'm a good girl.

There's a tap at the door: Robin.

I've been ignoring his knocks, but I can't bear these four walls any more.

'Just a minute!' I call out.

I run to the kitchen and put the book I've resurrected, plotting all the numbers of my life – weight, calories, waist and thigh measurements – in a drawer, then open the door.

'Howdy, stranger,' Robin says.

'Hey,' I say, and it sounds more like an admission of defeat than a greeting.

I go into the living area and slump on the sofa.

Robin follows, his nose wrinkling.

'It honks in here, I know,' I say.

'Well … maybe a bit. Do you need me to take the bin down?' he says.

I go to shake my head, but then turn it into a tight, embarrassed nod.

'Won't be a sec,' he says.

He rustles around in the kitchen then disappears with the stinking bin bag. In a few minutes he's back, flicking on the kettle, then goes into his flat for some milk when he sees I'm out.

'The cupboards are a bit bare, Ms Hubbard,' he says.

I don't answer.

Rose is now asleep. I ought to put her down for a proper nap, but recently she's started waking up when I try and move her and it's not worth the screaming fit she'll pitch if the transfer goes wonky.

'I heard Rose crying earlier,' Robin says, his voice gentle. He hands me a cup of tea and sits down. 'Actually, I heard her quite a bit last night too. And the night before that.'

'If you're here to complain, you need to get in line – the other side's got in first,' I say. I'm aiming for light-hearted, but it comes out knackered. Also, I'm pretty scared of the man next door.

'You know I'm not. I just thought perhaps it would do you good to get out for a bit?'

'Can't. Lift's busted. Sling's no good.' My eyes are burning like I doused them in bleach or something. They keep closing on their own. I force them open and try and focus on what Robin is saying, then realise he's not saying anything, just staring at me.

'OK. Right, here's what we're doing. I'll watch Rose while you get your head down. When was the last time you had more than a couple of hours' sleep in a row?'

'Dunno. Don't remember.'

'Give her to me. If she wakes up, I'll take her for a walk in the buggy. Here we go, come on, Rosie Posie.'

I try to protest but it comes out in a mumble.

The next moment, Rose's weight is lifted off my lap and I sink thankfully into sleep.

When I wake up, I'm in bed. Robin must have carried me. I hope he didn't think I was too heavy. Or too light … Right now, it seems there's no weight it would be OK for me to be.

It's dark. I feel like I just slept for twenty-four hours straight. I lie there, listening to the sound of Robin moving around the kitchen, chatting away to Rose. I think he might be telling her about some geeky sci-fi programme. I really ought to go and rescue her, but I'm enjoying the feeling of waking up on my own. For what seems like the first time in eternity, no one else is in the room. No one wants me. For a minute, I actually smile.

The need to simply lie here on my own battles with the knowledge that I have to get up, that I'm nearly out of nappies and formula and it's not fair on Robin, though he doesn't sound like he's bothered. He's so good with Rose. It seems easy for him, unlike me. How's that fair? I mean, most nineteen-year-old boys would be breaking out in a cold sweat at the thought of dealing with a baby, not making it look so simple. But then Robin's pretty capable.

I roll out of bed. I feel stiff all over, like I slept in one position and now I'm having trouble remembering how to move again. Like the dead, as they say.

'Hello!' Robin says. 'I was going to come and wake you. Your dinner's nearly ready.'

Rose spots me and goes from mildly diverted by whatever lecture Robin was giving her to a howling rage machine in approximately three seconds flat. So much for no one needing me. But today it's not a comforting thought.

It's more like a scarf tied too tight around my neck, the ends trailing on the floor, ready to trip me up.

I plug a bottle into Rose's mouth and she hooks her hand round mine. She's so warm and soft. How can I be having doubts about her?

'Right, I just need to grate some – woah!' Robin shoots an impressed look at Rose, who's up and over my shoulder and has just let out an epic belch. 'That's a big noise for such a sweet little baby,' he says and touches her on the cheek. 'Oh. I think she got some sick in your hair.'

'Figures,' I mutter and lay her down to wriggle about.

Robin's made chilli wraps with bowls of salad, Parmesan and mayo to mix in. He ladles his filling on and brings the wrap up at the sides, then folds it under, like an envelope, before taking a huge bite. I look at my own plate doubtfully, then copy his, minus the cheese and mayo. Mine falls apart as soon as I take a small bite, orange grease coating my fingers. I hold the wrap up and watch the drips glisten on the plate.

Fat, Nia says, and her voice pinches at me. But it also gives me this familiar feeling, like too-small shoes moulded into second feet.

I wade through a few mouthfuls and can feel them lodged under my ribs, like they're trying to work themselves back up. I hate this feeling more than anything.

Robin is staring at me, with this fake-casual expression, head on one side.

'So … I was thinking,' he says. 'Why don't we go somewhere tomorrow? Get out of here and take Rose someplace new?' It's there again, that confidence. How come he's not terrified at the prospect of taking her somewhere new?

'Like where? Hang on a sec.' I go to the bathroom and rinse my mouth to get rid of the chilli taste, then look in the mirror. There's a greasy orange streak on my chin. I scrub it hard

When I go back into the living area, Robin politely ignores my red chin and says, 'What about Sharland Wood? We could have a wander around, take a picnic.'

I'm about to make an excuse – I need to get some shopping in and finish tidying up properly – but something makes me glance up at the wall we painted what seems like a million years ago, and there's a swooping sensation inside, like a gap is opening up and I'm falling into it. All the rain has brought the damp back. Black patches of mould are starting to reappear through the paint in the top corners of the room. I look at the mould, and the yellow stain on the blue rug, right near Rose's head, and then turn to Robin.

'OK. Why not?' I say.

He grins.

Then I add, reluctantly, 'But first, would you be able to help me with the buggy? I'm kind of out of, well, everything.'

'I did notice,' Robin says.

Robin takes me shopping with the buggy in the morning. He steers like a pro round the shops, making revving noises while I stock up on nappies, formula, cleaning stuff and, grudgingly, food. Mainly noodles and fruit.

'Are you sure you've got enough? There's not much here,' Robin says.

'Oh yeah, I'll pop out again in the week,' I say.

Robin doesn't look convinced and I wonder when I became so … unconvincing. It used to be so easy. But he lets it slide.

At the till there's a woman with a little boy of maybe three. She stares into space while he writhes in the trolley.

'Want Bob the Builder,' he whines, fingers stretched out towards the exit where there's a tatty yellow digger ride.

The woman sighs and hands him a bag of apple slices.

He hits out and they scatter on the floor.

'Oh for heaven's sake,' she snaps, then bends to pick them up.

The little boy starts crying harder and Rose's eyes flutter open.

'Don't get any ideas,' I tell her, and I'm only partly joking.

I watch the woman push the overflowing trolley and the screaming boy, her back hunched over. I try and fast-forward through time, to when Rose might be crying for a stupid ride, but can't. Is this what it will be like? It seems impossible. The future seems so frightening with her in it, and she's changing so fast I don't know if I can keep up. Her neck seems less wibbly now; the other day when I was holding her she pulled right back and stared at me, and just as I was marvelling at her, the effort of holding her head up got too much and she crashed nose first into my collarbone. I nearly cried along with her, thinking I should have been ready for it, should have caught her head before she hurt herself.

Back at the flat, I get out stuff to make a Marmite sandwich to take on the picnic.

Robin shakes his head, saying, 'I already got some stuff from Aldi. We're having a proper picnic.'

I don't want to speculate on what that involves so I let him disappear off to his flat while I feed and change Rose and pack her bag.

Robin reappears after a while and hovers in the doorway.

'Sorry,' I say. I double-check I have two changes of

clothes for Rose, in case her nappy leaks. Actually, for when it leaks. A fold-up changing mat. Sun hat and sun cream. And nappies, sacks, wipes, muslins, bottles, socks, a blanket. A stuffed elephant I noticed she seems to like looking at. My phone, not that I'm expecting any calls. I zip the bag up.

'It all takes so long,' I say. I try and smile, but all I can hear is the whine in my voice.

'Yeah, I … can imagine,' Robin says.

'What's that?' I say, my head in the changing bag.

'Nothing. Shall we get going?'

Finally, laden with the buggy, car seat and what seems like enough luggage for a week's trip, we get into his knackered old Vauxhall.

Robin pats the steering wheel and turns to me, his expression stupidly proud. 'Hedda, meet Belinda. Belinda, this is Hedda.'

'Seriously? You seriously named your car? People actually do that?'

'Yup.'

He starts the engine and the rust bucket – I mean, Belinda – rattles and lurches into life. It sounds like the exhaust is about to fall off. Or possibly already has.

'Well, I've gotta say, it's a bit weird,' I say.

Robin doesn't answer, his focus on the road. He drives

like someone a few decades north of his age. Like, fifty decades. It's slightly terrifying, seeing as he does about ten miles under the speed limit yet still seems to brake the way he accelerates: very slowly.

'You sure you've passed your driving test?' I say.

'Oh yeah, I did one of those intensive courses straight after my seventeenth birthday,' he says.

I'm not sure it was intensive enough. I shut my eyes as Robin comes out of a street at a snail's pace, oblivious to the large van bearing down on him. The driver flicks his middle finger up then drives really close behind us, the engine a roar.

When I've managed to find my voice, it comes out shaky. 'Robin. Do you think you and Belinda could get us all there in one piece? Please?'

'Erm, sorry, what was that?' Robin says. He fiddles with the radio, only about a third of his attention on the road.

I decide I'll shut my eyes and hope for the best.

The next thing I know, Robin is whispering in my ear, 'Wake up, sleepyhead. We're here.'

Being dragged out of sleep before I'm ready feels a bit like I'm about to have heart failure these days. And it's a sensation I'm getting way too familiar with. I suck in a huge breath through my nose, suppress a groan and crane my head around the back of my seat to check on Rose.

She's fast asleep. I sit back, everything pounding, shaky and unreal.

We're in a little car park on the edge of the woods. It looks like we've outdriven the rain, because sun filters through the trees above the car, making patterns that dance across the back seat, a lattice of leaf shadow playing over Rose's face.

'Shall we picnic now by the car? It seems a shame to wake her,' Robin says.

'No, let's stretch our legs first.' I get out and reach up to the sky. It's nice to feel the breeze on my face and breathe in damp from leaves rather than mould.

'Are you sure? Shouldn't we … ?' Robin trails off when I go to the back of the car and open the boot to haul out the buggy.

We pick a wide, bumpy path and after a few moments the car park disappears and we're surrounded by cool, green pine trees, their needles forming a cushion that swallows our footsteps and the wheels of the buggy. Everything has that just-rained smell to it. Rose's eyes are open and she seems to like the breeze on her face. We walk, not aiming for anywhere in particular, Robin's shoulder a little way from mine. In the space between us, I sense Molly faintly, watching Robin.

When we get to a little clearing, Robin perches on the

massive trunk of a tree which looks like it was yanked out of the ground and tossed there by some huge creature. All the roots are in the air, naked and trailing splotches of mud. I turn Rose's buggy away and climb up on to the other end. The bark is rough and pitted under my fingers. I flake a piece off.

'So. How are you?' Robin says.

It's such a Felicity question, it takes me by surprise. I pick at more bark, consider how to answer.

'All right, I guess. Bit tired, you know. But then, what did I expect?'

The question hangs in the pine needles around us. Wind whistles through the tops of the branches and they seem to make a hushing sound.

'Do you know what you're going to do? When Rose is a bit older, I mean?' Robin says.

For a second it seems like my eyes go blurry, but then I realise it's just the sun dipping behind a cloud, making the clearing shadowy. I think about Molly, and the List, imagine her smiling gently over Robin's shoulder, saying, '*What **are** you going to do, Hed?*'

'You OK?' Robin says.

'Sure.' I smile at him. 'You mean college? Job? All that stuff?'

'Something like that.'

But I'm not convinced that was the question he was asking. He's giving me a look that seems both worried and something else. Interested, maybe, like he wants to know more about me. I consider what to say, leave it too long. He drops his eyes. Underneath the strips of bark I've flaked away, the tree trunk is pale and smooth.

'I don't know. I'm not thinking past the next feed and when I'm going to get some more kip at the moment,' I say.

I had a brief email conversation with college last week. Turns out all the spaces in their crèche are full, and besides, Edward the maths tutor said I've missed too much to catch up now. So on top of everything else, looks like I'm a drop-out. I suspect, given how fast she fired a terse email back, that the principal wasn't too sorry to see me go. Probably mucked up their attendance stats for one.

'You could ...' He leaves it hanging when he spots my look.

'What could I do? I've got no qualifications. There's nothing I'm good at.' I'm discounting Nia here so it's true. 'There's nothing I'm bothered about doing. I just want to look after Rose, and then ...' I break off.

I've been counting up all this time, counting how old Rose is, how many weeks we've been together, but it hits me now: somewhere deep inside I'm also still counting down, like I was before Rose was born, to the day everything goes back to normal.

To a place where it isn't me and Rose at all.

I never had any plans except for Nia.

So then, what is Rose? A stopgap?

'... helping other people like you? You could do psychology or counselling or something.'

I tear my eyes from the soft white tree innards, wishing I could put all the bark back. Robin is all hopeful, sparkling eyes and flashing teeth in a big smile, like an overenthusiastic puppy.

I narrow my eyes. 'You know what I think about people who've had "troubled pasts" and then go on to "save" other people just like them? I think that's a pile of crap.'

Robin blinks.

'I mean, when I was on a unit, it seemed to me like half the staff had their own problems. Why else would they want to work somewhere like that?'

'Maybe they wanted to help.'

I snort. 'Bollocks to that.'

'OK. I was just saying.'

I sigh. 'I know, I'm sorry. But I'm no Mother Teresa and I never will be.'

Robin looks like he's about to say something, but I've had it with the spotlight on me. Molly, Felicity, now

Robin – all of them asking questions and never giving any answers. Maybe it's time to turn things back the other way.

'What about you? Why did you end up at the Yewlings? Really?'

It's a shot in the dark, except that the little alarm I sometimes get about people, when there's something going on underneath, is blipping away, and it seems I have this need to pull back all the layers, even if I don't like what's underneath. There's something else too. I guess Robin's the first person since Molly who I really want to get to know properly.

Robin pushes himself higher on the tree trunk and looks away. 'I told you. My parents and I were fighting –'

'What about?'

'About … well …' He stares down at Rose's buggy like some answer might be found in there. Then he looks at me, and his eyes shimmer. 'I just … can't go into it. It's too …' He spreads his arms wide, lets them fall.

Painful, I think. Whatever it is, I know that look. I've seen it on Molly's face, for one.

'All right then, Mystery Man,' I say and smile, because I don't want to see that look any more – not on Robin.

Robin smiles too. He scoots up close to me and nudges his shoulder into mine. Then he hops to the ground and before I can tell him to get off, he's grabbed hold of me round the waist and lifts me down too. A frown flickers across his face. He puts me down super slowly, like he's worried he's going to smash me, and holds on a second longer than he needs to.

I freeze – I'm not used to anyone close to me except Rose, or the feeling of Nia – but then he lets go and grabs Rose's buggy and steers it in the direction we've just come from.

'Time to picnic,' he says.

Before I follow him, I pick up a long strip of bark and try to slot it back into the hole I made, but it curls at the edges and won't fit at all.

Chapter 21

5 WEEKS

'Well, it looks like Rose is getting on very well.'

Joanna passes me back Rose's red book from the health visitor which lists all her weights at the clinic, plots her growth on a line. She's right where she should be – exactly, in fact. I make sure I take her down to the clinic to be weighed twice a week, even though the health visitor said I could start coming less frequently now. I have another notebook for Rose as well as her red book, listing all her feeds, to make sure she's getting the right amount. I don't want to overfeed her.

Joanna snaps a file closed while I pretend I wasn't trying to look at what she's written in it. I don't know whether to be relieved the assessment I've been dreading is finally happening, so I can stop worrying about it, or if I just want to curl up as small as possible and pretend I'm somewhere else. I put one hand on Rose's head.

'But I'm more interested in you,' Joanna continues. 'How are you doing?'

'Fine. I'm good.'

'What about your support network?'

'Oh yes, I'm getting out and about plenty … Would you like some tea?' I say.

I catch her eye and work to keep my face from falling. Joanna is one of those ones. Sees too much for my liking.

'No thank you. Are you attending your counselling?'

'Yes,' I say, which for once is the truth.

We go through a questionnaire and it's like a game of Russian roulette. I'm trying to work out what to say and what not to say, and not to take too long over any of the questions. When Joanna asks about my plans for the future, I'm stumped for a moment and then I remember the conversation with Robin.

'Well, I was thinking about an Access to Nursing course. I just think …' I take a big breath and look up at her, my eyes wide, put as much sincerity into my voice as I can muster. 'I've been through a lot and I think I could really help other people. I *want* to help other people. And of course, it would be a stable income.'

Joanna holds my gaze and I keep absolutely still until she purses her lips like she's considering it.

'I did some research. There are bursaries. And there's help with childcare on the course.'

'How would you manage with shifts?' Joanna asks.

'I read that some lone parents …' I'm mastering the lingo, 'find childminders who can cover unsocial hours. And once I was qualified and in a job, I could find something with fixed shifts perhaps.'

'Well, I can see you've given it a lot of thought.'

'I have. I'm going to put an application in for September,' I say. 'The college has a crèche and Rose will be older by then and sleeping a bit more.'

Joanna nods, but I can't tell if she's convinced. 'Finances OK?'

I'm suddenly very glad she didn't want a cup of tea. No opportunity for her to get an eyeful of the empty shelves in the fridge.

'Yes,' I say, but she must catch my expression because she produces a slightly crumpled photocopied leaflet.

'There's a course on managing money at the community centre – budgeting, that sort of thing. Though it's in the evening and it doesn't look like there's childcare provision. Oh, it says here it's for the over-eighteens actually.' She pushes the leaflet back into her leather folder. 'Well, as you're coping, I'm sure you won't need it anyway, but I could see if there's anything for younger people. Or we could ask if they'd make an exception for you.' She looks doubtful about this.

'Don't worry, I'm fine,' I say.

I'm too scared to check how much money is in my account.

Before she goes, Joanna stops to examine the mould around the window.

'I'm going to speak to someone about that. Maybe make a complaint,' I say quickly.

To my surprise, she nods and says, 'I might be able to have a word with someone at the council.'

I shut the door after her and stand holding on to the handle. Remind myself to breathe. I can't tell if the assessment went well or not.

I go back in and scoop Rose up from the play mat. I sit her on my lap and just look at her, like she's a map I'm trying to read so I don't have to ask for directions any more. Her palms are so soft, the lines on the backs of her fingers like mine in miniature. I stroke her head and across her eyebrows, which are light blonde and very neat. Her lashes are long and curled, her eyes a deep blue with a darker ring around the edge of the iris. She's so beautiful she makes me breathless.

Rose looks at me.

I stare right back, and say, 'Well, we're doing all right, I think, aren't we?'

And suddenly, her lips stretch up and her whole face lights into a smile that's just for me. It lasts only a couple of seconds, but I know it's a real smile, not a wind-related one, and something in my heart opens and rushes like this shining river that could wash away anything that's ever been bad in the world, until there's nothing but the two of us.

Me and my girl.

My beautiful Rose.

6 WEEKS

'Awww, she smiled at me!'

Laurel has lost weight. She's been disappearing at lightning speed while I looked the other way. I'm worried about her, obviously. Also, a bit jealous. I've come out with Rose to meet her in a coffee shop, but Laurel won't have anything except water, not even black coffee. I go in for a cup of tea but, conscious of Laurel's eyes on me and the way she felt when we hugged hello, I don't put in any sugar. Laurel's cradling Rose, but her arms don't look strong enough to hold on.

'Here, pass her over. She probably needs a feed,' I say.

Laurel drops her eyes and looks for her phone when I plug Rose in.

'Does she always make those *noises*?' Laurel says, and I can tell she's trying not to sound disgusted.

'Only sometimes,' I say.

Laurel fiddles with the sachets of sugar in a bowl on top of the table, pinching them at one end and running the sugar along. She leans forward, a furtive look on her face. 'What's it like?'

'What's what like?'

'All of it. Being pregnant. I wish I could've seen you pregnant!'

I bet you do, I think.

'Giving birth must've been something. Did it kill?'

'In more ways than one,' I say.

'It's just so weird. Every time I look at you with her, I can't believe it. I mean, you were always so … focused,' Laurel says.

She means on Nia. I start to feel like she's enjoying it, seeing me like this, feeling like she's finally winning after all this time. And the worst thing is, I have no idea which one of us really is.

'Well,' I say. 'I guess I'd better get up to the unit to see Felicity.'

We say our goodbyes and arrange to meet again even though I'm stuck now, between admiration and envy, between hatred of her, of myself. I gaze at Rose in the buggy, remembering how I felt the other day looking at her, like there was nothing else in the world except her, and I try to reach out and scoop that feeling up. It works for a moment. Then a flash of Laurel's narrow shoulders pushes back, and I feel that sense of Rose being the only thing that matters slipping through the spaces between my fingers until only a tiny piece remains.

I sigh and push Rose's buggy through the coffee-shop door.

I've barely got off the scales and sat down before I'm saying to Felicity, 'I hate this.'

Felicity makes a disapproving noise before she writes down the number. She doesn't bother to go 'Mmm?', but waits for me to arrange the words in my head into some sort of order that will make sense.

'I don't know what I want any more,' I say. 'Nothing is the same. It's not just Rose. Well, it is. Everything was so clear before and now it's … complicated.'

There's A Silence.

Then, Felicity says, 'I wonder if it would help if you tried to consider your eating disorder in a different way?'

I don't really know what she means.

'I know you like research and lists. Why don't we make a list of everything you can think of about your anorexia? What you believe you've gained from it and what it's cost you.'

I give her a suspicious look, but Felicity ignores me and gets out an actual flip chart and marker pens.

I go over, rolling my eyes, but when I write *NIA* in big letters at the top, she stops me.

'No. I think you need to detach from your eating disorder. Despite what you think, it is not a person. It's not. And it doesn't have to be a part of you either. I think you know it, deep down.'

I stand with the red pen in my hand. The fumes from it are making me feel sick. I stick my chin up and stare. I'm not doing this.

Felicity lets the silence stretch for a while, then sighs. 'Let's just make the lists, shall we?'

I stare for a while longer, then turn my eyes up to the ceiling. 'Whatever. Fine.'

NIA

Pros:

(Felicity is already grumbling at this)

~~Pros:~~

What I believe I get out of it:

- Being thin
- Being safe ('What does safety mean to you?' Felicity says. I stare at the word 'safe' for a long time, then write the next point)
- Nia keeps the world away
- Being in control – I'm in charge (Felicity makes a noise about this, but then I remind her I'm supposed to be making the list, not her)
- Attention (this is Felicity's suggestion, which I only add after a long argument)
- Having A Purpose
- A distraction
- Makes me special, different
- I'm good at it
- I don't know how to do anything else

Cons:

(Felicity sighs again)

~~Cons:~~

What it has cost me:

- Nothing (another argument)
- ~~Nothing~~

- Missing school
- Losing my friends
- Having to be in hospital
- Hurting my family
- Hurting myself
- It ~~might~~ will kill me one day

(Long, long pause. And then I write:)

- It might hurt Rose

'Can you tell me a little more about this last one?' Felicity says, but I fold my arms and glare at her, and wisely, she doesn't push.

My hour is nearly up. It's taken me this long to get those few points and they don't begin to cover everything. Not even close. I think about the notebook in my drawer at the flat again, my own personal unit crap and not-so-crap list. It's starting to occur to me I never actually thought about why I was in hospital in the first place, about what put me there. Or that maybe there's other crap things about Nia apart from being in the unit. I grip the sides of my arms hard enough that it starts to hurt. No way am I saying that out loud.

'I think we should revisit this next week,' Felicity says.

I bite my lip, because what I really want to do is take a

huge black marker pen and scratch lines all over the words on the flip chart. This is all stupid. Except, it's also made me think a bit. Trouble is, from where I'm looking I have no idea which side is winning. And even though I know that Rose should count for so much more than anything on that list, somehow it's not as comforting a thought as it should be. It also makes me feel a tiny bit … trapped.

7 WEEKS

Rose is crying. The sound of it fills the flat, my head. My arms ache with holding her, pacing in tight circles around the poo-stained rug. It feels like we've been here forever, her and me.

The guy next door bangs on the wall.

'Come on, sweetie, stop crying, please,' I say.

I don't know what's wrong with her, with me. I can't seem to sleep even when she does. I wish there was a remote control for life so I could put it in reverse. I wish I was the baby and someone would come and look after me.

Rose keeps crying and I can't help it; a horrible rage is building inside me, along with the noise, until I think I might explode. I suddenly have a vision of letting Rose fall to the floor, anything to stop the crying. I put her down very slowly on the rug and go into the bedroom and lean over the bed, trying to shut my ears against her piercing cries, pulling air in and out of my lungs and wishing with everything I have for sleep.

I can't do this.

I've tried everything: feeding, changing, burping, songs, TV to distract her. Nothing is working. Maybe she hates me.

Another bang on the wall; he's really hammering at it.

A shout: 'Shut that baby up.'

I feel like battering his door down, thrusting Rose into his hands and shouting, 'You bloody try!' and then running far, far away, getting a train and just disappearing.

Maybe I hate her. How can this be possible when I love her so much?

I just need some sleep. My head is so fuzzy.

Rose is still screaming in the other room, but I can't make my feet move. And I think, *I don't want this. I never wanted this*. I was right all those months ago, when I thought I should get the abortion. Why did I change my mind in the hospital? Why did I think I could look after her? I can't even get her to bloody sleep.

The sound of it builds to a crescendo and there's nothing but white noise in my head.

Nia joins in, the usual chant: *Fat, disgusting bitch*.

If I believed in God, I'd be praying round about now.

But I don't. I go back into the living area and I put my face close to Rose's and I hiss, 'Shut up! Just shut up.'

Needless to say, this makes her cry more and I pick her up and slump down on the floor with her, appalled at myself. She wriggles and screams in my arms.

What is wrong with you?

I feel like Nia is watching me, watching and laughing in a dark, smoky voice, snaking around the light fitting, floating in the mould flecking the walls.

I think I might be losing my mind.

There's banging on my door now, then voices shouting in the corridor. I think I hear Robin. I open the door, chain on, Rose in one arm, and see Robin's profile, the guy from next door squaring up to him. Robin's as tall as the next door man, but way skinnier and he looks so young, like his namesake in *Batman*. Too young to step up and be a superhero. Rose is still crying, but quieter now, exhausted little bleats like a lamb. The next-door man says something and then goes back into his flat, slamming the door so hard I feel the whole flat shudder. Robin's shoulders slump and he leans against the wall for a second, his chest going up and down quickly, then turns and peers through the gap in the chain. He has shadows under his eyes. It's nearly one in the morning.

'I'm sorry. Are you OK? I'm sorry. She won't stop

crying,' I say in a voice that sounds like death and then I burst into tears.

Robin comes in, takes Rose and settles her down. I feel sick and shaky. Dried out. I sit on the bed, knees hunched up to my chest, and pinch the fat all the way down the backs of my thighs. I'll have bruises in the morning, but it serves me right.

'She's down,' Robin says in a whisper from the doorway.

'Thank you.'

He sits next to me on the bed. 'It will get better.'

'Will it? How do you know that? What if … ?' I can't finish the thought. It's one thing to think I've made a mistake, keeping Rose; it's another to say it out loud. And I do love her. I do, I do, I do.

Robin puts an arm around me and I let him pull me close, so my ear is resting against his chest. I wonder if that's what Rose likes about him: his heartbeat is steady, not stop-start-splutter like mine.

After a while his other arm comes across my shoulder. I look up into his face, the moonlight glancing over it through the open curtains. He pushes my hair back from my forehead and then leans down and touches his lips to mine, only for a second, then pulls back.

'Robin …' I begin.

'Get some sleep. I'll pop round tomorrow,' he says.

I lock the door behind him and drag the Moses basket inch by inch through to the bedroom, then finally lie on the bed and fall asleep without bothering to close the curtains.

When I wake up, Rose is making cooing noises in her basket. I scrub at my face with the back of my hand. It's already nearly morning, the dawn light making everything warm and orange. I look at the clock: 5 a.m. That can't be right, can it? That means Rose has slept for four hours.

I lean over and steal a glance at her. She's gumming away at one fist, looking delighted she's managed to get it in her mouth. She fills up the whole basket; I really need to get Dad to come over with the cot. Like he said he would ages ago.

I risk leaving her there while I go to the loo, and then come back and scoop her up, resting my cheek on her warm head. It strikes me that she's not even classed as a newborn any more. Maybe this is the start of something new.

'Sorry,' I whisper.

I make a silent vow I'll never lose my temper with her again, never question my decision to keep her.

We fit together, Rose and I. We have to.

We watch the sun come up together.

* * *

I wait until eight, as it's Saturday, and then send a text to Dad.

Hi Dad. Any chance you could drop the cot off sometime? H x

I'm surprised when my phone beeps almost immediately.

I'll be there in a bit, Dad x

He must be wanting to escape home.

It feels like Rose and I have been up for years when he finally knocks on the door, though it's only nine.

He has one end panel of the cot in his hands and looks a bit red in the face.

'Your lift is out of order,' he says.

'Oh yeah. Probably should have mentioned that,' I say.

He gives me a wry look. 'Where do you want this?'

I get him to put the end in my bedroom – there's nowhere else for it to go.

'Might be a bit of a squeeze,' Dad says. 'Any chance of a cuppa before we get the rest? And a cuddle with my granddaughter, of course.'

I plonk Rose in his arms and watch them out of the corner of my eye as the kettle boils. Dad is holding Rose up at an angle which is asking for trouble. I want to say, '*watch her head*' and '*don't drop her*' and '*careful*', and I hear echoes of Mum's voice over the years, telling me not to do this and to be careful of that. A tiny, tiny part of me might be starting to get why she says some of the stuff she does; that need you get with a child, to protect. Maybe a little bit.

The next moment, Rose has puked on Dad's trousers. I rush over with a packet of wet wipes and he mops himself down good-naturedly.

'I forgot they do that,' he says.

'Did I?'

'You were always being sick,' Dad says. 'You had colic or whatever they call it; you'd scream for hours. It's no wonder …' He stops and I look at him, my head on one side. 'So, shall we see about the rest of this cot?'

'You haven't had your tea yet.'

'Ah yes, perhaps in a bit. What about asking that young man from next door to lend a hand?'

I feel a bit guilty going to Robin so soon after last night. Also awkward because we sort of kissed and I'm not sure if it was a spur-of-the-moment kiss, or a pity kiss or what. And I don't know if I liked it and whether I'd like to kiss him again.

Robin's up though and happy to help. It takes them a couple of trips to get the cot up the stairs and then there's a bit of banging and mumbled swear words as they try and put it together. Finally, it's done. I'm practically going to have to climb over it to get in and out of bed and I'd have to move it altogether to open both wardrobe doors.

'Looks great!' I say, because it's no one's fault except mine we're in a minuscule flat in the crappy bit of town.

Dad seems to be having the same thoughts because he frowns. Though he doesn't suggest we come home. Probably for the best.

He wanders off to look for more things to fix and Robin turns to me. 'You like it?'

'Yeah, I do. It makes everything seem more … permanent.' I say it absently, without really realising what I've said, then want to suck those words right back inside, where they belong.

Robin gives me a shrewd look. 'That's a good thing?'

Maybe it's because of that sort-of kiss, or his heartbeat last night, steady as a metronome, but for once I don't talk around, and just say, 'I think so. It's scary though.'

'I guess it must be. I can't imagine all the responsibility.'

'Ah, I'm sure you'd make a great dad.' I smile.

'I need to get off – lots to do,' he says, and he's off out of the bedroom with me staring at his retreating back and cursing myself for being stupid. He must have thought I was fishing for a father for Rose … I put the back of one hand against my cheek and it comes away hot.

With Robin gone, it's just me and Dad, with Rose on his lap.

'Any biscuits?' he says hopefully, when I hand him his tea.

He nearly drops Rose when I produce a packet of Rich Tea. I don't have the heart to tell him Robin brought them over a couple of weeks back, in case I needed a snack when I was feeding her. They've stayed in their packet ever since.

'You having one?'

'I'm all biscuited out,' I say and drop my eyes to drink my tea.

Dad fusses with Rose, jiggling her about on his knee and straightening the bib she's got around her neck to catch all the spit-up milk and drool.

'Dad?'

'Mmm?'

'Do you think I could have had reflux or something? When I was tiny?'

He's still looking at Rose, not me.

'It's just you said I was sick and screamed a lot. Perhaps it was reflux – I read about it online. Maybe I wasn't a difficult baby,' I say.

He looks at me. 'Who said you were a difficult baby?'

'Mum did. Loads of times.' I'm pretty sure Dad's heard her say it at least once. I try and remember which Family

Therapy sessions he actually showed up to, and what he said, but get only blank space.

'Well, I suppose you did cry a lot and your mother didn't … Well, it was tough for her. She had a touch of the baby blues – I think that's what it was. And it didn't help that I had to be away for work so much.'

'You mean like the baby blues day-four thing?' I say and shudder, remembering how I turned into a ball of tears. Stupid hormones, making you feel stuff.

'I think it went on longer, a few months maybe,' he says.

'She had postnatal depression? Why did no one tell me about this? Why do you think she had … ?'

Dad's gaze, which has been split between Rose and me, sharpens and he sits up straighter. It seems like he's trying to look everywhere but into my eyes, like he doesn't want me to read what's in his. 'I don't know about all these terms – reflux, post-whatever depression. She had a difficult time. Things were … difficult. But she was fine after a while. And she adored you.'

I snort.

'She did. She does. It's not been easy for her, you know. She –'

'It hasn't been easy for me!' Suddenly my voice is getting louder and higher, all the years of not talking scrambling over themselves, trying to get out. 'Do you have any idea what it was like on all the units? How scared I was? My best friend died in front of me.'

It's the first time I've said it so bluntly and the words seem to swing back round, smack me between the ribs.

But Dad's face is careful, remote.

I take a deep breath, about to go on, but then I stop. What's the point?

Dad hands Rose back to me silently. 'It's not been easy for any of us, love,' he says, with a final tone in his voice. Then he turns to look at the ceiling. 'Are they going to do anything about this damp?'

I open my mouth, then shut it. Part of me wants to finish raging, to hurl every insult I can think of at him, so that he'll stop and listen. So he'll see me. But I don't.

Instead, I say, 'I'll get on to the council about the damp. Get them to send someone out.' It's on my to-do list, except I hate speaking to them. Last time I tried phoning, the woman more or less laughed at me and said there was a backlog. I got the impression they'd be getting round to the Yewlings in 2050 or so.

'Great. It's not good for the baby. In the summer it might be all right, but you can't have her in a damp flat all winter. That's no place for a baby. She could get ill.' He stands up to go. 'Your mother misses Rose. You should call her.'

I grunt a non-committal response.

'Let me know if you need any money,' Dad says.

'I'm OK, thanks,' I say, even though this is not really true.

I catch a relieved look on his face.

As he goes up the corridor, all I want to do is run after him with Rose and shout, '*Don't leave us here alone. We need someone to look after us.*'

But there's only me. And I don't.

Instead I shut the door and finish the rest of the Rich Tea biscuits, then quietly, despairingly, get rid of them again, the only version of a binge Nia lets me do. I tell myself it's just this once.

Chapter 22

8 WEEKS

I go to the library to choose more books for Rose. The alien one got boring, so now I take the buggy and load it up with five or six at a time. She seems to like the rhyming ones best, or ones with really bright pictures. That's what I reckon, anyway.

On the way to the library I keep thinking about the look on Dad's face when I asked about Mum last week. There's something he isn't telling me, I'm sure of it. But I won't get anything out of him; he's barely replied to my texts except to offer more money, which I declined. Somehow, I don't want to take money from him.

I do call Mum though. Dad was right about one thing: Mum missing Rose. We meet up in a cafe in town because I don't want to go to the house and she hates the flat.

As soon as she sees Rose her face gets this starved look and she reaches out like she can't stop herself. Guilt twists in my stomach as I hand Rose over.

Mum cradles her and gazes down like she's forgotten how to speak. Eventually, she looks up at me, her eyes overly bright.

'She's grown so much. I can't believe how fast they change.'

Rose looks the same to me, but then I see her every day. I sit down. Mum is still stroking the side of Rose's head. Rose smiles at her and I can see the way it lights Mum up. She sits Rose on her lap and chats to her, showing her a napkin, jingling her bracelet in front of Rose's entranced eyes. Very faintly, I feel something inside me starting to soften, the way butter might if you take it out of the fridge.

'So, shall we order?' Mum says and gives me another look and I realise immediately: she knows. She knows I'm not eating what I should be. She probably clocked it straight away.

But because this is the only dance we know how to do, I make myself smile and say, 'Sure!'

I scan the menu, pulse racing, making calculations in my head, but I can't look for too long because that would be a giveaway – and so would ordering a salad and Diet Coke. A waitress comes over and Mum orders the soup of the day and a roll, and then it's my turn. I can't help it – I keep my eyes on the menu a fraction too long, while Nia screeches at me, wanting to know how the soup is made, is it with cream, what's the calorie content?

I speak through her, 'Same for me please,' in a voice that is so close to normal that no one but Mum would sense anything is up.

The waitress goes.

Mum shows no sign of handing Rose back.

I figure deflection is as good a strategy as any, so I say, 'How are Tammy and Dad?'

'They're both fine.'

I wait for the inevitable follow-up, what new marvels Tammy has produced, but Mum doesn't say anything else. I frown.

She's had her highlights done, I realise, but the colour is a shade off and, instead of flattering her, it makes her skin look sallow and old. And she's wearing a hell of a lot of make-up and perfume, more than normal, like body armour. Is it for me, or is something else going on?

I try and think of what to say, and settle on: 'I probably should've told Dad about the busted lift the other day.'

Mum looks blank.

'When he brought up the cot?'

'Oh! Yes, of course.' Mum shifts Rose on her lap. 'He's working away a lot at the moment.' There's a tightness to the way she says it, but there's no time to ask what's going on as the soup's arrived.

'Here, why don't I hold Rose so you can eat?' I say.

'No, that's fine. You have yours before it goes cold,' Mum says and gives me a hard look.

Bollocks.

I crumble the roll into tiny pieces, add salt to the soup. Take a sip of water. All the while, Mum watches.

There's nothing for it. I could just take Rose and go, but I'm afraid of what that means, of what Mum could say to Joanna. So I force it all down, make myself tell Mum it's lovely, and when she passes Rose over so she can eat hers, I pull Rose to me, against my stomach which is bulging out by a mile. I could lean down now and be sick, watch all that greasy soup slosh over the floor in one huge release.

I start to tap my foot on the floor, and maybe Rose senses how uncomfortable I am because she wriggles and begins to cry.

I pull her up and give a big sniff of her bum and say, 'Uh-oh, I think someone needs a change!' in one of those horrid sing-song voice people do when they're talking to babies.

Mum puts her spoon down.

'No, no, you eat your soup. I'll be back in a second,' I say and shoot across the cafe and into the disabled toilets.

There's nowhere to put Rose, and I feel another hard spike of guilt as I take off my jumper and lay her on it on the toilet floor. Then I lean over and let it all go, rinse my mouth and flush. I have to wait for my head to stop pulsing and my heart to go back to what passes for normal for me, before I feel safe enough to pick Rose back up.

Back at the table, Mum narrows her eyes. 'You forgot your change bag,' she says.

'Oh, it must have just been wind – she was only a tiny bit wet. But it took an age to get her poppers done up; she wriggles so much,' I say, and hope my breath doesn't smell like sick.

Mum gets this look, an old one I know well, her eyebrows going up in the middle.

But before she can say anything, inspiration hits and I say, 'It's such a shame they don't have a proper changing table in here. It's discrimination really. Someone should have a word.'

And Mum chooses to believe me, chooses to get indignant at the lack of facilities, asks to speak to the manager.

'We need to get off soon,' I say when the waitress has retreated to find her boss. 'Thanks for lunch.'

I strap Rose into her buggy.

'It's been nice to see you. Both of you,' Mum says. I have to strain to catch the last bit over the noise of the coffee machine in the corner. 'Don't be a stranger,' she says.

We hold each other's eyes for a second. I nod.

Then a woman comes up to Mum, her face flushed. 'Can I help at all?'

'Yes,' Mum says in a firm voice, and I know the manager is going to be there for a while.

I use the opportunity to make my escape.

The following day, I'm getting ready for another session with Felicity when the post arrives. It's A Brown Envelope. This means nothing good. I put it on the side carefully, like it may shoot out papery tongues and cover me in tiny cuts, but my problem is, I always want to know, even if it's bad.

'Let's get it over with, shall we?' I say to Rose, whose face splits into a grin that lights her whole being. Sunlight streams through the window, bathing her face. My throat catches. Times like these almost make up for the nights when she cries and I think I can't do it any more.

Reluctantly, I turn to the envelope and rip the end away in one go, like yanking off a plaster hard and fast. I scan the letter and swear under my breath. I've missed an appointment for my benefits. When did they send it? I spool back over the past few weeks, trying to remember any other letters, but can't. There's a helpline number to call but it eats credit and I hardly have any on my phone as it is. I'm going to have to go down the Job Centre and try to sort it out.

An hour later, I steer Rose's buggy into the benefits office. I hate this place. I've only been here once before, when I first got discharged from the unit and they had to assess me, which was a bundle of laughs. I had an appointment that time, but today I've just shown up. I look around and realise you've got to take a ticket. I get one, then sit as far away from everyone else as I can, so I can convince myself I don't really belong here.

The wait takes forever. People come and go over the stained carpet, the air thick and heavy with desperation and a side of anger. One wall is made of plate glass and it should make the place cheery but it only highlights the dinginess. I fret over Rose, sitting her up and sliding my hand down her vest to check how hot she is. According to my phone it's time to feed her, so I get out a bottle, which is the exact moment my number is called. Typical. I struggle to the front, ignoring Rose, who is not happy her meal just got interrupted and goes red as she works up to full scream mode.

When I see the woman behind the desk, I know it's

going to be bad. She has deep frown lines scored between her eyebrows and a mouth that turns down as she takes the crumpled letter I hand her.

'I really don't think I got any letter about an appointment,' I say.

She taps at her keyboard. 'Can you confirm your address?'

I do.

'We sent you a letter about your assessment on the twentieth,' she says.

'But I didn't get it. Look, I just had a baby and it's all been a bit crazy. Couldn't you just … ?'

But it's no use. I can already tell from the way she frowns down her nose at me and taps at her keyboard with hard clicks of her gel nails – which, by the way, are ridiculously ugly – that she isn't going to bend any rules for me.

'I'm afraid because you missed your appointment your Disability Benefit has been suspended,' she says, and there's this gleam in her eyes, like she's enjoying this.

'For how long?' My voice goes up in alarm.

She takes her time flicking through computer screens and checking boxes. 'It says here you should be claiming Income Support anyway, if you've had a baby. You can fill in this form.' She hands it to me.

'What? No one told me that. How long will it take?'

She all but shrugs. 'We can usually process a new claim within a month.'

'A month? What am I supposed to live on until then?'

Her face says it's not her problem.

I take the form and start to fill it in, but they need loads of info I don't have with me. I'll have to take it home. I consider asking for help, but Rose is making noises that suggest I've got three minutes, maybe four tops, before she lets loose and I can feel sweat running down my back. I steer her buggy out into the hot sun and find a bench to feed her on, then check my phone and swear again when I realise it's going to be really tight getting to my appointment with Felicity.

In the end, I'm ten minutes late, but Felicity is running behind. I didn't bring any water with me and a headache has my temples in a pincer grip. All I want to do is lie on the floor and go to sleep. I shut my eyes for a moment and don't open them until I hear Felicity next to me.

'Hello, Hedda. You feeling OK? You look rather pale.'

It's a struggle to force my eyes open.

I push Rose's buggy down the corridor after her.

Felicity has given up complaining about me bringing her. In any case, I've pointed out I've got no one to look after her, so if Felicity wants me to show up, Rose comes too.

'Can I have some water please?' I say and it comes out croaky.

Felicity has the flip charts out from last time.

I try not to groan. 'I'm not really in the mood for all this,' I say.

Felicity raises her eyebrows in a 'go on' expression.

I feel like it's not really me sitting here, with Rose now asleep in her buggy, like the past few months can't possibly have happened.

'Maybe it's a dream … or nightmare. Whatever,' I mutter. If I concentrate hard enough on one spot, my eyes blur and it seems like the room isn't real. Like I could disappear.

'Perhaps by making yourself physically smaller, you felt like you could somehow disappear,' Felicity says.

'Did I say that out loud? I'm losing track … Sleep deprivation. They do say it's a killer!' I'm aiming for a breezy tone, but I sound more like a zombie. The heat's not helping. 'Can I open a window?'

Felicity switches on a fan on her desk and I angle my chair so the breeze blasts me in the face and guzzle down the cup of water she passes to me.

'I thought you said I was after attention.' I nod at the flip chart, which is back up in the corner, remembering Felicity adding the word to the list.

Felicity raises her eyebrows.

'I don't know … Maybe I was, when I was younger. But now … well, there's other reasons to disappear,' I say. I think about running from the room, leaving Rose and everything behind and finding some cottage up in the hills where I could be a shepherd or something, away from civilisation.

'We've talked about disappearing before – about what it means to you,' Felicity says.

The room is so hot, my brain is struggling to process.

Felicity goes on. 'There are all sorts of pressures: exams, family, career, social media …' She doesn't say 'looking after Rose'.

'… Growing up, friends, people's expectations. Yeah, yeah, I know. Anorexia as an escape from all that. I've read the books.' I mean it to be sarcastic, but I'm really tired.

Felicity is giving me an odd look.

'What?' I say.

'That's the first time I've ever heard you refer to your eating disorder without personifying it.'

I didn't notice. 'So?'

'Don't you think that's important?'

Silence.

Felicity gets up and, very deliberately, scores through the *NIA* at the top of the flip chart.

I don't move to stop her.

'I'd like you to do some more work on this before your next session. Perhaps you could write down what your eating disorder means to you, the reasons why you feel you developed it in the first place.'

I want to roll my eyes, or argue that this is ground she's tried to cover with me before and why bother yet again? But I'm too tired to do anything except give a nod.

'I'll try. That's all I'm promising,' I say.

Felicity smiles and it reminds me of seeing Rose's smile, like maybe this is something of Felicity I'm seeing for the first time.

'That's a start,' she says.

Back at the flat, I struggle to make sense of the benefit forms, which need their own twenty-page booklet to explain them. I get through half, then give up for the day. My headache is still drilling. I check my account online and realise the payment I was supposed to get today from the benefits – sorry, *welfare* – lot is missing, which means I have about a tenner to my name. That Job Centre woman worked fast, I'll give her that.

Looks like there's only one choice.

I pick up the phone to dial Dad, but it takes forever to pull his number up in my contacts, like my thumbs don't want to obey me. He doesn't answer and I listen as it goes through to voicemail. I don't leave a message.

Instead I get on the net and start looking at payday loans, the ones where you can borrow a few hundred, no questions asked, and pay it back the next week. I looked at them ages ago, before I found out about Rose, but never actually went through with getting one once I realised the interest rate was gigantic. I just sat in the dark for two days instead when the electricity ran out. Not really an option now, with Rose. It's stupidly easy – there's even a little dancing pound sign egging you on – but still my hand hovers over the final button for a long time, before I hit it and the payday loan wings its way to my account.

Chapter 23

9 WEEKS

'Is this oven on?'

It's Robin's birthday today and I'm baking him a 'surprise' cake that turns out not to be a surprise at all, because Rose is in super-whiny mode and won't be put down. I tried my hardest, but after half an hour of attempting to stir one-handed and then realising I'd forgotten to buy eggs, I gave up and knocked on Robin's door.

He answered in just his joggers, which was a bit of a shock. Not in a totally horrible way, I have to admit.

'Been napping, have we?' I said, and it was really cute, the way he went red.

'Sorry … Hang on, I'll just …' He disappeared off and came back, pulling a T-shirt over his head.

'What's up?' he said.

'Well, I just wanted to say happy birthday,' I said, and handed over a pot plant I'd picked up for a couple of quid and a card.

He pulled the plant to him, opened his mouth, but I said, 'I don't do thanks and all that. Anyway, you need to come and bake your birthday cake. Also, bring eggs.'

Robin's laugh echoed behind me.

Twenty minutes later, he showed up with eggs and a dubious expression.

'Yes, the oven's on … Hang on … No, it's not. Bugger,' I say.

'And what's happened here?'

I have to admit, the 'cake' does look a bit sketchy, half-mixed in the bowl. I've never made one before and it doesn't look like I'll be going in for *The Great British Bake Off* any time soon.

Robin gives it a sniff, then coughs. 'Perhaps we ought to start again?'

He scrapes out the bowl into the bin before I can stop him, which means he gets an eyeful of the half-congealed noodles from last night.

'Getting sick of noodles?' he says. 'I'll bring over some of that spicy chicken to put on them when I next make it.'

I nearly say 'no need', but it feels too rude, so I just smile instead.

I pop Rose on her play mat in the doorway so she can still see us and this time she doesn't fuss. I swear it's Robin's voice that does it. I guess we both like listening to him talk.

I'm checking the amount of flour on the scales, when Robin says, from close behind me, 'Hedda …'

'Yeah?'

'I wanted to … I need to talk to you about something.'

'Uh-huh,' I say, and shake a bit more flour in.

There's a pause.

I stop and turn towards him. 'What?'

'It's just …' He pushes his glasses up his nose and looks out of the window, like he's hoping the right words will float through or something.

I feel my body go stiff.

'What?' I say again, and my voice is all wrong, rough and suspicious. There's a sudden avalanche of flour which hits the scales in a big *whumph*, sending a powdery cloud up into the air and all over the floor.

We both start coughing, then Robin leans over. 'You've put too much in,' he says, with a funny sort of smile.

Before I can reply, he's spooned some out and then starts sifting the flour, holding the sieve up really high.

'What are you doing that for?' I say, coming up next to him.

'I read that it gets all the air into it, makes the cake lighter,' he says.

'Oh. OK, Delia Smith.'

Robin flicks his wrist and a light dusting of flour scatters over my head.

'Hey!'

I go to grab the sieve off him, but he's too strong and we wrestle for a second, then I poke him under the armpit and he curls up to one side.

'Ha! I knew you were ticklish.' I snatch at the sieve and manage to knock it up out of his hand and into his face. I freeze.

Robin gives me a startled look, then starts to laugh. He dips his hand in the bowl and flicks more flour at me, and the next thing, we're having a full-scale flour fight in the kitchen. It's everywhere, in our hair, coating our shoulders, even a bit on Rose, who kicks her arms and legs out like an excited starfish. Neither of us can stop laughing. Then Robin picks up what's left of the bag and holds it over my head.

'Don't even think about –' I break off because he's started tipping.

I reach up and feel the softness of it, like warm snow-flakes, tickling my fingers. I go still and so does Robin. He lowers the bag, then reaches out with a white-coated hand and brushes my hair back.

He takes a step forward, and suddenly I want to press into him, to feel his big heart, and his arms holding me tight. I want to kiss him properly.

'You look like a tiny snow angel,' Robin says.

And that's it. One minute I'm with him; the next I'm gone. I'm in the unit and Molly is playing her sax, the long, low notes of it keening as I watch from the doorway.

I never did get jazz, not really. Everything sounded jumbled up, like someone had snipped a load of random words from a newspaper and dropped them on the floor and she'd play first one phrase then another, yet nothing connected. Except it did that winter's day. I heard her playing from my room, and even though I wasn't supposed to, I crept down the corridor and eased her door open. The notes were long, a minor key. Less frantic than normal. She met my eyes, but didn't stop playing. Get-well cards from family and friends were plastered all over her wall. Photos too. But none of Molly. Some had snipped edges, a hole in the middle of a laughing group of people around a barbecue where she'd erased herself.

I went to the window, watched the trees shake frosted leaves in the wind. Molly kept playing. She played, and it seemed those leaves were in her music, beautiful but iced over. I might have made a movement, or sighed, I can't remember. The next moment, Molly put down the sax. I felt the air behind me shift with her breath.

Her fingertips pressed my shoulder blades, light as a flower. 'They're like angel's wings. Don't let them fly you so high you can't get back.'

I didn't say anything. In that winter place, with everything normal stripped away, what was there to say?

She knew it too, because she grabbed her sax again and started playing something else, something more upbeat. The moment was over, and they were calling us to the table for dinner.

'Are you OK?' Robin says. His eyes are so warm.

I blink, trying to dislodge flour from my eyelashes. It's only the flour that's making my eyes water. Just the flour.

'I think we've run out of ingredients. Looks like we'll have to do the cake another time,' I say. I take a step back, but my heart is going hard.

Robin's hand drops to his side.

'Happy birthday though,' I say.

Robin's face falls slightly, then he looks around the flour-spattered kitchen. 'You sure you don't want a hand clearing up?'

'Nah, I'll do it.'

'OK.' He hovers in the doorway for a second longer, then says in a rush before leaving, 'Thanks for the plant.'

It isn't until after he's gone that I realise he never finished whatever he'd been about to say. I tell myself it's nothing, but still it bothers me, like a sock that's twisted wrong under your foot, but I end up walking on it anyway.

Running late. Be there in ten. Hed x

I'm meeting Laurel in the park a few minutes' walk from the flats. Without Rose. Laurel sounded pretty upset on the phone and Robin offered to have Rose and I realised I haven't left her with anyone else yet. But it's harder than I thought to step out of the door.

'Do you think I ought to leave more nappies? Just in case?'

'She's fine. Anyway, you'll only be gone an hour, won't you?' Robin says.

Right. I can do this.

'OK,' I say. 'Be good for Uncle Robin. See you soon.' I kiss Rose's head and walk out of Robin's flat fast, before I change my mind.

Outside I feel naked without a sling or a buggy in front of me. There's all this space I don't know what to do with. I keep running my hand over my phone in my pocket, as though a bomb might go off in the flats behind me, or a flood, or fire, or …

I spot Laurel on one of the swings, trailing her feet on

the floor. How has she lost so fast? She's going some, even for us. She turns a white face to me as I sit on the swing next to her and loop the tops of my arms round the chains. She has a piece of paper in her hand.

'What's that?' I say.

'My "transition plan".'

Oh. Laurel's eighteen now. She's still an outpatient at Dewhurst, but she must have known they'd be moving her into Adult Services sometime soon.

She crumples the plan in her fist and chucks it on the ground. 'It's a pile of crap anyway.'

'When are you transferring?'

'Don't know. Soon. It'll be good. They don't bother with you as much, anyway. I'll be able to do what I like.'

I spent a week in an adult unit once, when there were no beds available at Dewhurst and the children's ward at the hospital couldn't have me either. It's a place I try hard not to think about. It's not somewhere I ever want to go back to. But it seems Laurel is heading there soon by the look of her.

'So what are you doing these days?' I say.

'Arguing with Mum mainly. I applied for a job though.' She tries to smile.

'Oh yeah?'

'Topshop. I'd get a staff discount.'

Figures. Laurel loves her clothes. Today she's got on a jumper slashed at the neck to show off her collarbones and skinny jeans that are wrinkled up round her thighs because there's nothing much to fill them. I wonder what size they are.

'I hope you get it,' I say, like there's really any chance she'll be able to take up a job even if they do offer one to her.

She leans her head against the chain of the swing. 'Do you miss it? The way it was before?' she whispers.

I push my head down to mirror hers, but I don't answer.

'I miss Molly,' she says.

Me too. All the time.

'Do you remember Dr Lishman?' Laurel says.

I smile. Dr Lishman was a locum who showed up one day last year on the unit, in mega heels and the sort of hair you only get if you spend hours with the straighteners. Molly took a dislike to her on sight.

Two days in, when Dr Lishman arrived during dinner time, which up until then had been a bit of a tense affair – I seem to recall Laurel chucking her roll – Molly looked up with a massive grin and said, in a reasonably good Bugs Bunny impression, 'Eeh, what's up, Doc?'

Dr Lishman's red lips disappeared.

Then Molly flicked her eyes to me, and I couldn't help

myself. I sat up straighter and said, 'All right, Lish? How's it going?'

Dr Lishman went pink and said, 'Yes, thank you, girls,' then sat and picked at a spare tray of food with extremely bony fingers.

Molly watched her for a bit, then said in a conversational tone, 'So how's *your* BMI, Doc?'

At which point I lost it. This massive snort came out of nowhere. That set off everyone, and before you knew it we were all in hysterics. It was one of those unit moments, where we all forgot we were supposed to be ill. Lish was pretty pissed off. I still think it was funny though.

'So do you? Miss it?' Laurel says.

I think about my list of crap stuff about the unit; how it's ended up with things that were not so crap on it. The list Felicity's making me write; how I said it made me safe, being in there, away from the world. Molly's face on that last night, when she said I liked it there. And I wonder what the truth is.

'Yeah. Sometimes I do,' I say softly.

But it's too much to think about, sitting here on these swings, with the sky blue above us, and the tower block in the distance, light flashing over all its windows. I look up, trying to pick out mine, spot Robin's flowers in his window box.

'Well. You know, there's really only one thing for it,' I say.

'What's that?'

'We need to find out who can swing the highest.'

I push off with my feet and lean back and in a few seconds I have a rhythm going. Air whooshes in my ears and my stomach dives, but I push my legs out to go higher, hear Laurel giggle, an odd, high-pitched sound next to me. She swings until she's caught me up and then our legs go in and out in time, higher and higher until I feel like I could take off like one of the fat pigeons round our way and soar into the sky. Laurel is a swallow next to me.

'I'm beating you!' I yell out and lean back the furthest yet, and as I do I realise Laurel's gone quiet.

Her legs drop. Then I see her slump sideways and on the next backwards swing, she rolls off and hits the ground.

'Laurel!' I scrape my feet once, twice, along the ground, trying to slow down, and then jump off, jarring my knees and pelvis where I land.

I crouch down and turn her over. Her eyes are closed and she's completely grey and suddenly all I can see is one of the nurses, pushing hard on Molly's ribcage. Sick scrapes at the back of my throat and I turn and spit a mouthful out, then reach a shaking hand to the side of Laurel's neck.

I can't feel a pulse. I put my head to her chest, feel the hard ridges of her ribcage. I think there's a flutter there. I pull out my phone, listen to a man's voice on the other end.

'Ambulance,' I say. 'I'm not sure if she's breathing.'

I manage to explain where we are and then Laurel lets out a noise between a cough and a sigh and her eyes open, then roll back shut.

I grab her hand and it's not until we get to the hospital and she's been whisked into a cubicle and the curtains shut, with me on the other side, that I realise I've left my phone in the park.

On the bus home, guilt burrows between the ribs, over my crappy heartbeat, which is going too fast. I will the bus to go faster, but every light seems to be red, each stretch between roundabouts a million miles of cars and bikes and people stopping me from getting back to Rose.

I couldn't remember Robin's phone number. I stayed at the hospital as long as I could, until Laurel's mum arrived, but they wouldn't let me see her. They were doing tests on her. Laurel's mum recognised me from the times she's seen me on the unit and gave me this look like she was holding me personally responsible for Laurel collapsing.

'Will you call me and let me know how she is?' I said.

She didn't bother to reply, and then I realised my phone will be long gone by now even if she does remember to call me. I suspect she won't anyway.

I'm out of breath, and there's a stabbing pain in my pelvis, which is still not right even after all these weeks, but none of it matters, because I've left Rose. I've left her for hours. Robin must be out of his mind.

I stagger up the stairs as fast as I can, but it feels like the bones are grinding together inside and I have to stop four flights up to catch my breath. By the time I reach my floor, I'm hobbling like a duck. I strain my ears for sounds of Rose crying, but everything is quiet – scarily so.

What if he called the police? Or social services?

I waddle faster up the corridor and thud on Robin's door. When it swings open, I'm already saying, 'Sorry, I'm so sorry,' and it takes a while for my brain to work out what's happening.

A girl is standing on the other side, holding a baby.

My arms have started to reach out automatically, when I spot the dark hair, the blue babygrow with tractors on, that he's much bigger than she should be.

It's not Rose.

'I take it you're Hedda,' the girl says.

Chapter 24

10 WEEKS

Rose is gone.

Gonegonegonegone.

This is your fault, you stupid cow.

Nia.

Why won't my brain work?

Rose is gone. Where is she?

I take a step towards the girl in front of me.

'I'm Jade and this is Ellis.' She smiles down at the baby on her hip, his arms clinging to her.

I nearly push her to the floor. It's only the baby that stops me. The baby that's not mine.

'Where's my baby?' I practically scream in her face.

She steps aside and behind her I see Robin putting out

a hand with a warning look. In the bend of his other arm, fast asleep, is Rose.

I run to him and snatch her out of his arms, pulling her close to me. She wriggles, opens her eyes and gives me this chilled-out look like she's not at all bothered I've been gone, then settles back down to sleep.

'What the hell is going on?' I hiss.

Robin takes off his glasses and passes a hand over his eyes. 'I could ask you the same question,' he says, but it's weariness rather than anger in his voice.

'Laurel had an accident. I had to go with her to the hospital and I left my phone … It all happened really fast. I'm so sorry. Did I leave any formula? She must be hungry.'

Jade speaks from the corner. 'No need. I gave her one of Ellis's bedtime bottles.'

I look at Robin. 'I don't … Who's Ellis?'

He pushes his glasses back on, avoiding my eyes, then says, 'Hedda … there's something I need to …' He can't seem to finish.

Jade is watching us both.

Jade, I realise now, is beautiful.

Jade is also thin.

Thinner than me?

Perfectly shaped legs. Hip bones peeking over the top of her leggings, framing the flat space where her top doesn't quite meet them. Huge dark-lashed eyes – falsies? I don't think so – and a shaped top lip, braided hair. She looks like she almost feels sorry for me.

'Ellis is our son. Mine and Robin's,' she says.

Sometimes, I think my heart will stop. At night, I wake up with a start and lie there feeling the way its beats change rhythm, like Molly's jazz. It does it now, thudding, faltering, speeding back up. I keep hold of Rose and try to make my brain process properly, but all I can hear is a rumbling sound.

I stare at Jade. She has studs in her ears that reflect the light bulb in tiny glints. I put one hand up to my own bare ear. Did I even brush my hair today? My teeth? I stink of hospital and sweat.

My arms ache from holding Rose so tight. My heart is squeezing in on itself. I imagine it in my chest, like a shrivelled walnut after years of Nia, hard and dry. Except there's a spot somewhere in there that's warmed and expanded these last few weeks, for Rose, and partly for Robin too.

'Robin's just been telling me about you,' Jade says, and I see the mixture of vulnerability and jealousy in her eyes. How in other circumstances I might quite like her.

She still loves him. I can tell.

I knew it. I knew he wasn't telling me something, that I

shouldn't have thought … My face starts to heat up. Why didn't I listen to myself, to Nia?

'Me and Ellis, we've come to bring Robin home,' Jade says in this firm voice, gazing at Robin like she's confirming something they've been talking about. Then she gives me a long look, like she's working something out about me, and adds, 'He doesn't belong here.'

I turn to Robin. I need him to say something, anything, to tell her she's wrong. But he can't meet my eyes.

I sway, Rose still in my arms, and lean back to steady myself against the wall. Jade hands Ellis to Robin and he takes his son smoothly, with that practised air he had when he first picked up Rose. I remember thinking how good he was with her, how natural he was.

Well, it makes sense now.

I've been so stupid.

As Jade stands back, I realise she's wearing an engagement ring and the little splinters of pain wriggling under my skin seem to sharpen and multiply until I'm crawling with them.

Robin is still sitting there, and I think that hurts the most. Why didn't he tell me? He leans forward, opens his mouth, but I shut him up with one look.

'Thank you for looking after her,' I say with as much

dignity as I can, and then that's it, I'm out of there, keeping my back straight though my arms are killing me.

Nia chants in my ear all the way back, and I let her words comfort me in a familiar chatter, like she's narrating my life for me.

Open the door.

I'm going.

Shut it, quietly, behind you.

Going, going, going.

Don't you dare think about crying.

Gone.

PART FOUR

NIA

Chapter 25

The Reasons Why

So, Felicity, you want me to tell you Why I Think I Developed An Eating Disorder. It would be great, wouldn't it? To come up with a lovely simple reason wrapped up in shiny paper you can open and then you will have fixed me. Go, you. Have a gold star.

But what if life's not as simple as that?

Maybe I developed an eating disorder to even the score up. I'm thinking of all those people buying food then chucking it away, or eating more than they need even though some people don't have enough. Perhaps I thought if I took less, it would all balance out. I was a girl on a noble mission. I could make a case for it. Why not?

Or maybe it was something more boring than that. Maybe I simply liked being small. I wanted the other girls in the playground to put their arms around my waist and lift me up and squeal, 'You're tiny!' I liked the attention.

I could cut myself some slack, tell you there's a big trauma in my deep dark past – you lot love all that stuff, don't you? But since when do I like things neat and easy?

We could pin it all on evil culture, if we wanted to. You know, red circly magazines, diets everywhere, how if you're a girl there's no way to look anything except wrong, wrong, wrong. You pick it all up pretty early on. Or, ooh, we could blame Barbie and, let's face it, pretty much every Disney princess ever.

Or Peer Pressure.

Or School Pressure.

Or Family Dynamics – I know you're keen on that one. Let's pretend I was jealous of my perfect sister.

Or maybe it was nothing.

Maybe it was just me.

Isn't the more interesting question the how, not the why? It's easier and harder than you think. And perhaps there's a price. But maybe I simply didn't care if it was high or not. Before Molly, I figured I could keep paying forever anyway. People do, you know. Just look at the Walking Woman.

Felicity scans through the pages of notes, which look more like a spider has dunked itself in a pot of ink then wandered across the page than actual handwriting. Anorexics are supposed to have tiny, neat handwriting. But then again I don't want to be a complete walking stereotype. And I guess it's fair to say I was pretty pissed off when I wrote it.

'Very clever,' Felicity says, and I think part of her means it, under the exasperation. 'Do you believe any of this?'

I shrug and try to give her my old hard stare. But I can't keep it going. Maybe not all of it was BS. I pick at my sleeve which is pulled down over my hand even though it's in the high twenties outside. I'm cold, on account of doing some extra cutting back since the Robin-is-a-dad-and-engaged-and-forgot-to-tell-me-about-either revelation. If I keep telling myself he's just a bastard, that I don't care anyway, it doesn't really hurt. Much. But I can't stop the same question spinning on repeat: why, why, why didn't he tell me?

I look at Felicity looking at my pulled-down sleeves, her face concerned, and try to care. Rose is snoozing in her buggy. That girl does nothing but sleep some days, especially if she's doing a growth spurt. It's just never all in one go, or when you want her to. That's why I ended up scrawling those pages at 6 a.m. this morning, because Rose was up and I basically had nothing else to do, no one to talk to.

I may as well admit it. I miss Robin. I miss him trying to tempt me to eat, and our stupid talks about nothing at all.

I miss that we never had a lightsabre fight, or took Rose to the beach like we planned, so we could all build sandcastles. But they'd only have been smashed up by the tide anyway.

'Who's the Walking Woman?' Felicity asks.

'She's just … someone I see.'

'Mmm?'

I nearly laugh. Does she ever get tired of that noise? Apparently not.

'She's an anorexic, I think. I've never actually spoken to her. She walks around and around all day like there's nothing else in the world.'

'You sound like you admire her.'

'I do. I used to.'

'And now? You're not so sure any more, are you?'

I nearly do it. I nearly agree with her. But Nia is still here, stronger than ever some days. Like she knows I'm having second thoughts. I go for the old standby instead. 'Maybe …'

Silence. The clock ticks.

In her buggy Rose lets out a teeny, adorable snuffle. I look over at her and smile, despite myself. But it doesn't last.

'Can't I have them both? Nia and Rose?' I say, my eyes pleading. 'Plenty of people do for years.' I think about the

Ana videos I've been watching and decide Felicity would probably tell me off if I mentioned them. 'I could have them both, maybe. If I control Nia.'

Felicity smiles again, but it's full of sadness. 'Control. That's the biggest self-deception of them all, don't you think?'

For once, when I walk away from the session with Felicity, I'm not thinking about how clever I was, or who won this time, but about control and who has it, exactly. I always thought it was me. But, if I'm being honest, even I know enough by now to realise there's a tipping point, a place where Nia reaches out and grabs you and then you're a rocket heading for the sun with no way to turn back.

What if it's been Nia in control all along?

The thought nearly makes me steer the buggy into a lamp post.

I stop by the benefits place to give in my forms and then wander to the shops, counting how many steps I take. I need a new phone and manage to find a PAYG I can't really afford at a market stall near the old golden arches. The sickly burger smell reminds me of the day I found out about Rose. It seems more than one lifetime and also like it happened five minutes ago. I still don't think I quite believe it.

They're digging into the pavement nearby; the drilling is loud and sounds in my ears even after it fades. Everything seems sharper and further away, and I realise I haven't actually eaten yet today. It makes things clear and blurry round the edges at the same time.

Outside the Methodist hall there's a huge ugly clock with cherubs around it – at least I think that's what they're supposed to be, except their eyes are so blank and their smiles seem to be pulled back in fear, not contentment. The hands on the clock tick slowly and I can hear some answering tick somewhere deep inside, but I'm not sure what I'm counting to. Numbers have been the backdrop to my life for so long. I look up at wriggly lines of cloud and imagine a vast hand parting them, reaching down and grabbing handfuls of numbers until there's none left in the world. Would it be a better one, or worse?

I store this thought up, thinking I might tell it to Felicity or maybe even Robin, when I remember I'm not speaking to him.

I go to the library to change Rose's books, hoping that if I keep moving I can stop thinking, but my thoughts still carry on zooming back round to Robin and Jade and Ellis. I grab six books for Rose, but I barely look at them, because my eyes are blurring with tears. I suddenly can't bear the thought of going back to the flat to sit there with

Rose, knowing Robin is next door. I do my old trick and swipe two books from the to-be-shelved section and shove them on the self-checkout under Rose's books. I hear a clicking noise and turn to see a woman giving me an odd look. I glare at her, then leg it out before she can say anything.

I don't bother with the bus, but take my old walk back to the Yewlings, through the underpass and out across town. I bump the buggy methodically up all eight flights of stairs, feeling the burn in my arms as I go. In my head a faint clock ticks with each jolt, counting the calories.

Inside, the flat feels so empty. I read a couple of books to Rose, put her down for a nap, then pace the blue rug in circles. Music blares from the flat next door – the dodgy side, not Robin – bass thumping the walls so I can hardly think. In desperation, I tip out the rest of Rose's books and find the two I grabbed from the to-be-shelved section.

Despite everything I find myself smiling. No wonder the woman in the library gave me a weird look.

I'm seventeen, skint, alone, with a baby I can barely keep in clean nappies and all I have to distract myself with are *Birdwatching for Beginners* or *Fifty Shades of Grey*. With pages turned down at the corners and everything.

Seems like the universe has a sense of humour even when I don't.

Chapter 26

Jade and Ellis are still at Robin's flat. I know this because I've heard Ellis crying, late in the evening, and also conversations that rise up to a crescendo, then fade away when Ellis adds his voice. I think, *Screw you, Robin*, and put music on to shut them out, until the other side wallops the wall. Seems the rules about being quiet only apply to me, not him, which isn't exactly fair. Then again, he's a lot bigger than I am.

A couple of days after I get my new phone, I'm coming out of my flat as Robin's door opens to reveal him in the doorway holding Ellis. We stand there in a freeze-frame, watching each other. We've got our babies slung up over our shoulders like we're on either side of a really weird mirror. They've even got on similar babygrows. Spielberg couldn't have staged it better. Even if he was a sadist or something.

'So, this is your son,' I manage.

Robin looks at the baby in his arms like he's still trying to figure that one out.

'Might have been nice to mention it to me,' I say.

'I know. I'm sor–'

'Don't.'

I turn and I'm about to bang the door shut, when Robin says, 'Hedda, please.'

The desperation in his voice makes me stop, my back still to him.

'Can we … find somewhere to talk?'

'Five minutes,' I say.

I sit cross-legged in the hallway, Rose on my lap, and after a moment, he sits too.

There's A Silence.

'Four minutes,' I say.

'OK.' Robin takes a deep breath, lets it out in a whoosh. He fiddles with one of Ellis's poppers. 'I never meant … didn't want …' He sighs again, like he's given up. 'I was going to tell you.'

'Oh yeah? When was that? Before I had Rose or after? Slipped your mind, did it?'

'I'm sorry.'

'That it?' I uncross my legs, about to go.

'Wait. Please.'

I sit back. 'Three minutes. I'm serious.'

'OK.' He sighs again, then starts talking in a speedy monotone, like he's going over lines he's had in his head for a while. 'Jade and I grew up together. Our parents are best friends. We lived on the same street. We all went on holidays together –'

'Is this coming to a point any time soon?'

'I'm trying to explain. Give me a second,' he says, and it's the first time I've ever heard him raise his voice.

I tilt my chin and stare at the door of the flat opposite. The hard floor is beginning to hurt my bum. I swivel Rose so she's leaning against my other arm, away from Robin.

'Maybe it was inevitable, considering how close we were, but eventually we started dating. After about a year together, things … progressed.'

I wince.

'And … Well, we were stupid. Not careful. She was on the pill, but … you know.'

'Mmm.' I bring out a Felicity Session voice.

Now Robin winces.

Rose is playing with my fingers, her tiny hands warm and soft. Comforting.

'It was … well … a shock. And it was the worst possible time too. I'd already been thinking … We were about to break up. Well, I thought we were … I was going to uni, you see, to do Law. I had this idea I'd be a human rights lawyer, you know, for Amnesty or something. I'd already said I wanted to take a break. She was so hurt. But I knew I didn't …' He pauses and rubs at his forehead. 'I didn't love her. But then she found out she was pregnant and she didn't want to … She wanted to have the baby. Her parents were furious at first, of course, but then they started making plans, about how we'd get married, then they'd help us get a place. I could get a job. Mine on the other hand …'

'I'm guessing they didn't take it too well?'

'Not exactly. My mum thought we were both far too young to be parents, that there was no way we'd cope. She wanted Jade to have an abortion. They had this massive fight, my mum and Jade's mum, and stopped speaking to each other. Then when Jade said she was definitely keeping the baby, my mum was on at me all the time, telling me I should go to uni, that I could still stay involved with the baby in a different way. God, that sounds so harsh, but I think my parents were just worried, you know? But I didn't listen to them. I let Jade and her parents sweep me up in it all. We moved in together. Her dad got me a job in his office.'

He pauses again, remembering. 'At first, it went OK, but as she got bigger, it was like she was getting further away. We started having these awful fights, Jade screaming at me, telling me to leave. It was like she couldn't forgive me for wanting to split up before I knew about Ellis. One argument, she threw a bowl of cereal at my head.'

I raise my eyebrows. 'What did you do?'

'I ducked.'

A ghost of a smile flits over my face, then goes. I nod at him to go on.

'And cleaned it up. She was really pregnant by then.'

There's another pause. 'So, what happened then? She obviously had the baby.'

He ducks his head over Ellis, sprawled fast asleep on his lap. I think Robin's crying. 'Yes. She wouldn't let me stay with her for the birth – she had her mum with her – but I waited outside in the corridor and they let me in afterwards. She was sitting up in bed holding Ellis and when I saw him, how tiny he was, how perfect … I can't explain it. Everything leapt inside. And I knew I'd make it work somehow.'

I know what he means; I felt it too, with Rose, when I decided to keep her. I give a tight nod.

'We had a couple of weeks all together, but then I had to go back to work. Jade started spending more and more time at her parents' house. They still weren't speaking to my mum and dad, and neither was I. Ellis never slept. We started to argue again. I tried not to, but ... well, you know what it's like.'

I stare at him. It looks like the ghosts of all those sleepless nights are sitting on his shoulders, pulling them down. And part of me flares in anger. Yeah, I know what it's like.

But then he says, 'One day I came home from work and they'd just ... gone.'

'Holy shit,' I say. It just slips out.

His face contorts. 'She found a letter from uni. I'd told her I wasn't going, that I was staying with her and Ellis, but actually I'd deferred my place.'

My mouth drops open. The last few weeks I've tried to make everything fit, but I still can't square this Robin with the one I thought I knew.

'I hadn't decided to go for sure! I just ... I didn't know. I didn't know what I wanted. I was scared, you know? I wanted to –'

'Keep your options open?' My voice is laced with sarcasm.

He drops his head. 'Something like that. I couldn't explain it to Jade. She took the money for the rent and went back to her parents to live. I went there, I called, but she didn't want to see me and her parents backed her up. Her dad sacked me, told me I was pathetic. I didn't know what to do. I couldn't go home, even if Mum and Dad would have had me back. I was angry at them too.'

'So where did you go?'

'To my grammy's at first. I slept on her sofa. Then she heard a friend of a friend was moving out from the flat here and she sorted it all out. Paid the deposit and the first month's rent. I thought it would only be for a couple of months. I kept on hoping we'd sort something out. I still thought we could try and make a go of it somehow, for Ellis. I missed him. I didn't really know how to do all that legal stuff so I could see him, and I didn't want to put Jade through that. And anyway, I had no money for a solicitor. She never answered her phone but I kept writing her emails and letters, hoping she'd reply, but she didn't. So I guess I just sort of … left it. Once I got here.'

I'm frowning, trying to process all this. Part of me wants to shout at him, to tell him I agree with Jade's dad; he's pathetic. That he should have fought harder if he really loved Ellis that much.

I remember the pictures on his wall. The two girls who must've been his sister and Jade. And the one I thought was Robin as a baby, but instead was his son who he never once mentioned. How can this be Robin? This boy who's … what? A coward? A liar? Or scared and alone?

I'm all of those things.

I weigh it all, feeling Rose, solid in my lap. I look at Ellis's sleeping face, Robin's hand stroking his head absently.

In the end, I simply say, 'Your grammy could've picked a nicer location. This place must've been one hell of a shock.'

Robin snaps his head up and gives a short laugh. 'Maybe a bit. But then, well … I met you and –'

'Oh well, that must've made it all better.' I say it sarcastically, but Robin shakes his head.

'It did. Don't you see that? You, and Rose, you both did,' he says.

And suddenly something clicks in my brain. How supportive he was once he found out I was pregnant. The way he looks at Rose.

I push myself up. 'Screw you,' I say over the top of Rose's head.

'What?'

'It was Rose, wasn't it? You saw her as some sort of, what, substitute?'

'No. God, no, Hedda. That's totally not what I mea–'

'You did! It was Rose all along. That's who you –' I break off. Shake my head. 'No wonder you didn't tell me.'

'I tried to. I really did. That day in the woods, I was going to tell you then, but you were so tired. And when we made the cake. But it was like it had grown into this enormous thing, and I didn't know how ...'

'You could've just told me straight away.'

'I know that. But ... it hurt, OK? I wanted to forget all about it.'

I remember the look he sometimes had, when I first met him. That he still gets. The one I ignored because I didn't want to see him as anything other than Robin the sorted guy, the one who looked out for me. Someone I could lean on. But I can't help it; I'm still furious, angrier than I've let myself be in a long time, and I have to hold on to it, because underneath is this feeling in my chest, like someone's replaced my real, crappy heart with one made out of tissue paper.

I don't know if I believe him. Don't know what I want to believe.

'Jade says she wants to try again. That she's sorry, she wasn't thinking properly. She wants to stay until I've had a chance to think and decide what to do,' Robin says.

I turn it all over, trying to work it through, but it's like a light bulb on overload and the only thing I can do is shut down before I explode. I pinch at my forehead.

'So have you? Decided?' I say.

'I'm not sure. I mean, I'm angry with Jade. But there's ...' He looks down at Ellis, who stirs in his sleep, then pings awake like a little bouncing monkey, that cheeky smile on his face that's so like Robin's. Robin smiles back for a moment and bumps him up to sit upright, letting Ellis play with his hands.

I sigh. A massive wave of tiredness hits me. 'Well, you'd better get sure.'

'I know. Jade and I need to talk. Properly talk.'

'Yeah.' I look down at the dark curls on Ellis's head, his little fingers rubbing over Robin's nails like he's feeling their smoothness. 'Then you shouldn't be talking to me.'

He opens his mouth like he's going to argue, then closes it again and nods.

'Jade's right, you know,' I say quietly. 'You don't belong here.'

I go into the flat and listen to his door click shut. My chest is still tight and I'm breathing so fast I have to put Rose on the floor. I sit next to her. A big part of me wants to run back to Robin's door, to scream at him, or to kiss him, tell him he has to stay here, with us. But I know I have to leave him alone.

I try and push thoughts of Robin out of my head, shove deep down the urge to cry.

What now? I can't stay in forever. Rose needs nappies and I need some food for the flat, even if it is for display purposes only.

I've got yet another headache. I shove down some pain-killers and a pint of water and bump Rose's buggy down the stairs. By the last flight, my arms are shaking really badly, and for a moment I am terrified I won't be able to hold on to the buggy, but I make it into the sunshine which is too bright – I don't care if it's supposed to be summer or not. Even the tarmac is sweating.

I managed to get another loan from a different company last night, to pay off the first one and have some left over, but what started as a few quid has now spawned debt babies all over the place, a whole roomful of them. I queue at the benefits office for an hour to find out what's going on with my claim, only to be told it's still being processed.

'What am I supposed to do about food?' I say.

'We could refer you to a food bank,' the man behind the counter says.

He's barely older than me, red in the face over a nasty tie that looks like he last wore it to school. There's no sympathy in his eyes, only a glazed kind of boredom that whispers, '*Get me out of here*' with an undercurrent of terror because he's seen us lot in here, knows how bad it can get if he loses his job. Probably has targets to hit.

I could feel sorry for him. I choose not to.

I have to give all sorts of details, including Joanna's,

which makes me pause, but now I've started it seems too late to stop in case he reports me anyway.

If only Dad would respond to my texts. I could phone Mum, but I guess I'm too proud or whatever. Sue me.

I walk through town and watch the crowds stream past. I assess the sizes of the women. I don't care about the men. No one looks at me twice. Now, with the buggy, I'm just another teenage mum, invisible to everyone except those who get a kick out of disapproving. Nobody sees me with Rose in tow, only her and what I represent: a lazy, hopeless scrounger who had a baby to get the benefits.

The food bank is up a maze of alleyways between houses set at a slant on a steep hill not a million miles away from the unit. The sun is hot on my back and I'm struggling to breathe when I get to the top. Dots gather at the edge of my vision. I fight them, but they're getting stronger, and I have to lean over the buggy and hold on for several minutes until they pass. When I straighten up, my whole body shakes.

Inside, a woman in her thirties with a mass of laughter lines around her eyes welcomes me.

'Hello, I'm Vi. You look like you could use a sit-down and a glass of water.' She goes off and gets one, then sits next to me. 'And who's this?'

'Rose,' I say.

'What a beautiful name. She's lovely.'

'Thank you,' I say, even though I didn't have anything to do with it. It seems the done thing, and Vi has a level of warmth – genuine warmth – you don't see that much.

'So, do you have a form?'

I hand it over.

'Lovely. Well, we can certainly sort you out with a few things. We have some nappies and wipes too,' she says. She begins to load my buggy up with bags of stuff: tins of economy beans and pasta and tomatoes, nappies, tea bags, some shower gel and toothpaste, formula.

'I think we have a little chocolate too,' Vi says.

It seems rude to refuse so I let her put it in. I don't quite know whether to feel ashamed, relieved or sad. I settle for smiling gratefully.

'Would you like a cup of tea before you go?' Vi says.

I nod, suddenly close to tears.

She brings one and settles in a seat next to me. 'I don't mean to pry, and of course you don't need to tell me anything, but occasionally it helps to share, if you have anything on your mind?'

'Doesn't everyone, if they're in here?' It comes out with more acid in it than I wanted. I can't seem to help myself. I want to pull it back, to tell her I am grateful, but she doesn't seem to care.

She smiles. 'Yes, I suppose they do.' She makes no move to ask me any more questions, but sits with me in silence while I drink the tea.

I asked her to put a sugar in it, for the way back, and as I sip the last sugary dregs, I hear Nia stir and sigh, like a coiled snake.

I want to talk to her, this nice woman who seems like she has some time for me, but I don't know how. I form different sentences, but everything feels too complicated and they end up sliding away before I can get them out.

'Thank you,' I say in the end, and stand up.

'Any time. You can come back to us again if you need to.' She puts one hand on my arm and a brief frown passes over her face. 'You remember to look after yourself too, as well as Rose.' She really means it.

I turn away fast, before she can see the look on my face.

My phone goes off as I'm careering back down the hill, trying not to let the buggy go. I'm counting the steps like always, to forget about the food bank and money and Robin. I put the brakes on and sit on a wall to catch my breath, drink some water.

Maybe it's Dad, finally.

But it isn't. It's Laurel. I emailed her my new number the other day.

'Hey.' Her voice is small and high, like a little girl.

'Hey. How are you? You out of hospital?'

'Yes,' she whispers. 'They kept me in a few nights then sent me home. I'm at the park in the Yewlings. Are you at home?'

'On my way back now.'

'I thought I'd check, before ...'

She means before she climbs all those stairs, I realise. What sort of state is she in?

'Are you OK?' I say.

'Yes. You must be busy. I'll go.'

'No, don't. I'll be half an hour. Stay put, all right?'

'Yes.'

I hang up.

I'm not sure if she's still going to be there or not, but when I reach the park, she's huddled into one of the swings, a ball of oversized jumper, with nothing much inside.

I wave and she raises one hand, then drops it back to her lap. I listen to a squeak that's developed on one of the buggy wheels as I go over, counting footsteps so I don't need to really take her in until the last minute.

It is and isn't a shock. She's booked herself a ticket back to a unit, and it looks one way to me. I see Molly on the floor again, the nurse slamming her hand down hard on her chest.

I turn my head to one side, trying to dislodge the memory, and say, 'How are you?'

'Fine.'

Her voice is disappearing. And I have nothing to say to her. I scan my mind, sitting on the swing. I don't try and swing this time, but keep my feet planted on the ground, arms ready to catch her if she goes off. Or let her fall, I don't know which. I'm angry with her too.

'Do you remember Molly's jazz?' Laurel says.

'Yeah, course. Who could forget?' I say, and smile a little because Molly's playing was awesome. She was so talented. Grief lands like some creature on my chest and burrows in, spreading tentacles out through my body. It bloody hurts. I swallow hard, drink some water. Keep breathing.

Rose is looking around, bright-eyed. She likes being outside.

'Can I hold her?' Laurel says.

I hesitate, then say, 'Come over here then.'

We go over to a bench and I sit Laurel down, then pop Rose into her wasted arms. She smiles, looking down on Rose's face.

'She's so beautiful. I can't believe you made her with your body.'

Neither can I.

'Yeah, maybe it's good for something after all,' I say.

It's meant to be light-hearted, but Laurel's eyes are huge and sad. She's put on make-up, but it only serves to accentuate bone. Perhaps it was on purpose, who knows? Or maybe she is actually trying to cover up, to be normal, but it's far, far too late.

I take Rose back when I sense Laurel's getting tired. She sighs and straightens herself up.

'Are you getting the bus back?' I say.

'No. I'll walk.'

I want to argue, to tell her to just get the damn bus, but I know she won't listen. She's retreated back into Planet Anorexia before she's even kissed Rose goodbye. I watch her sudden burst of energy as she gets into a rhythm and wonder if I'll see her again. Part of me is still jealous. Laurel turns her head to catch a glimpse of her reflection in a clapped-out car she passes. I wonder why she asked me here to the park, where we can only talk about days that are gone and people who won't come back. Where Rose has split us on to two planets and I don't know any more which one is my home, which one I want to belong to, so I float in space, weightless, veering first towards one, then pulling back again to the other. Why does Laurel even care?

But then, I see. I see her. It's not about me, or even Rose. Laurel glances into another car window as she passes, brings her elbows up to check the narrowness of her shoulders. The air around her seems to shimmer, like in *The Matrix*. One minute I get a flash of her: slim, balletic, white. Control in motion. The next she's horrific, a walking skeleton. I don't think either of us knows which one it is any more. But I do know now what she's after. She wants me to watch.

Because what's the point of disappearing if no one's around to notice?

Chapter 27

'What do you think would happen if you didn't have your eating disorder? What would life look like?' Felicity has the flip chart out again.

I try to focus on what she's saying, but all I can do is stare out of the window to where a magpie is pecking at the ground under a tree. I look around, but can only see one. I salute it anyway.

'What are you doing?'

I nod towards the window. 'One for sorrow.'

'Yes.'

I turn back to Felicity. 'Yes, what?'

'Emotions. You would have to feel emotions. You would have to grow up, to take responsibility for your life. And that's scary.'

My jaw tightens up and I feel my back teeth grind

against each other, so tight they might crumble away. I imagine my bones, soft like playdough, easy to break. 'What do you think I've been doing with Rose? I am taking responsibility for her life.'

'Mmm. And is that the same thing?'

'Anyway, what's so great about emotions?' I'm aiming for flippant, but it's not coming. I keep thinking about Robin.

Felicity holds my gaze and it's me who looks away first, down at Rose on my lap. The scales weren't good today. Or they were excellent, depending on your perspective.

'There's love,' Felicity says.

'I do love her. I never knew how much I could love anybody before. But ...'

'Mmm?'

'Is love something you feel or is it something you do?'

'I think it's both,' Felicity says.

When I emerge, it's raining. I don't have a coat or a rain cover for Rose's buggy, so I take my jumper off and loop that over the top. I can see the double bones of my wrist and my knuckles that look oversized compared to the flesh around them, white and streaming with water on the buggy handles. I think about the tipping point, like Laurel the other day, where the anorexia takes over and you're gone. I remember Molly telling me not to fly so high I can't get back.

What if I'm already there?

I turn my head up into the rain, trying to clear it, but everything is opaque, like the world is going into monochrome. My chest hurts. My pelvis grinds. Walking sends hard stabs of pain up my shins. Shin splints, that's what they call them. And it feels it too, sometimes, that there's something splintered inside. I go towards the shopping centre, because being anonymous in a crowd is better than being alone at the flat, having to stop myself from knocking on Robin's door. I don't look at the cherub clock when I go past, but I can feel it anyway, the ticking feeling inside.

Inside, I get a Starbucks and sit on a bench, feel the caffeine race through my bloodstream. I manage half a flapjack and the sugar sprints alongside the coffee. There's a free soft-play area in the shopping arcade and I sit with Rose on the edge of a seat, watching her watch the children screaming and jumping from plastic cars. I knock back the dregs of my coffee, feeling a bit clearer. *It will all be OK. It's under control. Everything is fine.* If I say it enough, it might even come true, like in fairy tales.

A group of girls a lot younger than me is coming towards me and I realise it's past school kicking-out time. I wonder what I'd say if I got in touch with Sal or Natalie now.

'That's so basic,' one girl says.

I don't even know what language to speak any more. Actually, I suppose I never have. I never learned. I imagine myself, Rose free, Nia free, wandering around a shopping centre, talking about films and music and clothes. Eating a Maccie D's without worrying about it, moaning about school and boys I like, and I could keel over with grief at everything I've missed and will never get back.

I stare at the girl, who's wearing all black, a heavy fringe and very bright lipstick, and I realise she's staring right back at me.

Plus, she's not any girl out with her friends. She's Tammy.

'Later,' she says to the others and walks slowly over to me. She takes Rose out of my arms and gives her a big kiss, then hands her back.

'Hi,' I say.

'All right?' Tammy sits next to me.

I think desperately of something to say.

'How are you?' I come up with, eventually. Sometimes I seriously despise myself.

She sniffs and shrugs in one movement. 'Fine.'

'Uhh … School all right? Friends?'

She snorts at this, like my attempt to be a big sister has come about seventeen years too late. She has a point.

But because this is me and I don't let things go when I should, I say, 'How are Mum and Dad?'

Tammy looks at me properly then, through her fringe. How can she have changed so much in just a few weeks? But she's fourteen now. I should say sorry for missing her birthday, but it seems too late to apologise. Yet another example of my general crappiness as a sister. Maybe this is what fourteen-year-olds look like, what they do. How would I know?

'You don't know,' she says, and for a moment I think she's developed some voodoo mind-reading trick and is echoing my thoughts right back at me.

Her expression is hard.

'Know what?'

'Dad left. He's been having an affair for years, turns out. He moved out a couple of weeks ago.' I hear the ice in her voice. God, she sounds like me.

'What?' I say.

She looks at me. 'Don't know why you're so surprised. It's what you wanted, isn't it?'

'What the hell are you talking about? No. It's not.'

Tammy shrugs again and stands up. 'Got to go.' She gives Rose another kiss on the forehead. Rose blinks. Then Tammy's face softens, gets younger as she looks down at me. 'Maybe you could take her to see Mum? She's a bit … you know.'

I don't know, but decide I ought to look like I do.

Tammy starts to walk off.

'Take care of yourself,' I call after her, feeling stupid.

She holds one arm up, either in a 'yeah, OK' or a 'stop' or a 'go screw yourself' gesture, and keeps going.

Chapter 28

I stand outside Robin's door, hand raised. I've been getting these sudden impulses to knock on his door more and more, even though I know I shouldn't. Inside I can hear voices, Robin's low tone and then Jade answering. They both laugh and I drop my hand, turn away to lug the buggy down the stairs yet again.

Rose and me are going on an outing with Lois and Ethan. I don't know why I got in touch with her really, only that everything feels so empty and not in a good way, not any more. I keep thinking about control and how it used to be so simple. Before, I loved that blank space it gave me, but now it feels like it goes down forever, like those underwater lakes you get at the bottom of an ocean.

I nearly called the whole thing off, but I was surfing the net and reading all these things on parenting boards and realised I've never taken Rose anywhere much, if you discount the woods and the weekly thrill-fest which is my sessions with Felicity. So when Lois texted to ask if I wanted to come, I said yes. It's something to do that isn't sitting in the flat and not knocking on Robin's door. And maybe ... well, I like Lois.

Lois is waiting at the bottom of the road in an Audi, of all cars, and I realise I've never found out what she does for a living. I've never asked her anything much. Maybe I should.

We pack Rose and all her stuff in and twenty minutes later we're on the way out of town.

Lois puts on some music and sings along. After a moment, I join in.

Lois falls silent and when the song finishes she glances over at me. 'You have a lovely voice,' she says.

'Really?' I never knew that. I like singing though.

I open the window and let the warm air rush over my head.

'It'll be autumn before we know it. I love it when the leaves are turning,' Lois says.

I give her a sideways look. 'Why?'

'I suppose it gives me a sense of things changing, dying and making way for something new,' she says.

I sit back in my seat. I never thought of it like that. I

only ever saw naked branches and dead leaves. Molly liked autumn too. Maybe that's why I feel so comfortable with Lois; she reminds me of Molly.

'I'm thinking of going back to work early,' Lois says.

'Oh yeah? What do you do?'

'I'm an accountant.'

'You're not!'

She takes her eyes off the road to look at me for a second again. 'I certainly am. And I can tell you one thing: making the numbers work is far easier than looking after a baby.'

On second thoughts, maybe I like Lois because she doesn't pretend. She tells it how it is. Unlike some. I think again of Robin, holding Ellis, and of Molly too.

'I was supposed to have a whole year off, but that's still twelve weeks away. Or eighty-four days if you want to –'

'You count too!' I twist round in my seat to face her. It seems really important, somehow.

'I suppose so. Doesn't everyone?' Lois says in a light voice.

'That's exactly what I told Fel–' I stop myself short.

'Sorry?' Lois says, her eyes on the road.

'Never mind,' I say.

We turn off the main road and up a drive that leads to a stately home, long and low, with a lake in front of it. To the side on perfect lawns two arenas have been roped off. One is full of people dressed up like medieval soldiers, fighting pretend battles. We get the babies out and wander over to watch.

'Now that's what I call a sword.' Lois nods to a man swinging a huge broadsword.

I listen to the metal clank as the two soldiers clash, but to be honest, it's not really my thing. In the other arena, there's a falconry display going on. I push Rose's buggy over to watch. A woman stands with a huge leather glove on, the bird perched on her wrist. I can't take my gaze off its talons, or its eyes, which look intent, wily. Dead. It opens its hooked beak and calls out, a desolate, gaping sound.

'These birds are extremely intelligent hunters,' the commentator says.

A shiver runs down my back.

The bird spreads its wings and soars up into the sky, and then plummets with deadly accuracy before swooping away in another loop. And I see it. The bird's nature.

Lois comes up next to me.

'It's not meant to be caged up and trotted out for people to stare at. It's meant to be free,' I say. 'It must hate it, living like this. Trapped.'

And then everything stops.

I think about Nia, about Rose, and I see it's not just the bird that's trapped.

I hate living like this.

There are tears in my eyes.

Lois doesn't ask if I'm all right, but puts a hand on my shoulder.

After, we explore the house and stare at tapestries and four-poster beds with intricately carved headboards. But Ethan starts to fuss before we've seen half the house.

Lois gives a sigh. 'Abort mission?' she says.

'Yup.'

In the car on the way back, Lois says, 'Are you good with numbers?'

I start to laugh and worry for a moment I won't be able to stop.

Lois casts sideways glances at me.

I get myself under control. 'Not bad. I was doing maths A level,' I eventually manage.

'You were?'

'Yeah. I had to quit … Well, I decided to quit, to look after Rose. Maybe I'll go back in September, I don't know.'

Lois drives a little way then says, 'I might need someone in a few months. I'm thinking about setting up on my own. If you'd be interested, I could do with some help. It would only be basic admin at first, but I could train you up.'

I watch the fields fly by, feel how smooth the car is, how comfortable.

'I'll definitely think about it,' I say.

Two days later, the conversation I had with Tammy is still looping round my head. I decide I can't put it off any more. I have to go and see Mum. I need to check she's all right. And also, I have to admit, because I'm hoping she might lend me some money.

I run my fingers through my hair, which yet again I forgot to brush, before I press my finger to the bell of the house. I hear it sound, chirpy and bright through the rooms. I always hated that bell.

I'm about to turn away when Mum opens the door.

She looks … the same. I don't know what I expected. For her to have wild hair, be rending her clothes? We watch each other and I see Mum take in my frame under the baggy clothes. I scan her eyes for signs of crying and don't see any.

She looks past me, to Rose, and her face softens, but I catch something wide and hungry in her eyes. I reach into the buggy and pass Rose wordlessly to her.

Mum holds her close and blinks a few times, then says, 'You'd better come in. You can leave the buggy in the porch.'

She disappears into the kitchen with Rose while I park it and shut the front door.

I sit at the table while Mum bustles about, putting a cup of milk and some biscuits in front of me, like I'm twelve again. Good old custard creams, I have missed you. Though I have no intention of eating any, obviously. Mum sits opposite me, but doesn't comment on my untouched plate. I realise we've gone back in time, to after-school snacks, and a sticky sense of her in the background – always knowing where some toy was when I asked, or ironing school uniform and nagging me about homework – rises up and I want to push it away, scrub it off me, all that care sucked tight like cling film.

'Tammy told me about Dad. I'm really sorry,' I say.

Mum shifts Rose on her lap to face her and says, 'She's grown. Her face has changed.'

I look at Rose, really look at her, and see that what Mum has said is true: she's emerging, her face widening out, tiny curls appearing at the back of her head, which also has a large bald patch from where she sleeps on her back. I stressed about it at first, but the health visitor at the clinic said it's totally normal and she definitely wasn't going to end up all baldy like the baby I saw that time at the antenatal class. She looks more solid, more girl-like now.

In a weird role reversal, I'm saying, with an approximation of Felicity's Listening Face, 'How are you?'

'Yes, fine, thank you, Hedda. Your father and I, as Tamara

has told you, are spending some time apart. He has so much work at the moment. Truthfully, I think perhaps he's having a little midlife crisis. I'm sure it will pass.' She tries to give a laugh, but it's not coming out properly.

'Tammy said he's been having an affair. She said he's moved out.'

Mum stiffens, but doesn't answer.

'How long has it been going on?' I say.

I think about how Dad was at my flat last time, what he said about Mum being depressed after she had me, and I'm suddenly sure of something. It rises up, new and shocking, making things fall into place with a sharp click.

'You knew, didn't you? He's done it before, hasn't he? After I was born.'

Rose senses the change in atmosphere because she begins to wriggle on Mum's lap.

I go around the table and reach for her. 'Can I warm a bottle?' I say.

'I don't really want to discuss this with you, Hedda,' Mum says, and there's a hint of weariness in the way her shoulders slump as she goes to the microwave with the bottle I hand her.

When it's done, I say, 'Would you like to feed her?'

Mum nestles Rose in the crook of her arm and plugs her in. Rose chugs solidly to start with, one hand gripping the bottle, one holding on to the edge of Mum's hand. Then she slows, and her eyes start to open and shut more heavily. Mum sits her up so she can let out a burp, and then Rose is asleep, cradled in Mum's arms. Mum's face looks older, under the make-up, but more real as she gazes at Rose, like she's surrendering something.

'She reminds me of you. You used to hold on just like that,' Mum says.

I think of all the hours I've spent, learning Rose, her cries, the way she moves, memorising the way her hairline goes and I realise then, that whatever's happened since, Mum must have sat here and done the exact same thing with me. It's like cream on a burn; it might not take away the sting, but it helps.

'It must have been so hard for you,' I say to Mum in a soft voice.

Mum pops Rose back in the buggy and then begins tidying away my untouched biscuits and milk.

'Mum?'

She keeps her back to me, rinses the plate in the sink. 'Well. You have to get on with things, don't you? It's the only way.'

I follow her through the hall, past rows of pictures of me and Tammy. Us at the seaside, at parks, making a snowman. Both of us in Dad's lap next to the Christmas tree. Mum is in hardly any of them; she was always the one taking pictures, always moving, cleaning, organising, tidying. In the bathroom is a framed copy of her degree certificate, part of the wallpaper all my life.

'Do you regret it? Not having a career?' I say.

Mum straightens some cushions. 'We never needed the income.'

I stare at the way she moves and suddenly this burst of images comes at me, like paparazzi: Mum in the front row at school plays, while Dad was at work, and behind the PTA cake-sale stall, as a parent governor, a reading helper, a charity bucket shaker, the centre of a large group of women in the playground at pick-up time. The day I came home from getting the bus to school all by myself the first day of secondary school, proud and excited, to find her crying in the kitchen, the washing-up still in the sink.

'You all needed me,' she says, and I see how desperately she needs this to be true, for it all to have been worth it.

'You did a good job, Mum,' I say and she meets my eyes, then looks away, but I mean it, I really do. She did what she could do, what she thought was right.

'I'm sorry,' I say quietly.

'What for?'

'For all of it. For the units … For what I said that time I asked you about my name.'

Mum looks straight at me, and she seems a bit broken. 'Perhaps you see more than people your age are meant to,' she says. 'Maybe you always did.'

It's as close to an admission that all is not right in her world, that it probably never was, as I'll ever get. My heart hurts for her. There's so much I want to say, but I don't know how. How can we move past a lifetime of never saying what we mean, at least not in words?

Then she says, 'Hedda, your shoes!' And she rushes off to get the Dustbuster.

I look at my grubby trainers, which are starting to come apart at the seams, and I don't know how to ask Mum for money she probably doesn't have anyway.

That evening, I really try to eat a proper dinner, but all I can manage are noodles. I think about knocking on Robin's door, like in the old days, getting him to do one of his omelettes for me, but when I listen at the wall I can hear Jade's voice calling to him and I know there's no way to get that time back – if it was ever really mine.

Chapter 29

Another week drips past. Rose is four months old. She can roll, flipping over and over, looking delighted when she winds up somewhere new. Still doesn't blinking sleep though and sometimes, when I'm trying yet again to settle her, I realise why they use sleep deprivation as torture. Then I feel bad that I blame her for not sleeping more, but it's hard not to take it personally. She's trying to push herself up on her arms already and reach for toys. I take this as a sign that she's clearly a genius, then tell myself off for being like Mum with Tammy.

Rose is growing as I shrink.

At night, Nia seems to expand and fill the room, swooping, her wings like they could almost reach down and smother me.

You're disgusting, she says, and I lie there, trying not to listen, holding the pillow over my head, attempting to drown her out with Rose's deep sighs and grunts, but the only thing that works is getting up to pace round and round, or exercise, falling into an old routine as I count push-ups and lifts and crunches. I get the sense again and again that there's a giant clock ticking through me, that Nia is growing alongside Rose.

I haven't heard from Laurel.

I dream about money and things chasing me through empty streets. Of wandering the aisles of a deserted supermarket where everything is too bright and hurts my eyes, but the checkout keeps getting further away so I can never find what I need and get out of there. When I wake, my heart feels faint and jerky. Temporary. The two ridiculous books I got out of the library the day after I found out about Robin are now overdue and I can't afford the fine. At least they don't fine you for overdue kids' books.

There's no word from Dad. It's as though he's melted away, like he was never really there.

I speak to Mum a couple of times on the phone.

'How's Rose?' she says, and I tell her about the latest cute thing Rose has done, like when she laughed at a teddy bear, but it's as though someone else is speaking, and somewhere inside I understand I've crossed the tipping point and now there's no way back.

White noise starts to crowd the edges of the room.

The more I try to eat, the less I can manage.

The nappy situation is getting desperate; I'm almost out again. I switched to a new, cheaper formula and it doesn't seem to agree with Rose. She's done about twenty poos in one day. I put the last nappy on her before I go to see Felicity.

I let myself out of the flat as quietly as possible, so I don't annoy the man next door. I think about his hard knuckles, his face that pushes out into a dark frown whenever he sees me and Rose. I glance at Robin's door as I shut my own, then look away fast. The other day when I looked out of the window, I noticed all the flowers he planted have gone brown and brittle through lack of water. It scratches at my heart, but I won't give in, I won't knock on their door.

Off we go on the long walk to the unit. By the time I push Rose across the car park, past the usual cohort of girls smoking outside, I'm panting. I give them a proper look, comparing, but they don't even see me, their ranks closed into a different, private world. I want to run and join them, to tell them I'm one of them, and I want to run away too.

I tell this to Felicity, sitting in the same chair I've sat in a thousand times, with the same books and pot plants, and ticking clock. 'I want to go and give them a shake, you know?'

'Why?' she says.

'I don't know. To tell them to stop. To make them understand getting back isn't as easy as you think it is. To ask them to let me in. Who knows?'

Felicity considers me. 'You're losing weight.'

Rose is on my lap. She's getting so big. She coos and stuffs her fist in her mouth, chewing so hard I worry she's going to hurt herself, but every time I pull it away, sticky with drool, she calmly and firmly slots it right back.

I nod. I'm tired of the BS. 'It's not on purpose.' OK, maybe I am still a BS factory. I meet Felicity's eyes. 'It's half on purpose and half … like it's coming from outside of me. It's Nia. She won't shut up.' I find I'm crying, tears plopping on to Rose's head. She carries on chewing her fist. 'I just want … Sometimes I want her – it – to … to leave me the hell alone!'

Felicity hands me the tissues.

She's smiling, a small smile. But her eyes are sad and worried.

'We talked about control last time,' she says.

I give a laugh at that, a strangled sound. 'You know what? I always thought it was me, or that Nia and me, we were a team. Both in control. But these days, I don't know who I love more, Nia or … or …' I don't want to finish that sentence. 'Hate is another form of love, isn't it?'

Felicity is silent.

'Well, I guess it's safe to say when it comes to who's in charge, all bets are off, because ... I don't think it's me,' I say.

Finally admitting it gives me a feeling like there's a chasm inside. With sharp spikes at the bottom. I'm not in control. I haven't been for a while. And for the first time I want to scream, to make it stop. The fear rises all around, filling up the room, beating me down in my chair, battering Rose's head.

'I used to be so sure,' I whisper. 'When Rose was inside me, I was doing it, I was eating, for her. Why can't I do the same now she's out? I do love her.' I breathe in Rose's smell, feel the weight of her fitting just right in my lap. 'I do,' I whisper.

'I don't doubt you. But, Hedda, have you considered that being well needs to be about you too, about loving yourself, if it's going to be sustainable?'

'Maybe,' I say.

Right now, I don't know if I can even do it for Rose, let alone me, and the unfairness of it all threatens to choke me.

'She's so small,' I say. And what I mean is: too small to hold me up. How can I even make her try? How can I put that on her? And Nia has grown so big.

Felicity looks at Rose, happy in my arms, not knowing any of this. Yet.

A shadow goes over Felicity's face, one whose meaning I refuse to interpret.

In the morning, there's a faint tap on the door and I know it's Robin.

When I open it, I see he's come to say goodbye. Jade is at his shoulder with Ellis. I know it's wrong, but I want to smack the sympathetic look out of her eyes.

'I just wanted to say goodbye, and good luck,' he says.

I thought this was going to happen, but still, it's a shock.

'Yeah. OK. Bye then,' I say it fast, so it hurts less.

'We're going back to Leeds,' Robin says.

I nod.

We hold each other's eyes.

'You look … Are you OK?' he says.

I keep still.

Robin reaches out and puts a finger on Rose's cheek and it's like he's touching mine. 'I called the council, about the damp in the flats,' he says.

Jade coughs. 'I'm going to wait in the car. Take care, Hedda.'

I nod, say 'Thanks' so quietly I'm not sure she heard me. Then I look at Robin and try to keep myself steady.

'So … I guess you made your decision then,' I say.

Robin's eyes have dark semicircles underneath them. My heart is going fast. I think again about what Felicity said about feeling emotions. I stand by my previous thought; I don't see what's so great about this.

'Yeah.'

I swallow hard. 'But you don't love her.'

'No,' he says and holds my eyes for a long time and I read a whole universe there. Then he sighs and says, 'But I love Ellis. He's my son. I have to try.'

I put one hand up in front of my face, like I can block out the path we might have taken, together.

'I'm sorry,' he says.

I look up at him, at his silly glasses, his eyes, which are shining and so tired. Why did I never stop to think he had stuff too? I try and think of a way to tell him that I'm sorry, that I should have asked properly, not just skimmed over the surface of things for the sake of it, but in the end I just say, 'Good luck. I hope it works out for you.'

He touches his fingertips to mine, then lifts up my hand and runs one finger along the bones of my knuckles. 'I'm worried about you. Will you be all right?'

I want to say, '*No, I won't be.*' Because I don't think I will.

But he has Ellis and Jade to worry about. Rose is my responsibility.

'I'll be fine,' I say.

'I made you something.' He leans down to pick up a box at his feet. 'It's the spicy chicken you liked.'

I don't know how to tell him it's too late, that I can't eat it, so I take it from him.

'Keep in touch?' he says.

I nod then shut the door before he can see the tears in my eyes.

I put the box of chicken into the empty freezer and then look at the damp that's spreading on to the ceiling now and remember what Dad said about the winter.

That this is no place for a baby.

Chapter 30

My phone rings from far away. I open my eyes. White tiles overhead and a dull pain spreading across the back of my head. It takes me a while to realise I've fainted, the unreal aftermath like a familiar song. It's the first time since I was pregnant with Rose …

Rose.

I roll over and push myself up in panic, and immediately there's a sound like when you put a seashell to your ear filling my head and I have to wait it out, helpless, my heart going because I can't hear Rose.

I finally manage to stagger to the bedroom and she's still in her cot, fast asleep, her face serene. I lean over and kiss her, very gently so I don't wake her up, then go and drink some water and try to get my heart rate under control, but I'm too panicked for that. Rose is already pushing herself up, and can move across the room by rolling. What will I do when she's crawling? Walking? Can open the door?

Will she eventually become yet another person begging me to eat?

My phone goes again. I reach for it, and miss.

I blink a few times, trying to clear my head.

It's Mum.

'Hi, Mum, how are you?'

It's quiet on the other end.

'Mum?'

'Sorry, Hedda, love ...'

Love? Why is she calling me 'love'? And why is her voice so muffled? Cold prickles run down my arms.

'Are you all right, Mum?'

There's a sound of her nose being blown and then her voice comes again, steadier now. 'I apologise. I didn't mean to worry you. I wondered whether your father has been in touch at all? And also how you and Rose are, of course.'

'We're fine,' I say, trying my best to keep my voice steady and ignoring the fact we are, apparently, an afterthought. 'I haven't heard from him. Actually ...' I take a breath, then say it as fast as I can, 'I had a little issue with the benefits people and I was trying to get in touch with Dad. I was hoping he might be able to give me a loan until it all gets put right.'

Mum gives a bitter laugh. 'I wouldn't bother asking your father for any money. I've just got off the phone to the bank. He hasn't paid the mortgage in two months. And …' she pauses again and I sense her fighting to keep herself under control at the other end of the phone, 'he filed divorce papers.'

'Oh crap.'

'Hedda! Language,' Mum says. Which is sort of reassuring.

'Sorry,' I say.

'Well, if you do speak to him, tell him … tell him he can contact my solicitor,' she says, and for a second I almost laugh because she sounds like me when I go in to bat in my Felicity sessions.

I get off the phone, feeling stranger than ever.

Then I ring Dad's phone and leave him six different messages.

Later, when Rose is awake, I sit in front of a plate of food. It's safe food, it's impossible food. I take a mouthful.

Nia whispers at me: *Fat bitch*.

'Shut up,' I say out loud through gritted teeth.

She laughs, the sound of it a roar.

Rose rolls over on the mat and turns large, bright eyes up to me.

Another mouthful.

I've been here forever.

I finish what I can and pick Rose up, trying to find comfort in the weight of her.

She watches me exercise from her place on the mat. When she cries, I ignore her and carry on, until I've completed everything Nia is telling me to do, listen to her voice insisting, *More. Do more*, so that I feel safe, and then I pick Rose up and scatter apologies all over her silky hair. They slide off and hit the floor; cheap, plastic, worthless.

I'm too tired to get to the library, so instead I tell Rose a story.

Once there was a little girl who lived on a page in a tiny dot. She sat curled up looking at her round arms and her scruffy hair. The dot was small and it stayed in one place, surrounded by an ocean of white. The corners of the page were far, far away, in another realm. Sometimes, she would catch the faintest glimpse of their long, hard edges and wondered what lay over them. When she was hungry, she ate black ink, bitter and hard. There was no day or night inside the dot, but a many-layered warm darkness. She lived for years in her dot so it got hard to see where the dot ended and she began. Ages passed. Over time she became obsessed with the edges of the dot world and the wide space beyond. In her dreams she saw the clean lines and longed to know what she might find there. She spent many days and nights in her warm dot, wondering how she could cross the white sea. She pushed at the inky blackness, and it pushed her hand back.

One day, after she had pushed harder than usual, a finger of ink pulsed into the white and then spread out to form an oar. She did the same again and another sprang up, and then, laughing, she took hold of the oars and began to row across the whiteness. But though she rowed and rowed, she found she only went in circles.

Chapter 31

Dad finally calls.

The messages must have done the trick. About fricking time.

'Hello, Hedda,' he says. My name sounds strange coming from him. I realise now how rarely he says it. It's usually just 'love' or something like that. Like I'm not actually a person at all.

'Dad, I need a favour,' I say. 'Could you –'

'I've been meaning to call you and see how you both are,' Dad says in his 'jolly' voice. 'I'm in town actually – perhaps you could pop along and see me? I could take my girls out for lunch.'

It would be so easy to say no. To tell him where to go. But underneath the fake jollity is something like iron. I know I'm going to have to play it his way.

'Sure,' I say, forcing my voice up, 'that would be great.'

We fix a time for the following day and I spend an age doing clothes and make-up to try and hide how thin I've got – bit of a turnaround for me.

I push Rose through town, my feet feeling too heavy to lift. A few heads turn as I go past and I know those looks so well. But now, I only partly want them. I'm running late because I have no money for the bus fare and it's taken longer than I thought to walk; I keep having to stop and catch my breath. I get to the pub where he wants to 'treat' me to a meal and wheel Rose's buggy in. I scan the dingy interior and spot Dad in the corner.

At least, I think it's Dad, but he looks different. Younger. Like a man let out of prison. And with him is a woman I don't recognise.

I pull the buggy back a few paces, but he's already seen me and waves. 'Over here!'

I trundle over slowly and force a smile. 'Hello.'

'Come here, sit down. There's someone I'd like you to meet. This is my eldest and the little one.'

Rose, I think. *She has a name.*

But he's already turning back to the woman, a dowdier version of Mum, with badly dyed hair and an unfriendly look in her eyes, though she's showing a lot of teeth as she smiles.

'This is Meg,' he says.

'As in *Meg and Mog*?' I say, one eyebrow notched up, thinking about the witch in the books I used to read when I was little.

Meg's smile gets even bigger and her eyes go so hard she reminds me of the bird of prey I saw with Lois. 'That's right. How clever of you.'

Dad doesn't seem to notice anything amiss and he beams at us. 'How lovely to have all my girls here,' he says.

'Except Tammy. And Mum,' I say. 'And I'm not actually a girl, though the "little one" is. Your granddaughter. Rose.' I'm not quite shouting but I'm speaking loudly enough for a couple of people at the bar to glance over.

Dad's face darkens, but before he can say anything, Meg says in a high, trilling voice, 'I've always said you're far too young to have a granddaughter, Peter.'

Vom. Then I realise she's looking rather pointedly at me, and actually she's probably right. He's too young. I'm too young. This whole thing is a complete mess. How can I ask him for money with her watching? Her eyes are the same as the woman's in the charity shop, the one who called me a scrounger.

I stand up. 'I just remembered I have an appointment,' I say.

'At the "unit"?' Meg says. Her eyes say she knows all

about it. She puts her hand on Dad's arm and turns sappy, fake-sympathetic eyes up at him.

'No, at the bookie's. Got to do something with all that lovely benefits money. Then I was planning to go out and see if I can't get myself duffed up with another one. I hear you get extra,' I say as sarcastically as I can manage, and then start to push Rose away.

But not before I hear Meg say, 'I shouldn't imagine so in that state. No, let her go, Peter. She's a grown woman.'

Which one is it then? I nearly shout it. I'm always stuck in this space between what everyone expects me to do, to be. Too young and irresponsible for a baby; too old and hard for help. I consider going back to give her a good slap, or at least tip her drink into her roots, but I don't. I keep walking.

It takes everything I have to get home again. I manage to feed and change Rose, and then I put her on her change mat and pretty much collapse on to the sofa.

Someone is really hammering on my door.

At first, swimming back up through layers of night-mares, with Nia whispering through them, I think: *Robin*. But he's gone.

I turn my head, wondering where Rose is, what the time is, did I pass out or just fall asleep or into some form of daydream?

I'm on the sofa and Rose is kicking on her mat. She looks fine. I can't have been out of it for long.

The door is still going. What if it's the man from next door? But we're being quiet.

Then I hear a voice call, 'Hedda?'

I try and reply and it comes out in a croak. I stand up in slow stages, because if I go faster I know I'll go down, and make it to the front door.

Tammy is in the corridor, swamped by a duffel coat. By the light, it's early evening.

I pull the door open and she swivels round.

'Hey,' she says.

'Hey.'

'You look awful.'

'Yeah.'

I let her in and we go into the living room. Rose is still on her mat, not looking at anything in particular. Has she simply got used to her mum sparking out now and again?

'Can I hold her?' Tammy says.

I hand Rose over and Tammy gazes down at her in her arms.

She puts a finger on Rose's nose and says, 'Beep.'

Rose giggles. It's an amazing sound, this low chuckle that's too big for her. Tammy and I both smile at each other.

Rose is like candyfloss, making the air between us gentle and soft.

'She knows who her auntie is,' I say.

'Yes, you do, don't you?' Tammy says and beeps Rose's nose again.

I go to the kitchen to check Rose's book. The clock says seven, which means she's not due a feed for a while. Her weight is still on exactly the right percentile.

'What's that?'

Tammy has followed me into the kitchen and is staring over my shoulder at the book.

I flip it closed. 'How's Mum?' I say.

Tammy gives the book another hard stare then follows me back to the sofa. 'She's cooking stuff. Think she's worried I'm aiming to fill your shoes.'

'Are you?'

She looks at the ceiling as if she's considering, then says, 'No. One's enough for the family, don't you think?'

'You're sure?'

Tammy looks me straight in the eyes. 'I'm sure.'

And I know it's true. A tiny breath I never realised I was holding releases.

Tammy's still looking at me. 'How about you? You look half dead,' she says.

I flinch.

Tammy waits.

Where did this version of my sister come from? She seems old, suddenly, older than fourteen.

'I guess … I guess I am.' I say it so quietly I wonder if she's heard me.

She strokes Rose's face with the back of one finger.

'Hedda … what about Rose?'

'What about her?'

'What are you going to do, when she's older? Is she going to watch you like … like this? What will that feel like for her?'

And I realise that if anyone should know, it's Tammy. I drop my head. 'I'm sorry.'

Tammy sighs and I think for a minute she's going to go, but instead she wriggles closer, Rose still in her arms. She hesitates, then puts her head on my shoulder. For a moment, I don't move at all. Then, very slowly, like I'm trying not to scare away some wild animal, I wrap my arm around her shoulder. We stay like that for a while, my heart skipping all over the place.

'Wanna watch something?' Tammy says. She grabs the remote and flicks through channels, until she gets *Strictly* on.

'Seriously?' I say.

'Oh just shut up and watch,' Tammy says, but not in a cross way.

The couple are going some, hands and feet flying all over the place. Rose stares at the TV, mesmerised by all the glitter and fake tan.

'Those two better be going out first,' Tammy mutters.

'Never knew you were into this,' I say.

'Well, don't tell anyone.'

We watch a few more dances, and then there's a waltz, the woman's dress drifting behind her like she's floating. It's kind of beautiful. Tammy stands up and starts dancing Rose around. Rose's eyes go wide and she stares at Tammy with such a cute look my heart pushes out and opens. For some reason the matching music boxes Tammy and I got one Christmas, with two dancers on them, pop into my head.

'Come on,' Tammy says, holding her hand out to me.

'What? No.'

Tammy ignores my protests and pulls me up and then we're dancing, me and her and Rose, in a strange circular waltz and that warm opening in my chest seems to lift like the lid of a music box until there's a tiny space for my angry, annoying, little sister, right next to Rose.

But when she's gone, the flat is so empty.

For once I do try to eat dinner, for Rose, for Tammy, but I just can't.

* * *

The next day, the noise in my head only gets stronger. Nia is everywhere, seeping through the walls, echoing through the flat: *Fat, fat, fat.* It's like a battering ram that won't stop.

I run on the spot for half the night and in the morning I take Rose for a walk, away up and out of the town, and find myself at the gates of the cemetery.

I didn't even know I was coming here, and yet part of me did.

It's the first time I've been here and I search for an age, walking up and down under the quietly rustling trees.

Somewhere in all the static, I know what day it is. It's a year since Molly died.

I find the grave finally, marked by a black marble slab. I trace Molly's name and the dates of her short life and then take Rose out of her buggy and sit cross-legged with her in my lap.

'Hi, Molly. This is Rose. Rose, Molly,' I say.

Rose giggles.

I remember a night on the unit. Molly and I had gone into the garden to smoke. Above us, tall trees, I don't know what kind, swayed in the wind.

'It sounds like the sea,' Molly said. She took a big sniff in through her nose and let it out again. 'When I die, I want to be reincarnated as a tree.'

'Thought you didn't believe in that stuff?' I said.

'Oh, I believe in something all right.'

'Like what?'

'I don't know. The way a butterfly looks, its symmetry. The smell of conkers. Cut grass. Snow. How much better the world would be without people in it.'

She looked up at the sky and that look was so dark and full of despair. 'I love the world, you know.' Then she stood up and shouted to the sky, 'I love you!'

'Settle down,' the nurse watching us said.

Molly turned her back on her.

'If you love it so much, then why … ?' I left it hanging.

A week or so before, she'd run away and been brought back by the police a few hours later, but not before she'd necked a load of something that meant she needed her stomach pumped.

'Because I'm not good enough for it,' she said.

Nothing I could tell her would make her believe it wasn't true. And I tried, back then. Believe me, I tried. Oh, they went on at the unit, trying to ferret out a why, but the most she'd ever say was that she felt like a black hole, that she'd pull everyone and everything she loved into it. And I wonder now why she would never explain. Was it because she wouldn't or because she couldn't?

From this distance, I realise I'm angry with her, that I've been angry for the longest time, but it's faint under the Nia haze, like a memory of being scalded, when all you can see is the shrivelled skin left behind.

'Molly, you have to tell me what to do,' I whisper. 'She won't let me go. Or I can't let her go.'

I look at the black stone and think about Molly's fingers dancing on the sax, conjuring sadness and joy out of some deep place inside her. The blackness she carried around, the way she loved dark films and storms. How destruction was what she did best in the end. About fairground rides and tipping points and numbers.

'I don't know what to do. Tell me what to do,' I whisper.

I think about the pages I scribbled during those long weeks when Rose was still inside me, my 'Crap Things about the Unit' list. When I was writing it, I felt like Molly was really there, sitting by my side. And suddenly, I know. It was never about why I shouldn't go back. I was writing for her. So I didn't have to say goodbye.

I wait and wait for a sign, a feeling, anything that isn't black emptiness, but any sense of Molly looking over me is gone.

She's gone. This whole time I've been fooling myself.

There's nothing left of her but cold stone and memories.

Chapter 32

A few days later, I have a cold. Rose has a cold. We cough and sneeze through the night and in the morning I'm so weak I can barely lift her. My head is thick and stuffy. When Rose cries, I put a pillow over my ears, and think, *Shut up, shut up, shut up,* then I'm overcome with remorse. Sometimes she stops and gives me this sideways look, like she can't figure out if she should trust me, which makes two of us.

There's no food in the house, no money, no nappies. I fold up a tea towel inside her vest while I take her down to the shops. On the way back, I can't get her buggy up the stairs; I can't lift it any more. I unstrap Rose and my arms and legs tremble all the way up. I put her down in the flat and gasp for breath.

There's a crushing feeling in my chest, and I think, *This*

is it. This is the day my heart gives out.

I've been waiting for this moment since the day Molly died, probably before.

My vision blurs. I scream Rose's name so loudly in my head, but I can't make the sound come out. And there's no one to help. Robin isn't here, Laurel's in hospital. Mum's used to me not answering my phone. It could be days before anyone realises anything is wrong.

I stumble and fall to my knees.

'Rose.' I half sob, half whisper her name. She's just a faint outline now, everything fading away. I reach out again, and know it's no good; I can't get to her …

I wake up to someone banging on the door. I feel sore all over, but my chest hurts less. I roll on to my side and see Rose is fast asleep on her play mat, her fists screwed tight like she's protecting herself. The door bangs again, and I haul myself up, feel for my heartbeat, which still seems to be going, after a fashion. It was a panic attack, that's all. Maybe.

I look out of the door and see one of the girls who sit on the stairs, chatting and drinking cider. I open the door a crack.

'All right? You left your buggy. I brought it up,' she says.

'Oh. Right. Thanks.' It's all coming out in staccato.

'No worries,' she says, then looks me up and down. 'No offence, but you look like shit. You ought to get yourself to the doctor's or something.'

'Thanks,' I say again and take the buggy from her.

She gives me a worried look over her shoulder before clattering back to her cider.

I walk slowly over to Rose. She seems OK.

I try to ring Dad, but it goes on to voicemail.

I check my account and see a benefits payment has come through, finally, but most of it has to go on the payday loan. I make lists but no matter what I do the numbers won't add up. They wriggle and blur in front of me. I realise once I've bought nappies and formula, there's no more money for food and I'm in no state to make it to the food bank.

When I look out of the window into the dull grey concrete park, I see the Walking Woman circling it, like she's always been there.

My jeans are hanging away from me now. I feel like I'm suffocating, like I can't get enough air. I read the same books over and over to Rose, until the words dance on the page. I even try the bird one, but stop when I get to the page about cuckoos and how they sneak their eggs into other birds' nests to hatch there and massacre the real chicks. Brood parasites, they're called. My mind snags on the word 'parasite'.

Joanna calls round, and I hide with Rose in the bedroom, waiting until she goes away. She leaves a voicemail on my phone, telling me to be in when she comes back and I know from her voice the clock has run out.

That night, the thoughts expand and grow until all the walls are dripping with them, thick and black. I'm afraid to sleep, because what if I don't wake up again? I keep thinking about Molly's grave. If something happens to me, what will happen to Rose? Will anyone even find her before …?

I fling my head to one side, get out of bed. I put my earbuds in and turn up rock as loud as I can. I start to run on the spot, pumping my arms frantically, trying to outrun the voices. The room spins and I feel sick rising up, but I shut my eyes and run on. In my head, Nia chants: *Too late, too late, too late*, or is it *Fat cow, fat cow, fat cow*? I push the volume up until it screeches in my ears.

Then there's a crash and a blaze of light and the man from next door is right in front of me, splinters of wood on the floor where he's kicked in the door.

He grabs my wrists and one earbud pops out so all I can hear is thrashing guitars in one ear, and him shouting, 'I told you to keep that baby quiet!' and Rose screaming, screaming, screaming, like she's been crying forever, but I didn't hear, I didn't hear her and the man has his face pressed up close to mine and I can smell the sourness of his breath and I realise how dangerous his eyes are. I try to twist away, but his hands are crushing my wrists like he's trying to snap them, and I'm so terrified I can't get a sound out and all the time the rock music plays on and Rose screams and my heart flutters and goes still in my chest.

He lets go and I stumble and fall, heavily, into the wall. Pure white pain flares over my ribs, taking the breath out of me. The other earbud falls out and tinny rock skids over the carpet. He kicks out and sends the iPod flying against the wall. It bounces back and continues to play and then he stamps on it hard and there's a cracking sound and the music stops bleeding out into the room. Now it's just Rose, whose cries have turned to frightened whimpers.

I push up to my knees, though my ears are ringing, and there's a colony of ants tracking across my vision, and crawl into the other room. He follows and leans down close to my ear as I try and pull myself up using the bars of Rose's cot.

'Next time, I'll fucking kill you.'

I think he really means it.

I freeze in place, staring at my girl, and finally he goes.

I stand and sway. Retch silently.

I reach into Rose's cot, pull her out. Smell an acrid tang coming off her.

Her nappy.

I turn on the light and see it's leaked everywhere, all over her cot, her legs. She was screaming in her own crap while I tried to outrun the voices in the next room. I shush Rose as best I can, terrified he'll come back. I get the door shut and manage to put the chain on, but the door frame is splintered.

I wipe her down in the shower, putting one hand over her mouth as gently as I can to blot out her cries.

'Shh-shh-shh, sweetie, please, shhh. Twinkle, twinkle, little star …' My voice breaks.

I find a sleepsuit, already worn and too small for her so I have to cut holes in the bottom to get her feet in. They stick out, tiny and vulnerable. I rub at them with my hands, but she flinches away from my cold fingers. When I put the last nappy on her, her bottom was bright red. No wonder she screamed. I feel sick with guilt.

I wrap her in the blanket and curl myself around her in my bed, and lie rigid until morning comes, listening to Rose's breaths and Nia talking on and on through the night, a symphony of horror I can't outrun.

Morning light shines weakly into the flat. I look at the stains, creeping everywhere, the wood splinters by the front door. I open cupboards and they're empty. Robin's chicken sits in the freezer, surrounded by white shelves.

I hate white, I realise.

I go into the bathroom and look at the way my eyes are sinking in, the dark hollows in my cheekbones. My hair that's coming out in fistfuls when I put a hand to my head. I see myself, the way I saw Laurel that day, a shimmer that focuses everything.

I see myself.

Finally.

Then I pick up the phone and make a call.

Chapter 33

Felicity arrives first. She takes in Rose and me and the state of the flat and sighs.

'Come on, sit down. Do you have any tea?'

'No.'

'That's all right. I brought some. And some milk and sugar.'

We sit and drink. I let Felicity put sugar in mine and it gives me the energy to repeat what I said on the phone.

'I can't do this. I can't look after Rose. I need … I need help.'

'That takes a lot of courage to admit, Hedda.'

I cuddle Rose tighter, as though I can take back the words, what I've set in motion. But I can't. I love her too much to keep pretending. She needs more than this, more than I can give. All down my side a huge bruise is forming.

I'm stiff with it, wincing whenever I move. My heart still feels strange and wrong, like parts of it might have died off. I can't trust it, can't trust myself.

'You need to be checked out. And we'll need to contact the police about the assault,' she says.

'I'm not going back to hospital,' I say. 'Not now. Not ever.' I know this suddenly, and there's grief in it, long and howling. Molly's gone, and so is the unit. I can't go back. Because if I do, I don't think I'll be coming out again.

'Then we need to work out a plan, to keep you out.'

'Like what? I've got nothing left.' I sort of mean that I'm exhausted, but maybe more than that. I try and get it straight in my mind through the Nia fog. 'It's too late, isn't it?'

Felicity's voice is very gentle. 'I think, for now, you need extra support, yes.'

I put my hands over my face and speak through them. 'It's like this war in my head. If I don't have Nia … I don't even know what I'm like without her … it. I don't know who I am. I've never done anything worthwhile. Except for Rose. But I can't make her my everything, can I? Like Mum? I can't ask Rose to carry all that.'

'No, you can't.'

'So Nia wins then.'

Felicity leans forward and touches my hand. 'Only if

you let it. Nia's not a person, Hedda, and your eating disorder is not you, no matter how comforting you might have found it in the past. And I think you know it too.'

I give a tiny nod.

She sighs. 'Maybe I've been in this job too long … I think you've worked very hard, and you've done a very brave thing, to call me. I don't think you realise just how strong you are.'

I look at her in disbelief, but she's not finished.

'All this power you have, all this destruction – you can turn it into something positive.'

I shake my head.

'You can. You are,' Felicity says. 'You just need some help. You have to let people help you.'

I think about Robin, and Laurel, and Molly. How they always asked about me, and never once admitted they needed help too.

I start to cry. 'I have to let her go, don't I?'

I mean Rose.

But also, Nia.

Felicity sighs. 'I think right now you need to work on your recovery, and I don't think you have the resources at the moment to look after Rose too. I know how much you love her, but you have to love yourself as well. When you're ready, I think you will be a beautiful parent.'

'Just not now.'

'No, not now. You need to be healthy first. And I believe you will be. I see you, and I believe that.'

When Molly died, I never thought anyone else would see me – properly see me and love me anyway. And now Felicity, of all people, the woman who's taken everything I've thrown at her – my lies, my insults and my silence – has. Then in a flash, I see her too. The apology in her eyes. How hard she's tried. And I want to tell her how much it means that she did. That she didn't fail me. I can't find the words, but I grab hold of her hand and she blinks really fast and I realise she's holding my hand back just as hard. We sit in silence with our fingers linked for a long time, until Rose stirs and begins to cry.

A while later, Joanna arrives. Felicity talks to her in a low voice, and then I do. Joanna makes notes and asks questions and I try my hardest to answer, but I want to sleep and sleep.

I tell her about Mum, and about Dad going AWOL.

'I think that rules out your mother as a placement for the time being,' Joanna says. She goes out for a bit to make calls and to buy nappies and formula.

Felicity stays with me the whole time.

I hold tight to Rose, my girl, my beautiful girl, my life raft I have to let go.

Because no baby should be someone's life raft.

All that need.

All my need.

It's too big for one tiny person.

Another while later, the police arrive. They take a statement and go next door. There's shouting and banging and then he's being done for assault and possession and carted off. But I know he'll be back. They say someone will come to fix the door later on.

I can't stop holding on to Rose.

Eventually, Joanna is back. 'I've found a foster placement. It's a wonderful couple, very experienced. I've spoken to Violet and they can take Rose today.'

'Today?' Everything is falling away. I hold Rose tighter, like Joanna is going to snatch her from my arms right now. 'What then? What will happen?'

'Well, you'll have contact, be able to visit Rose. And you will work on your recovery. This should be short term, until you're back on your feet. We'll need to sort out your accommodation. Perhaps college, or a job. If you weren't turning eighteen next month I might have been able to arrange a placement for you both together, but as it is …'

'I'll be on my own,' I say dully.

'No. I'll be here to support you,' Joanna says. 'This isn't the end, Hedda. I can't make any promises, and Rose's welfare will come first, but this isn't the end.'

Felicity squeezes my fingers.

Violet arrives as it's getting dark with her husband Rod, a big, carefully shambling man, with thinning hair and broad hairy arms. Through my haze I recognise Violet. It's Vi, the woman from the food bank.

She smiles at me. 'We'll take good care of her, I promise.'

She leans down to take Rose and I can't believe this is it: this is happening, she's going. I can't make my arms let go. But Felicity is there and she puts her arm round my shoulder, and I breathe in Rose's smell, and feel her warm against me, and I take what courage I have left and kiss her.

Then I let her go.

Vi holds her and says, 'She's a lovely wee thing. I can tell how loved she is.'

I want to scream and howl, but I don't because I can't frighten Rose.

Violet straps her into her car seat.

I start to gabble. 'She likes "Twinkle, Twinkle, Little Star". And this bear – she laughed at him. If she's tired, she likes you to stroke here between her eyebrows and that makes her sleepy. She likes going for walks. And books – she likes books.' Panic rises in me. How do I sum her up? If only I'd made a list ... Why didn't I make a list?

But Rose is the one thing I could never turn into a list.

I take a deep breath. 'She likes the bath quite warm, and if she has wind, rub this way.' I hold a hand up to demonstrate. 'Not this way.'

I take a breath, and Joanna says, 'Let's give her a couple of days to settle in and then we'll arrange a visit.'

The space where Rose was on my lap is cold.

I lean into the car seat and give her a kiss on her forehead. She's fast asleep, but I whisper to her anyway. 'Time to go, Rose. I love you. I'm sorry. I'll see you soon.'

And then they're gone.

Felicity says she'll stay but I just want to be by myself.

'I'll be back tomorrow. Early,' she says, and then she leaves too.

I run to the window and lean out to watch the car edge away slowly, like it's carrying the most precious object in the entire universe. I stare until the car gets to the end of the road. It waits a huge amount of time at the junction, and I imagine Rod dithering, his thinning head spinning from left to right and back again, Vi telling him to get on with it. Then the car turns the corner and its lights fade away.

I don't know how long I spend at the window as dusk turns into darkness. It seems the flat is smaller when I turn back around. Rose's spare blanket is still on top of the sofa and I take it with me and curl up, smelling it, trying to etch every line of her in my mind. And I want to run and not stop running until I find her and bring her home with me where she belongs, but then I remember not only her smile but the other times, when she cried and I thought I would do something terrible, the money running out and the man next door breaking in while she screamed. The Nia voice calling from the ceiling and my heart fading into nothingness.

I let the grief wash over me and as it deepens, Nia comes, like I knew she would, like she always has. She wants me with her, and right now in this bleak flat, with the one good thing that's ever happened to me gone, I can't think of any reason why not.

It gets darker still. Night is arriving. Words form, gathering strength and speed, like a train: *Fat, disgusting bitch. Hate you …* And there's a part of me that wants to sink into them, back to where everything hurts, and maybe it would hurt less than it does now, because all of a sudden I don't think I can breathe for one more second without my girl. Felicity was wrong. I'm like Molly after all; I've never been good for anything but destroying myself.

I stand up and go back to the window. Lean way out in the night air. It wouldn't take much to let go.

I think about Molly underneath that stone slab, how I told myself she had cast a spell, to keep me out of hospital. But she's not here. She never was.

The ground below is dark, wind rushing around my ears. If it wasn't Molly watching over me, keeping me out, then maybe that means something else.

Maybe some part of it was me.

And then, I think of Rose.

Rose who is still here. I might not be able to look after her right now, but I have contact. I'll get her back. If I can. I think about all the things I've counted over the years and realise I can't put a number on the love I have for Rose. It's bigger than infinity. Countless. Perhaps if I have that much love for her inside me, I can find a way to love myself too.

The saying comes back to me then, the one Robin's grammy said about life being a precious gift, and making it flower. I weigh it, try and find its size in the darkness. I don't know whether my life counts too.

The Nia train is near. I can feel her in the room behind me. I look down, at the ground that seems so close.

And slowly, I pull myself back.

I go to the kitchen. In the back of the cupboard is a packet of noodles. I leave them there. Instead, I take out the chicken Robin left me and heat it on the stove, watch it bubble.

I sit down at the table with the plate in front of me.

Nia chatters, but I know now. It's my choice to hold on to her or not. But if I let her go, it has to be for me, not Rose.

I look up at the ceiling, where Nia's watched for so long, and then at the darkness beyond the open window. I think about my daughter, my beautiful girl, who picked a mother like me, one she could trust to choose right. Then I gather Nia to me, and whisper in her ear.

'It's time for you to go now.'

I watch my hands release thin air.

And I begin to eat.

Epilogue

'Hello, Hedda. Come in. The birthday girl's in the garden.'

I follow Rod through the house and into the toy-strewn garden. Balloons and streamers hang from apple trees. At the bottom of the garden Rose is crouching over a sandpit, digging with a spade. I watch her for a while.

She looks up and smiles, then takes a few uncertain steps towards me. 'Heddy,' she says.

I force myself to walk, not run, towards her and pick her up. She's so heavy now, but she still smells the same. I feel her warm fingers at the back of my neck. I wonder for the millionth time how much she understands.

After a while, she wriggles down and I turn to Vi, who's carrying out a glass of lemonade. I drink half of it, carefully, and set it down.

'Ba-a,' Rose says, which is her word for 'balloon'.

Vi untangles one from a tree and hands it to her.

She totters over and passes it to me. 'Heddy.'

'Thank you,' I say, and bend down to kiss her again. 'I'll tell you what, shall we let it go? See how far it goes on the wind?'

Rose gazes up at me, her little face serious. I reach up and open my fingers, and we both watch as the balloon floats into the sky. Rose squeals. I pick her up so she can see and do my best not to hold her too tight. When it's a tiny dot in the distance, I put Rose down gently and turn to Vi.

'I'm not going to stay for the party. I'm due at work.'

Vi nods.

'I'll pop her present inside,' I say. 'She can open it later.'

'Or you could give it to her on Saturday?' Vi says.

Saturday is Rose's first home visit with me in my new flat. If it goes well, then eventually she'll come to live with me again.

Vi squeezes my shoulder. 'One step at a time. You can be a good mum to her, Hedda. You already are.'

I don't know about that.

Mum and Tammy will be here for the party soon. I see them twice a week and they visit Rose in between too. Tammy and me have a laugh actually and I think we've rubbed off on Mum because she's started to develop a sense of humour. She told us this joke the other week that had an actual swear word in it, and we were so shocked it took us a good minute to start laughing. Who would've thought Mum would tell sweary jokes? I wish I'd realised sooner. I think she's happier now Dad's finally gone and she can stop waiting for it to happen and get on with life. She's applying for jobs, inspired by me working for Lois, I think. I've been doing my A level maths in the evenings, alongside an accountancy qualification and I'm going to finish it this time.

The other day after work, I went to see Mum and Tammy. Mum was in the garden pulling up weeds with her bare hands. I went over to her, put my own fingers into the warm earth. Mum rocked back on her heels and looked at me for a while. Just a look taking me in, straightforward.

Then she said, 'You seem well.'

And I didn't flinch, or grimace. Instead, I smiled.

I was about to go inside, when she lifted up one muddy hand and said, 'Hedda, I've been meaning to talk to you … I wanted to say … to say …' And she stopped. Two tears dropped down her cheeks.

I held her eyes, and in them I read a thousand apologies.

Then she reached out.

And I let her hug me.

After a while, I brought my hands up and hugged her back, and neither of us was bothered that we were getting covered in all that earth.

'What you've been through ...' Mum started.

'It's OK, Mum. I know.'

Later on that day, Tammy and I watched *The Force Awakens* again. I loved the bit where Rey got hold of a lightsabre. It made me think of Rose growing up strong, and of Robin. We've been emailing, but I haven't seen him. It didn't work out with him and Jade, but he's staying in Leeds to be near Ellis. Sometimes I have this dream, where I hear his heart beating strong and slow and I feel calm. Warm. I'm still working out what that might mean, or if it means anything at all. I don't know if it should. Robin will always be the boy who was there when my own heart woke up. But maybe he belongs to that time, not the future.

Laurel writes occasional letters from hospital, but she lives in monochrome now. I tried to write back at first, but it didn't do any good. I don't answer any more, but sometimes I look up at the sky and think about her. I hope she makes it.

As for me? I guess part of me will always be left in that world. But I also have my new flat, my job, my books.

I've stopped swinging by the to-be-shelved section. Instead, I'm working out the things I like. Turns out I love fantasy.

I still go to therapy, twice a week, with a different counsellor now I'm under Adult Services, though I send Felicity the occasional message to let her know I'm OK. I stay away from scales. Sometimes I feel like I'm on a bike that's just had the stabilisers off and the smallest wobble is going to slam me straight back down. But maybe life's like that for everyone.

I don't feel Molly or Nia on my shoulders the way I did before, and it's so lonely sometimes, without them there. A few weeks ago, I visited Molly's grave one more time, to give her back the lists and the poncho. I sat in front of her headstone and watched them burn and thought about how little I ever really had of her. She could have had a beautiful life, but I'm not the one to live it for her.

I've got enough to do working out how to live my own.

'Saturday's still OK, isn't it? You're ready?' Vi says.

I look over, to Rose reaching her fingers up to the leaves. She sits down hard on her bottom and giggles. She's so happy here. Whatever happens, whether she lives with me or not, the fact that she's in the world still seems like the strangest miracle.

I realise Vi is waiting for my reply. I could count the seconds, wide as raptor wings, but I don't. Not this time.

'Saturday,' I say. 'I'll be ready.'

The things that matter the most can't be counted anyway.

Acknowledgements

I am incredibly grateful to all the people whose input and encouragement have helped shape *Countless*. In particular, a huge thank you to:

My agent, Claire Wilson, who has believed in my writing from the beginning. Thank you for your patience, calmness and always knowing exactly the right thing to say. This book would not have been written without you. Thank you, too, to Rosie Price and everyone at RCW for all your hard work.

Rebecca McNally for giving Hedda a home. Hannah Sandford, my fantastic editor, for bringing such care and insight to Hedda's story. You have made the editing process brilliant – thank you. Helen Vick for steering *Countless* through the final stages, Madeleine Stevens whose suggestions for amendments have been invaluable, and to all the

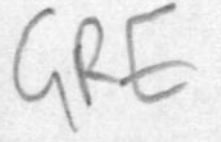

team at Bloomsbury. I feel so lucky to be working with you.

My thanks and love to my family and friends, especially Mum for all those library trips and hours of babysitting, and Emily for reading multiple drafts and cheering me on with grace at every stage. You will always be the first person I call. Thank you to Tom, Suki and the girls for your enthusiastic support.

The Coven, for your support and welcome, especially Lexi for fielding the panicky emails and for all that rhubarb!

I promised a shout-out to the PMO crew for putting up with all the book talk – sorry and thanks. Thank you, Vic, for talking me through maternity procedures for vulnerable young adults. Any remaining mistakes are my own.

Countless is fiction and Hedda is not me, however as I'm writing this, it's almost exactly twenty years since I began my own 'unit' journey. To the brave, wonderful people I knew during that time, I still think of you and hope we all made it. And for anyone who is currently there, please know you're not forgotten and that things can get better.

Finally, to Naomi and William, who picked a mother like me. Thank you for sharing me with the laptop and making me smile every day.

About the author

Karen Gregory has been a confirmed bookhead since early childhood. She wrote her first story about Bantra the mouse aged twelve, then put away the word processor until her first child was born, when she was overtaken by the urge to write. A graduate of Somerville College, Oxford, and a project coordinator by day, she's become adept at writing around the edges. Strong coffee and a healthy disregard for housework help. Karen lives in Wiltshire with her family. *Countless* is her first novel.